Praise for previous editions of Andrew Lownie's ~~~

'. . . a thorough job on the city's literary locations and characters . . . lovely quotes . . .'   *Sunday Telegraph*

'Andrew Lownie has done an exceptionally fine job . . . in a work which sets off history against geography, physical detail against imaginative transformation . . . For the literary tourist it will be indispensable, but it has revelations for residents, too.'   *The Herald*

'All the old favourites are here, including Scott, Stevenson, Boswell, Burns, Hogg, Fergusson and Garioch, as well as many more fleeting visitors, such as Mark Twain, Dylan Thomas and Daniel Defoe. Relating writers to parts of the city, Lownie marshals his facts well and presents them intelligently.'
   Scotland on Sunday

'The Edinburgh Literary Guide traces a fascinating historical path through the city, old and new, in the footsteps of numerous writers who have been associated with it . . .'   *Glasgow Evening Times*

'This guide is ideal for walks.'   *The Economist*

'Lownie's research is impressive . . . This is an informative and practical guide which will be of considerable interest to any tourist seeking out his favourite author . . .'   *Daily Mail*

'Andrew Lownie's definitive guide charts in meticulous detail the landmarks associated with some of our best-loved writers . . . A fascinating guide full of delightful anecdotes.'   *Mail on Sunday*

'. . . a comprehensive guide to this rich heritage . . . meticulously and thoroughly researched, the book is a useful and enjoyable asset to any fan of the city and its literature.'   *The List* (Glasgow & Edinburgh)

'. . . set to be yet another indispensable volume on the bookshelves, appealing to lovers of both literature and Edinburgh.'   *Scots Magazine*

'The Edinburgh Literary Guide should give pleasure and instruction to those who know and love the city . . . a salute to Edinburgh and Scotland's literary glory . . . If you are going to Edinburgh put this paperback in your pocket. It will add to the pleasure.'   *Catholic Herald*

'. . . this entertaining companion . . .'   *Spectator*

'. . . the ideal city guide . . .'   *Choice Magazine*

THE EDINBURGH
Literary Companion

ANDREW LOWNIE

Polygon

First published in
Great Britain in 2005 by
Polygon, an imprint of Birlinn Ltd
West Newington House
10 Newington Road
Edinburgh
EH9 1QS

9 8 7 6 5 4 3 2 1

www.birlinn.co.uk

ISBN 10: 1 904598 61 7
ISBN 13: 978 1 904598 61 9

British Library Cataloguing-in-Publication Data
A catalogue record for this book is available on
request from the British Library

Design and layout: Mark Blackadder

Printed and bound by Graphycems, Spain

Contents

Preface

Edinburgh's literary associations are so numerous, and her citizens often so possessive and knowledgeable about their history, that I should first of all explain my approach.

This is not a definitive guide to Edinburgh's literary associations, merely a personal selection. I have been quite subjective, concentrating on the last two hundred years and indulging my own particular loves, such as R. L. Stevenson and Robert Garioch, and largely ignoring important, but now little read, writers such as William Drummond of Hawthornden. Over a hundred literary figures have been covered in the following pages and it has not always been possible to fully describe them or assess their importance, outside the confines of their relationship with the city. I have attempted to strike a balance between those individuals who by virtue of birth, upbringing, residence or subject matter can be classed as 'Edinburgh writers' and the many visitors, who, if not influenced in their work by the city, have at least responded to the capital. I have tried to appeal to both the tourist, whose knowledge of the city and its literary past is necessarily limited, and to the resident whose knowledge will be much more extensive. The book is written to be used as a walking guide but I hope will also be read at home.

This is not a work of literary criticism but a mixture of literary guide and anthology, the story of writers in Edinburgh and how the city has been portrayed in literature, which grew from my own explorations of the city as a schoolboy and university student. Over five hundred novels have taken the city as their backdrop – a hundred of them published in the last fifteen years – and I have sought to give a flavour of some of them, and how writers have attempted to write about a city that can be paradoxical and inscrutable. As such I hope this is not just a literary companion but also a portrait of Edinburgh as seen by writers over the ages.

My thanks to the staffs of the British Library and the Edinburgh Room of the Central Public Library, to Martin Healey for his computer help and to Ken Begg (McClure), Carol Anne Davis, Joyce Holms, Quintin Jardine, Alanna Knight, John Skinner and Hunter Steele – who supplied information at short notice – and to all at Polygon: my editor Alison Rae, Jan Rutherford and Neville Moir, who worked on the first edition in 1992, and Hugh Andrew. My wife and two young children deserve a special thanks for their patience and help during the research and writing of this new edition. I would be grateful if any corrections or suggestions could be sent to me at 17 Sutherland Street, London SW1V 4JU, or by e-mail to lownie@globalnet.co.uk.

Andrew Lownie
May 2005

PART I

The Old Town

The train swung into the flat lands of the Lothians and as we hurtled at sixty-five miles an hour through fields of hidden grain I glimpsed the small hill behind which was Bernard's home. Soon the speed slackened and we were on the outskirts of Edinburgh, with Arthur's Seat looming larger until we skirted its base and plunged into the defile of scruffy tenements and squalid side roads that are the preamble to the largest, dirtiest and gloomiest station in Britain – Waverley.[1]

NEIL McCALLUM, *A Scream in the Sky* (1964)

Waverley is for many visitors their first experience of Edinburgh. In a city so rich in literary associations it is entirely appropriate that its railway station should be named after a famous series of novels, and that it is the Gothic monument to their author, Walter Scott, on Princes Street that first greets the traveller leaving the station.[2]

In few other major European cities is one brought so abruptly right to the heart of a city. To the north the steep Waverley Steps, often claimed as the windiest spot in Britain, rise from the depths of the station to Edinburgh's principal shopping thoroughfare, Princes Street. Alternatively the western exit takes the visitor almost straight into Princes Street Gardens, an oasis of carefully manicured lawns lying in the shadow of the Castle.

Edinburgh's most distinctive features are immediately visible for it is an intimate city. To the east Calton Hill with its cluster of monuments looking proudly down Princes Street, with the volcanic Arthur's Seat behind it. To the north the elegant, symmetrical streets of the New Town. To the west Princes Street with the Caledonian Hotel and the spire of St Mary's Cathedral in the distance. To the south the famous serrated 'crag and tail' skyline stretching from west to east, the jumble of buildings apparently hanging in suspended animation.

THE CASTLE

It is the Castle, however, that one notices first. Early in the morning its menacing presence looms out of the dark, at noon the sun may play upon its stonework casting giant shadows on the slopes below, while at night with lights blazing it stands out like some fairy castle above the city. At whatever time of day it dominates the city's skyline:

> In every point of view, however, the main centre of
> attraction is the Castle of Edinburgh. From whatever side
> you approach the city – whether by water or by land –
> whether your foreground consists of height or of plain, of
> heath, of trees, or of the buildings of the city itself – this
> gigantic rock lifts itself high above all that surrounds it,
> and breaks upon the sky with the same commanding

blackness of mingled crags, cliffs, buttresses, and
battlements. These, indeed, shift and vary their outlines at
every step, but everywhere there is the same unmoved
effect of general expression – the same lofty and imposing
image . . .[3]

Even when the haar, a raw mist, occasionally creeps in from the North
Sea, and the Castle is shrouded from sight, its presence is detectable,
providing a fixed point around which its citizens revolve. From almost
anywhere in Edinburgh it can be seen in all its chameleon splendour.
However obscured, it is the heart and soul of Edinburgh.

The American writer, Washington Irving, on a visit to Walter Scott
in 1817, wrote to his brother, Peter:

It seemed as if the rock and castle assumed a new aspect
every time I looked at them; and Arthur's Seat was perfect
witchcraft. I don't wonder that anyone residing in
Edinburgh should write poetically.[4]

The Castle also dominates the city's history. Originally it was a military
base for a tribe who named it 'Din Eiden' (the fortress on the hill).
Subsequently the Romans built a hill fort in order to protect the road
from the south and later invading armies from the south knew they had
to capture it to retain control of the eastern part of Scotland. Gradually
a settlement grew around it stretching down the volcanic overflow to
create the present distinctive skyline.

The views from the Castle ramparts are spectacular and illustrate
Edinburgh's position, like that of Rome, as situated on seven hills: to the
east Calton Hill, Arthur's Seat and the fertile farmland of East Lothian,
to the south the Braid Hills, Blackford Hill and in the distance the
Pentland Hills, to the west the suburbs spreading out past Corstorphine
Hill while to the north, lie, in R. L. Stevenson's memorable phrase, the
'draughty parallelograms' of the New Town and, beyond, the gleaming
waters of the Firth of Forth.

Its dramatic history has been reflected in literature. The Earl of
Moray's famous climb up the north wall to recapture the Castle from the

English in 1314 is described by Scott in *Tales of a Grandfather* (1828), while the central figure of R. L. Stevenson's unfinished novel *St Ives* (1897) was one of the French prisoners kept in the Castle during the Napoleonic Wars. The writer, George Borrow, was briefly quartered in the Castle about this time when his father, a captain in the West Norfolk Militia, was posted there as adjutant and the Castle figures briefly at the beginning of his autobiographical novel *Lavengro*.[5]

One of the best known artefacts in the Castle stands in the French prison. Forged in the fifteenth century, the power and range of the magnificent siege cannon Mons Meg was legendary, being able to fire a five-hundredweight stone at a target more than a mile and a half away. In 1681 it burst while firing a salute, a disaster recorded by the poet, Robert Fergusson:

> Oh willawins! Mons Meg for you,
> Twas firing crack'd thy muckle mou!

In 1754 it was removed to the Tower of London and only returned after Walter Scott had made approaches to George IV during his state visit in 1822. The history of the gun is given in a note to chapter 27 of Scott's *Rob Roy* (1817). Scott was also instrumental in putting on public display the 'Honours of Scotland', which included the crown worn by Robert Bruce, the sceptre and sword of state and the Order of the Thistle, after they had lain hidden in the Castle since the Act of Union in 1707, over a hundred years before. It has been Walter Scott who, perhaps more than any other writer, has drawn on Edinburgh's history for his writing and done most to popularise the Castle in the public imagination.

Eric Linklater (1899–1974), who was posted to the Castle to join the Reserve Battalion of the Black Watch, after being wounded during the First World War, has written widely about it both in his book on Edinburgh and in several of his novels. In *The Impregnable Women* (1938) the Castle is occupied by women determined to stop the Second World War, while in *Magnus Merriman* (1934), an autobiographical story of politics and literary intrigue in the Scotland of the 1930s with its mischievous portrayal of Hugh MacDiarmid as Hugh Skene, he gives a lyrical description of it:

> It is a castle of moods, now merely antiquated, now
> impregnable, now the work of giants and now of dreams; a
> fairy castle, a haunted castle, a castle in Spain … it has heard
> the cry of Flodden, the travail of queens, the iron scuffle of
> armour . . . it is Scotland's castle, Queen Mary's castle and the
> castle of fifty thousand annual visitors who walk through it
> with rain on their boots and bewilderment in their hearts.[6]

A number of Linklater's books or short stories have an Edinburgh setting. His story 'Kind Kitty', inspired by a poem of William Dunbar, concerns an old woman in the Edinburgh slums of the 1930s, while perhaps his most popular 'Joy as it Flies' also has some Edinburgh scenes. His satirical novel *The Merry Muse* (1959) revolves around the discovery of sixteen hitherto unknown erotic poems by Robert Burns, and the effect this find has on a cross-section of the capital's citizens.

Linklater noted that it was while drilling on the Castle Esplanade that his love for Edinburgh was first nurtured. Nowadays the best known drilling takes place there for the August Military Tattoo. Huge stands suddenly fill the expanse, overhanging precariously the gardens below, while the skirl of pipes can be heard wafting through the night air. Several novels have at their centre plots to blow up the Tattoo such as Angus Ross's *The Edinburgh Exercise* and Owen John's *Festival.* The latter has a splendid description of a tattoo:

> At that moment a great roar came from the Esplanade; the
> crowd clapped and cheered, then silence fell over the
> Esplanade. … A line of soldiers stood to attention. In a
> sudden brilliant flash the bugles went to their mouths. A
> hush fell over the arena, all eyes turned towards the great,
> curved bastion.
>
> The buglers sounded a magnificent fanfare, which
> reached out from the Castle over the ancient city. In perfect
> unison the bugles filled the night with their call. Then they
> stopped. The lights went out. There was darkness. The
> fanfare was over. The crowds burst into enthusiastic clapping.
> The Military Tattoo had started.[7]

In July 2005, the Castle's Great Hall became 'Castle Potter' for the publisher Bloomsbury's launch of J K Rowling's *Harry Potter and the Half-Blood Prince*.

ALLAN RAMSAY

Leaving the Esplanade one comes to the Outlook Tower and a steep lane which leads to Ramsay Garden. Rebuilt in the 1890s by the town planner Sir Patrick Geddes, the tall narrow flats, with their cross-slipped gables, are a familiar Edinburgh landmark and it is well worth the detour to see the attractive window-box displays and cast-iron staircases.

In 1738 the poet Allan Ramsay (1685-1758) built himself a retirement home here, which he called Ramsay Lodge, but which quickly became known as the 'Goose Pie' because of its octagonal shape. Ramsay, one of the most important literary figures in the city's history, came to Edinburgh in his teens to be apprenticed to a wig-maker. In 1712 he opened his own wig shop in the Grassmarket and helped found the Easy Club which met to discuss literary and political matters.

His first collection of poetry, the best of them in Scots and celebrating his love of Edinburgh's low life, and in particular the taverns and brothels of the High Street, was published in 1721. This collection and the five volumes of his pioneering anthology of Scots songs and ballads, *The Tea-Table Miscellany* (1724-37), and *The Evergreen* (1724), a selection of medieval Scots poems, did much to restore interest in an earlier Scottish literary tradition and led to the eighteenth-century literary revival of the Scots tongue.

By this time Ramsay had abandoned wig-making for a career as a bookseller and publisher, and in 1725 he opened what is generally understood to be the first lending library in Britain at premises in the Luckenbooths on the High Street. Eleven years later he opened the first theatre in Edinburgh in Carrubber's Close, off the High Street, but this was quickly closed by the city authorities who disapproved of the enterprise. As a result it was many years before a theatrical tradition was established in a city now renowned for its International Festival. Ramsay's own verse drama, *The Gentle Shepherd* (1725), which is sometimes compared to John Gay's *The Beggar's Opera*, was adapted by Robert Kemp for the 1949 Festival.

Ramsay spent the last fifteen years of his life at the 'Goose Pie' and on his death it passed to his son, the portrait painter Allan Ramsay. Later occupants included the writers Ann Grant of Laggan (1755–1838), best known for her reminiscences of Highland life, *Letters from the Mountains* (1803), and John Galt (1779–1839), whose *Annals of the Parish* (1821) provides a picture of Ayrshire rural life that was rapidly vanishing.

THE ROYAL MILE

Returning up Ramsay Lane one comes to the top of the Royal Mile, which in fact consists of several linked streets Castle Hill, Lawnmarket, High Street, Canongate and Abbey Strand and is so named because the distance between the Castle and the Royal Palace of Holyrood is just over a mile. Daniel Defoe, who spent several years in the city as a journalist, called it 'the largest, longest and finest street for Buildings and Number of Inhabitants, not in Britain only, but in the World', a view shared by the English traveller, Edward Topham, in his *Letters from Edinburgh* in 1774.

As the population of Edinburgh grew, shortage of space within the city walls meant that the houses or tenements became increasingly taller, giving the High Street its distinct appearance. This shortage of space also led to the various social groups living in close proximity, and even on top of each other, with the result that not only was Edinburgh the first city with multi-storey flats but from its beginnings one where the social classes mixed.

The central figure in William Boyd's novel *The New Confessions* (1987), John James Todd, was brought up in one of these tenements at the beginning of the twentieth century:

> Some of these old buildings contained up to twenty
> apartments, some small, some grand. Ours was one of the
> latter; I think at one stage two had been knocked into one.
> There was a large drawing room, a library, a dining room, six
> bedrooms and a bathroom. A large kitchen with a pantry, a
> scullery, and a sleeping closet constituted the servant's

quarters. There had been buildings on this site since the fifteenth century. From time to time they had fallen or burnt down and new dwellings had been constructed on the ruins. The architecture on the High Street had the character of an antiquated, stone shanty town. Houses had grown piecemeal, by accretion and alteration. Windows were all sizes – actually a pleasing diversity – and installing water closets and modern plumbing required real ingenuity.[8]

JAMES COURT

A few yards down the High Street on the north side is a narrow passage which leads into James Court, one of the last additions to the Old Town. An open square built between 1723 and 1727, much of it was destroyed by a fire in 1857. The philosopher David Hume (1711–76) lived in the court, most probably on the third floor of the western block. Hume was born in Edinburgh and briefly studied law at the University; finding it 'nauseous' he turned to a wider course of reading to prepare himself, as he put it, to be 'a Scholar and Philosopher'. In 1734 he left for London and then Paris where he wrote perhaps his best-known book, A *Treatise on Human Nature* (1739), in which he first advanced his arguments about the importance of reason.

After several diplomatic posts abroad, Hume returned to Edinburgh in 1751 as librarian to the Faculty of Advocates, living first at 322 High Street and then Jack's Land renumbered as 229 Canongate, both premises situated further down the High Street. He was a founding member with the artist Allan Ramsay and Adam Smith of the Select Society of a debating society which met in the Advocates Library and whose membership grew to include most of the leading literary figures of the Scottish Enlightenment.

His final address in the city was at the corner of St Andrew Square and South St David Street where he died in 1776. He is commemorated by a monument in the Old Calton Burying Ground and by the University's David Hume Tower, ironic given that he was passed over for the Chair of Moral Philosophy there in 1744 on account of his religious scepticism.

In turn Hume rented his flat in James Square, then a prestigious Edinburgh address, to James Boswell (1740–95). Though Boswell had been born and educated in Edinburgh and practised for seventeen years at the Scottish Bar, he made frequent visits to London to pursue his literary and political ambitions and it was there in 1763 he met Samuel Johnson, with whose name he has now became inextricably linked through his *Journal of a Tour to the Hebrides* (1785) and *Life of Samuel Johnson* (1791). It was at James Square that Boswell entertained Samuel Johnson (1709–84) on the Doctor's famous visit to Edinburgh in 1773 en route for the Western Isles.[9]

Johnson's initial impression seems to have been of the filthiness of the city, a concern shared by many visitors. He complained he could smell Boswell in the dark and his biographer relates how on arrival Johnson had asked for his lemonade to be sweetened, whereupon the waiter 'lifted a lump of sugar with his greasy fingers' and put it in the drink. The outraged Doctor threw the offending drink out of the window. The practice of discarding one's waste was not unique to Johnson. The cry of 'Gardyloo', a corruption of the French 'Garde l'eau', was often to be heard as slops were hurled from the tenement windows to the streets below and later became the name of Edinburgh's sewage ship.

DANIEL DEFOE

The city's dirtiness was one of the principal memories of Daniel Defoe (1660–1731), who had been sent to Edinburgh to report on Scottish attitudes to the 1707 Act of Union and who in his *A Tour Through the Whole Island of Great Britain* (1727) gives one of the best contemporary accounts of Edinburgh and its citizens:

> The City suffers infinite Disadvantages, and lies under such
> scandalous Inconveniences as are, by its Enemies, made a
> Subject of Scorn and Reproach; as if the People were not as
> willing to live sweet and clean as other Nations, but delighted
> in Stench and Nastiness: whereas, were any other People to
> live under the same Unhappiness, I mean as well of a rocky

and mountainous Situation, throng'd Buildings, from seven to ten or twelve storey high, a Scarcity of Water, and that little they have difficult to be had, and to the uppermost Lodgings, far to fetch; we should find a London or a Bristol as dirty as Edinburgh, and, perhaps, less able to make their Dwelling tolerable, at least in so narrow a Compass; for, tho' many cities have more People in them, yet, I believe, this may be said with Truth, that in no City in the World so many people live in so little Room as at Edinburgh.[10]

LADY STAIR'S CLOSE

James Court leads into Lady Stair's Close, named after Elizabeth Dowager Countess of Stair, a leader of Edinburgh Society in the seventeenth century and noted for being the first person in the city to keep a black servant. However, it is with her daughter-in-law Eleanor that the Close is most clearly associated. Eleanor's first husband was Lord Primrose, who so ill-treated both her and their four children that when it was discovered he was forced to flee the country. One day Eleanor consulted a foreign fortune-teller and is supposed to have seen in a mirror that Primrose had married bigamously. As she watched she saw her brother enter and draw his sword to prevent the marriage, whereupon the vision faded. Soon after her brother confirmed that what she had seen was true. The story made a strong impression on Sir Walter Scott who used it as the basis of his story 'My Aunt Margaret's Mirror'.

On the death of Primrose in 1706 she resolved not to marry again though still a young and attractive woman. The Earl of Stair declined to accept her refusals of marriage, and when all persuasion failed he secreted himself in her house, and showed himself half-dressed at her window in the morning. How far this slur to her reputation affected her decision is not known, but she married him shortly afterwards.

A plaque at the entrance to the Close commemorates the first visit to Edinburgh of Robert Burns (1759–96) in November 1786 drawn by the excellent reviews of his first collection, *Poems Chiefly in the Scottish Dialect*, published in Kilmarnock three months earlier. He stayed in lodgings kept by a Mrs Carfrae, 'a staid sober piously-disposed skuldudery-abhoring widow', in what was then Baxter's Close and now corresponds to the east side of Lady Stair's Close.

This first visit failed to secure a patron but Burns returned the following year with an introduction to the Earl of Glencairn, who persuaded the Caledonian Hunt to subscribe one hundred copies of an Edinburgh edition, for which Burns was paid one hundred guineas for the copyright. The Edinburgh edition includes his 'Address to Edinburgh':

> Edina! Scotia's darling seat,
> All hail thy palaces and tow'rs,
> Where once, beneath a Monarch's feet,
> Sat Legislation's sov'reign pow'rs.

It is perhaps fitting, given all these literary associations, that Wardrop's Court, off Lady Stair's Close, should now house a museum devoted to probably the three most important writers connected with Edinburgh – Robert Burns, Walter Scott and Robert Louis Stevenson.

In 1998 the area outside was designated as Makar's Court, where seventeen flagstones commemorate Scottish writers including John Buchan, Iain Crichton Smith, Naomi Mitchison and Sorley Maclean, and in 2002 the poet and playwright Stewart Conn (1936–) was appointed for a three-year term as the capital's first poet laureate, to be known as the Edinburgh Makar, with the responsibility of promoting the city's literary connections and the work of current writers. A former Head of Radio Drama at BBC Scotland and the author of several plays premiered at Edinburgh's Royal Lyceum Theatre, Conn has written numerous poems about Edinburgh, where he has lived since the 1970s.

DEACON BRODIE

Deacon Brodie (1741–88), one of Edinburgh's best known characters, lived in Brodie's Court, named after his father Francis Brodie. His house has now gone, and the nearest memorial is Deacon Brodie's Tavern opposite, at 435 Lawnmarket, where there is a life-size figure of Brodie beneath the stairway connecting the two bars. William Brodie was by day a respected cabinet-maker and locksmith and member of the Town Council, but at night could generally be found at the nearby Cape Club in Craig's Close or James Clarke's Tavern at the head of Fleshmarket Close where he would drink, gamble and indulge his mistresses.

Such pursuits did not come cheap and in 1786 he decided to turn to a life of crime. For two years he was responsible for a series of robberies around Edinburgh until in March 1788 he, and his accomplices, were surprised while attempting to break into the General Excise Office for Scotland in Chessel's Court. They managed to escape, Brodie making his way south to Dover and Amsterdam. However, he was betrayed when one of his colleagues turned King's Evidence and was traced through letters he had sent to his mistress. He was brought back, tried by Lord Braxfield – the inspiration for Stevenson's Weir of Hermiston – and executed that October near to St Giles on a gallows of his own design.

Stevenson was fascinated by him and wrote a play with W. E. Henley called *Deacon Brodie or The Double Life* (1880), while Muriel Spark in *The Prime of Miss Jean Brodie* (1961) makes her central character, a woman herself torn between her repressed nature and romantic longings, a direct descendant of the cabinet-maker. G.K. Chesterton has argued convincingly that Stevenson's *The Strange Case of Dr Jekyll and Mr Hyde* (1886) owes more to Edinburgh than its ostensible setting of London.[11]

GEORGE IV BRIDGE

On George IV Bridge, off the Lawnmarket, are Edinburgh's main lending library, the Central Library, and opposite it the National Library of Scotland, one of the United Kingdom's five copyright libraries. One of Edinburgh's earliest literary taverns, Johnnie Dowie's, supposedly frequented by amongst others Allan Ramsay and Robert Fergusson, was reputedly on this site.

PARLIAMENT SQUARE

Matthew Bramble writing to Dr Lewis in Tobias Smollett's *The Expedition of Humphrey Clinker* (1771) noted:

> All the people of business at Edinburgh, and even the genteel
> company, may be seen standing in crowds every day, from
> one or two in the afternoon, in the open street, at a place
> where formerly stood a market-cross, which (by the bye) was
> a curious piece of Gothic architecture . . .[12]

This was the Mercat Cross where bankrupts were brought, merchants met and crowds gathered to hear the news and exchange gossip. It was also for a time the place of execution. According to the legend preserved in Sir Walter Scott's poem *Marmion,* it was at the Mercat Cross that the names of those doomed at the Battle of Flodden (1513) were given, even before news of the defeat was brought to the citizens of Edinburgh.

Parliament Hall is entered by the doorway on the south side of Parliament Square. It is an impressive sight: 122ft long, 49ft wide with a 60ft roof of dark oaken beams with cross-braces and hammer-beams resting on curiously carved corbels. Apart from Mondays it is filled with advocates in their gowns and wigs pacing its length in consultation either with clients or their solicitors. A statue of Sir Walter Scott, an advocate and Clerk of the Court of Session between 1806 and 1830, looks benignly down on the proceedings. Thomas Carlyle on his first visit to Edinburgh in November 1809 was noticeably struck by it:

> An immense Hall, dimly lighted from the top of the walls, and
> perhaps with candles burning in it here and there; all in strange
> 'chiaroscuro', and filled with what I thought (exaggeratively) a
> thousand or two of human creatures; all astir in a boundless
> buzz of talk, and simmering about in every direction, some
> solitary, some in groups. By degrees I noticed that some were
> in wig and black gown, some not, but in common clothes, all
> well-dressed; that here and there on the sides of the Hall, were
> little thrones with enclosures, and steps leading up; red-velvet
> figures sitting in said thrones, and the black-gowned eagerly
> speaking to them, – Advocates pleading to Judges, as I easily
> understood. How they could be heard in such a grinding din
> was somewhat a mystery. Higher up on the walls, stuck there
> like swallows in their nests, sat other humbler figures: these I

found were the sources of certain wildly plangent lamentable kinds of sounds or echoes which from time to time pierced the universal noise of feet and voices, and rose unintelligibly above it, as if in the bitterness of incurable woe; – Criers of the Court, I gradually came to understand.[13]

Stevenson who had spent many unhappy hours there, while training to be a lawyer, was less complimentary:

A pair of swing doors gives admittance to a hall with a carved roof, hung with legal portraits, adorned with legal statuary, lighted by windows of painted glass, and warmed by three vast fires. This is the 'Salle des pas perdus' of the Scottish Bar. Here, by a ferocious custom, idle youths must promenade from ten till two. From end to end, singly or in pairs or trios, the gowns and wigs go back and forward. Through a hum of talk and footfalls, the piping tones of a Macer announce a fresh cause and call upon the names of those concerned. Intelligent men have been walking here daily for ten or twenty years without a rag of business or a shilling of reward . . .[14]

Stevenson had qualified as a lawyer at the insistence of his father, who felt he should have some qualification to fall back on if his writing did not prosper. The experience was not wasted for many of Stevenson's characters are lawyers: Prestongrange, Rankeillor, Stewart, Utterson, Mr Johnstone Thomas WS and the 'hanging judge' Weir.

The law plays an important part in Edinburgh life and there is a long tradition of lawyers also being Men of Letters. Lawyers often worked for only six months of the year and Henry Cockburn, himself a judge and journalist, thought it was 'this abstraction from legal business that has given Scotland the greater part of literature that has adorned her. The lawyers have been the most intellectual class in the country.'

Writers with strong legal connections include James Boswell, David Hume, Walter Scott, Francis Jeffrey, founder of *The Edinburgh Review* and Lord Advocate, and another Lord Advocate Sir George Mackenzie (1636–91), who is credited with writing the first novel published in

Scotland, *Aretina* (1660), a pastoral romance set in Egypt. Many of Scott's novels have scenes set around the law courts, a tradition continued to this day in novels such as *The Justice-Clerk* by W. D. Lyell, *A Judge of Men* by James Allan Ford (himself a former Registrar General for Scotland) and *The Hermitage* by Magda Sweetland.[15]

ST GILES

The western side of the quadrangle is occupied in all its length by the church of St Giles's which in the later times of Scottish Episcopacy possessed the dignity of a Cathedral, and which, indeed, has been the scene of many of the most remarkable incidents in the ecclesiastical history of Scotland. In its general exterior, this church presents by no means a fine specimen of the Gothic architecture, although there are several individual parts about the structure which display great beauty – the tower above all which rises out of the centre of the pile, and is capped with a very rich and splendid canopy in the shape of a Crown Imperial. This beautiful tower and canopy form a fine point in almost every view of the city of Edinburgh; but the effect of the whole building, when one hears and thinks of it as a Cathedral, is a thing of no great significance.[16]

The history of the High Kirk of St Giles can be traced back to the twelfth century, though the church itself has been considerably rebuilt over the centuries, with a final restoration in the 1870s.

The Provost between 1503 and 1515 was Gavin Douglas (1476–1522), best known for his loose translation of the *Aeneid* into Middle Scots which did much to widen the usage of Scots and introduce a wider audience to Virgil. Each of the books is prefaced by a prologue with original poetry by Douglas, that to Book VII containing a timeless description of an Edinburgh winter:

Bewte was lost, and barrand schew the landis,
With frostis hair ourfret the feldis standis,
Seir bittir bubbis and the schowris snell
Smyt on the sward a symylitude of hell,
Reducying to our mynd, in every sted
Gousty scaddois of eild and grisly ded.

There are a number of literary memorials inside the High Kirk. Beneath the oriel window in the west wall is a large memorial bronze to Stevenson by Augustus St Gaudens which pays tribute to Stevenson's 'spirit of mirth, courage and love' and quotes his 'Requiem' with its concluding words:

> Here he lies where he longed to be;
> Home is the sailor, home from sea;
> And the hunter home from the hill.

In the original version of the memorial the right hand holds a cigarette, but a pen was thought more appropriate in a church. The central west window, designed by Leifur Breidfjord, a former student at the Edinburgh College of Art, was dedicated in 1985 as a tribute to Robert Burns.

Muriel Spark in *The Prime of Miss Jean Brodie* uses St Giles to personify the Scots' former preoccupation with the Calvinist theory of the Elect. Sandy, the only girl to eventually see through Jean Brodie's division of the world into the *crème de la crème* and the rest, is frightened by St Giles:

> With its tattered blood-stained banners of the past. Sandy
> had not been there, and did not want to go. The outskirts of
> old Edinburgh churches frightened her, they were of such
> dark stone, like presences against the colour of the castle rock,
> and were built so warningly with their upraised fingers.[17]

Another passage spells out more clearly what Calvinism means:

> Fully to savour her position, Sandy would go and stand
> outside St Giles Cathedral or the Tolbooth, and contemplate
> these emblems of a dark and terrible salvation which made
> the fires of the damned seem very merry to the imagination
> by contrast, and much preferable. Nobody in her life, at
> home or at school, had ever spoken of Calvinism except as a
> joke that had once been taken seriously.[18]

A heart-shaped pattern of cobblestones known as the Heart of Midlothian next to St Giles marks the position of the doorway of the Tolbooth. Consisting of three buildings, the first of which was built in the mid-fifteenth century, it served in turn as the meeting place of the Scots Parliament, the Town Hall, chambers for the Privy Council and as the College of Justice. In 1640 it became a gaol for debtors and criminals,and among those imprisoned there were the rebels of the first Jacobite Rising in 1715. In 1817 the gaol was pulled down to be replaced by a new one on Calton Hill. The prison's heavy wooden door was presented to Scott, and can still be seen at his house, Abbotsford, in the Scottish Borders.

The opening chapters of Scott's *The Heart of Midlothian* (1818) centre around the Tollbooth, while in *Ringan Gilhaize* (1823), his contemporary John Galt (1779–1839) has a graphic description of the horrors the Covenanters experienced in the Tolbooth.

> It was a foul and unwholesome den: many of the guiltless
> inmates were so wasted that they were rather like frightful
> effigies of death than living men. Their skins were sinews
> in a manner very awful to see. Their eyes were vivid with
> a strange distemperature, and there was a charnel-house
> anatomy in the melancholy with which they welcomed a
> new brother in affliction, that made me feel, when I
> entered among them, as if I had come into the dark
> abode of spectres, and manes, and dismal shadows.[19]

Galt is increasingly being recognised as one of the best novelists of the early nineteenth century and much of his work has been reissued in recent years. Combining a career as a businessmen with writing, he wrote over forty books between 1812 and his death, many of them dealing with the major social, political and economic issues of his day.

Until their removal at the same time as that of the Tolbooth, much of the local trade was conducted in a series of timber-fronted tenements of up to six storeys that stretched along the north wall of St Giles. Matthew Bramble in *The Expedition of Humphrey Clinker* thought the High Street:

> would be undoubtedly one of the noblest streets in Europe, if
> an ugly mass of mean buildings, called the Lucken-Booths,
> had not thrust itself, by what accident I know not, into the
> middle of the way . . .[20]

This view was shared by Scott in his famous description of the Luckenbooths in *The Heart of Midlothian*:

> For some inconceivable reason, our ancestors had jammed
> into the middle of the principal street of the town, leaving for
> passage a narrow street on the north, and on the south, into
> which the prison opens, a narrow crooked lane, winding
> between the high and sombre walls of the Tolbooth and of
> the adjacent houses on one side, and the buttresses and
> projections of the Old Church upon the other. To give some
> gaity to this sombre passage (well known by the name of the
> Krames), a number of little booths or shops, after the fashion
> of cobblers' stalls, are plastered as it were against the Gothic
> projectments and abutments, so that it seemed as if the
> traders had occupied with nests bearing the same proportion
> to the building, every buttress and coign of vantage, as the
> martlet did in Macbeth's Castle. Of later years these booths
> have degenerated into mere toy shops . . . but at the time of
> which we write, hosiers, glovers, hatters, mercers, milliners,
> and all who dealt in the miscellaneous wares now termed
> "haberdashers' goods", were to be found in the narrow alley.[21]

Balfour, in Stevenson's *Catriona*, visits the Luckenbooths to be fitted out so 'that servants should respect me'.

Allan Ramsay had his bookshop on the first floor of the eastern Luckenbooths and it was there John Gay would sit watching the passers-by during his visit to Edinburgh in 1732. Below Ramsay were the premises of another bookseller and publisher, William Creech (1745–1815). Creech had served on the jury in the trial of Deacon Brodie and in 1811 became Lord Provost, but he is now largely remembered as a literary figure. While a student at Edinburgh University he founded the Speculative Society, which met for 'improvement in Literary Composition and Public Speaking', and which to this day has attracted to its membership most of the literary figures connected with Edinburgh. He printed many of the leading periodicals of time, wrote for a number of newspapers and was renowned for his literary salons at his home in nearby Craig's Close, known as 'Creech's Levee', while his shop was:

> the natural resort of lawyers, authors and all sorts of
> literary idlers who were always buzzing about the convenient
> hive. All who wished to see a poet or a stranger or to hear
> the public news, the last joke by Erskine, or yesterday's
> occurrence in the Parliament House, or to get the
> publications of the day, congregated there; lawyers,
> doctors, clergymen and authors.[22]

Creech published the Edinburgh edition of Burns's poetry – he was a close friend of the Earl of Glencairn – and initially relations between publisher and poet were cordial. When Creech had to go to London on business in 1787 Burns wrote a poem 'To William Creech' recording Edinburgh's sadness at the loss of 'her darling bird that she lo'es best – Willie's awa'. The poet soon grew exasperated, however, when he realised he had sold the copyright to Creech who took all the earnings and Burns' attitude changed:

> A little, upright, pert, tart, tripping wight
> And still his precious self his dear delight;
> Who loves his own smart shadow in the streets
> Better than e'er the faiest she he meets.

MARY KING'S CLOSE

Almost directly opposite St Giles was Mary King's Close and the scene of one of Edinburgh's best known tales. All twenty-seven families living there were killed by the plague of 1645 and, as was the custom, the close was sealed off, even while the victims lay dying. It soon gained a reputation for being haunted, even after the Royal Exchange was built on the site, and features as a murder scene in Ian Rankin's *Mortal Causes* (1994) and Iain Banks's *Complicity* (1993).[23]

ANCHOR CLOSE

A favourite haunt of Burns, during his visits to Edinburgh, was Dawney Douglas's Anchor Tavern in Anchor Close. This was the home of the Crochallan Fencibles, a celebrated drinking club founded by the printer William Smellie (1740–95), whose members read like a roll-call of the Scottish Enlightenment: Adam Smith, Adam Ferguson and Henry Mackenzie. Burns wrote his collection of bawdy lyrics, later published surreptitiously as *The Merry Muses of Caledonia,* for the Crochallans and his song 'Rattling, Roaring Willie' for the club's president William Dunbar.

It was Smellie, a sober printer by day but rabble-rouser by night, who introduced Burns to the Club and a world far removed from the Edinburgh drawing rooms the ploughman poet had hitherto experienced, and for this Burns seemed grateful. He wrote warmly of his host:

> Shrewd Willie Smellie to Crochallan came;
> The old cock'd hat, the grey surtout, the same;
> His bristling beard just rising in its might,
> Twas four long nights and days to shaving night;
> His uncomb'd grizzly locks, wild staring, thatch'd;
> A head for thought profound and clear, unmatch'd;
> Yet tho' his caustic wit was biting-rude,
> His heart was warm, benevolent and good.

Smellie made an important contribution to the Scottish Enlightenment, not least as the editor of the *Encyclopaedia Britannica* for which he wrote most of the entries. A founder-member of the Society of Antiquaries in 1780, he assisted in the preparation of the first statistical account of Scotland, was a regular contributor on literary and scientific subjects to the journals of his day and his memoirs *Literary and Characteristic Lives* (1800) give a wonderfully anecdotal picture of the Edinburgh of the Scottish Enlightenment.

CRAIG'S CLOSE

Craig's Close, on the north side of the High Street, has always had strong associations with the printing and publishing industries. During the reign of King James VI of Scotland the Scottish printer Andro Hart, best known for his edition of the Bible and *Psalms in Scottish Meter*, lived and carried out his business there and later Daniel Defoe is supposed to have lived there.

This part of the Royal Mile, with its warren of narrow alleys, cavernous walls stretching endlessly above one and the lingering smell of urine, has changed little. While some tenements have been restored as bijou flats, it is still an area of small bars much as Eric Linklater's eponymous hero Magnus Merriman must have known it in the 1930s:

> Like a great battlement the north side of the High Street
> confronted them. From their lower level a long flight of steps
> led upwards, a narrow passage between black walls whose
> farther end was invisible, and on whose middle distance a
> lamp shone dimly. Here and there on the steps, obscurely
> seen, were vague figures. Under the lamp, with harsh voice
> and combative gestures, two men were quarrelling. Another,
> oblivious to them and perhaps to all the world, leaned against
> the wall with drooping head. From the high remote darkness
> of the passage came the shrill sound of a woman laughing,
> and from the tavern whose door the lamp lighted there
> issued, muffled by the walls, the multifarious sound of talk
> and argument and rival songs.[24]

Close to both College Wynd and Old Assembly Close is the Tron Church, which took its name from its proximity to the old public weighing-beam, the Salt Tron. Traditionally the Tron Church was the spot to see in the New Year ('Hogmanay') and from which the revellers departed to first-foot, the Scottish practice of visiting friends immediately after midnight on 31 December. Founded in 1637 to house a congregation displaced from St Giles when the latter became an Episcopalian place of worship, it was destroyed by fire in 1824. Henry Cockburn, who watched the fire, gives a dramatic description in his *Memorials of His Time*:

> An alarm was given that the Tron Church was on fire. We ran out from the Court, gowned and wigged and saw that it was the steeple, an old Dutch thing composed of wood, iron and lead and edged all the way up with bits of ornament. Some of the sparks of the proceeding night had nestled in it, and had at last blown its dry bones into flame. There could not be a more beautiful firework . . .[25]

Robert Fergusson found the clamour of the Tron's bell so loud he felt it must be a trick of the devil:

> Wanwordy, crazy dinsome thing
> As e'er was fram'd to jow or ring,
> What gar'd them sic in steeple hing
> They ken themsel'.
> But weel wat I they coudna bring
> Waur sounds frae hell.
>
> Fleece merchants may look baul' I trow,
> Sin' a' Auld Reekie's childer now
> Maun stap their lugs wi' teats o' woo,
> They sound to bang,
> And keep it frae gawn thro' and thro'
> Wi' jarrin twang.

O! were I provost o' the town,
I swear by a' the pow'rs aboon,
I'd bring ye wi' a reesle down;
Nor should you think
(Sae sair I'd crack an' clour your crown)
Again to clink.

ROBERT FERGUSSON

Fergusson (1750–74), who was born opposite the Tron, in Cap and Feather Close (destroyed when the North Bridge was built), is regarded, arguably, as Edinburgh's greatest poet. In his poems, 'Auld Reekie', the first part of a planned comedy of Edinburgh life, 'Caller Oysters', 'Leith Races', 'The Rising of the Session' and the quoted 'To the Tron Kirk Bell', he gives a marvellous picture of life in the city during the mid-eighteenth century ranging from the taverns of the High Street and the legal world to the Leith Races and All-Hallows Fair.

Educated at the Royal High School, Fergusson became a Divinity student at St Andrews University. The death of his father forced him to abandon his studies and to begin work as a clerk, but he also wrote in his spare time. He first appeared as a poet with verses in English – correct and rather uninspired – in 1771 in the *Weekly Magazine and Edinburgh Amusement*, but in 'The Daft-Days', which the same periodical published a year later, Fergusson wrote in Scots, imaginatively and amusingly, and over the next two years revitalised the Scots tradition of verse. Prone to bouts of depression and rendered destitute by being unable to work, he was committed to an asylum where he died at the age of twenty-four. He is buried in the Canongate Churchyard.

Though his life was short and his output small, Fergusson had a considerable literary influence, not least on Burns, and his reputation has continued to grow in this century, particularly among the poets of the Scots Literary Renaissance. Sydney Goodsir Smith edited a collection of essays to mark the bicentenary of his birth with contributions from Hugh MacDiarmid and Robert Garioch while Ann Smith's one-act play *A Vision of Angels* was produced to mark the bicentenary of his death.

TWEEDDALE COURT
AND JOHN KNOX'S HOUSE

Tweeddale Court takes its name from the town mansion of the Marquess of that name. Daniel Defoe on his tour in 1724 was struck by a 'plantation of lime-trees behind it, the place not allowing room for a large garden'. It is difficult to imagine now, but later its gardens extended to the Cowgate. The Court now houses the offices of Canongate Books and for a time the headquarters of the Saltire Society, which campaigns for a greater awareness of Scottish culture, were there (now in Fountain Close, at 22 High Street), and the Scottish Poetry Library, now at 5 Crichton's Close in the Canongate.

Beyond Moubray House jutting into the High Street stands John Knox's House, with its unmistakable gables and outside stair. Knox (c.1513–72), one of the most important figures of the Reformation and the moral and spiritual leader of the Protestant revolt in Scotland, possibly lived here while he was minister of St Giles between 1559 and his death in 1572. Born in Haddington he lived abroad until 1559, during which time he spent two years as a French galley slave and four years as a minister in Frankfurt and Geneva. It was in Geneva he met the reformer John Calvin and there he formulated many of the doctrines, such as original sin, predestination and the elect, that would form the basis of Scottish Presbyterianism.

THE CANONGATE

The stretch of the Royal Mile from the top of St Mary's Street to Holyrood is called the Canongate, or more exactly the Canongate of the Order of St Augustine. Until 1856 this was a separate burgh and a refuge for those in debt. Running south off the Canongate is St Mary's Street. A plaque at No. 26 marks the site of Boyd's Inn where Dr Johnson stayed in 1773. Behind it is Chessels Court which for a time housed the Excise Office, where Deacon Brodie attempted his last burglary.

The street poet and storyteller James Smith (1824–87), now best known for his song-lyric 'The Cries of Edinburgh', an evocation of the life of the Old Town over the course of a year, was born in St Mary's

Street. A modern adaptation of one of his stories, 'Nancy Sleekit', was staged at the Netherbow Theatre at the 1994 Edinburgh Festival.

OLD PLAYHOUSE CLOSE

A little further down the Canongate, opposite New Street, is Old Playhouse Close which between 1747 and 1769 was the site of the Playhouse Theatre. A plaque records that it was here that John Home's play *Douglas* was first performed in 1756. Though now rarely performed, *Douglas* is important in any literary history of Edinburgh for it marked a stage in the development of a Scottish national drama and finally broke the taboos surrounding the theatre which had hampered Allan Ramsay's efforts some twenty years earlier in the neighbouring Carrubber's Close.

Home (1722–1808) was born in Leith and educated at Edinburgh University, where he was a friend of Adam Fergusson and William Robertson. He fought on the government side during the Jacobite Rebellion of 1745, was captured at the Battle of Falkirk and imprisoned in Doune Castle. After his release he became a minister in East Lothian but continued with his efforts to become a playwright. The first performance of *Douglas* proved to be a great success and provoked from a member of the audience the often quoted cry 'Whaur's yer Wullie Shakespeare noo?' The Church, however, took exception to a minister writing for the stage and Home was forced to resign his ministry.

Alexander 'Jupiter' Carlyle (1722–1805), himself a minister near Musselburgh, evokes the furore in his *Autobiography* (1860), an important chronicle of the Enlightenment:

> The play had unbounded success for a great many nights in
> Edinburgh, and was attended by all the literati and most of
> the judges, who, except one or two, had not been in use to
> attend the theatre. The town in general was in an uproar of
> exultation that a Scotchman had written a tragedy of the first
> rate, and that its merit was first submitted to their judgment.
> There were a few opposers, however, among those who
> pretended to taste and literature, who endeavoured to cry
> down the performance in libellous pamphlets and ballads (for

they durst not attempt to oppose it in the theatre itself), and they were openly countenanced by Robert Dundas of Arniston, at that time Lord Advocate, and all his minions and expectants. The High-flying set were unanimous against it, as they thought it a sin for a clergyman to write a play, let it be ever so moral in its tendency.[26]

The play was performed the following year in London by David Garrick, where it eventually became part of Sarah Siddons's repertoire and gave Charles Kean his debut role in 1827. Home wrote several more plays for Garrick and the two became so friendly Home was twice chosen as Garrick's second in two unfought duels. After the performance of *Douglas,* theatres were licensed and it is a sign of how it changed attitudes that the nearby Netherbow Arts Centre is run by the Church of Scotland.

ST JOHN'S STREET

Further down on the south side is St John's Street, once one of the most aristocratic quarters in Edinburgh. This was where Tobias Smollett (1721–71), the author of *Roderick Random* and *Peregrine Pickle,* stayed, at what is now No. 22, in the summer of 1766 while writing *The Expedition of Humphrey Clinker* (1771). This, his best loved novel, is told in epistolary form as a group of travellers journey through Britain and has numerous scenes around Edinburgh and many references to real people. The party visit Holyrood ('an elegant piece of architecture, but sunk in an obscure, and as I take it, unwholesome bottom'), the dancing assemblies and Leith races but the novel is most revealing in noting the existence of a Scottish national identity:

. . . they are far from being servile imitators of our modes and fashionable vices. All their customs and regulations of public and private economy, of business and diversion, are in their own stile. This remarkably predominates in their looks, their dress, and manner, their music, and even their cookery. Our 'squire declares, that he knows not another people upon earth, so strongly marked with a national character . . .[27]

One writer who more than any other did much to identify and romanticise this sense of being Scottish was Walter Scott, particularly in the Waverley novels. His printer, James Ballantyne, who was based at 10 St John's Street was one of the few people to know the true identity of their anonymous author. The two of them had been at Kelso Grammar School together and remained friends throughout their lives. James's nephew was to become the novelist R.M. Ballantyne, best known for his adventure story *Coral Island* (1858).

There is also a Burns connection with St John's Street. It was at the Canongate Kilwinning Lodge of Freemasons, which claims the oldest masonic chapel still in use in the world, that Burns was inducted a member in 1787, an occasion commemorated in a famous picture by William Stewart Watson.

THE CANONGATE KIRK

On the south side of the Canongate is Huntly House Museum, now home of the City Museum, while opposite is the unusual-looking Canongate Tolbooth. Next door and set back behind some railings is the Canongate Kirk. Built in 1688 to take the congregation ousted from the nave of Holyrood Abbey by James VII of Scotland and II of England when he converted it to a chapel for the Order of the Thistle, it was here in 1745 that Prince Charles Edward held prisoner captured English officers after the Battle of Prestonpans.

Among those buried in the churchyard, with its stunning views to Calton Hill and jumble of funerary monuments, are the economist Adam Smith (1723–90), who lived nearby in Panmure House for the last twelve years of his life; Mrs Agnes McLehose, better known as Burns's 'Clarinda'; and George Drummond, the 'father' of the New Town.

On the west side is the grave of Robert Fergusson. One of Burns's first actions on arriving in Edinburgh in the winter of 1786–7 was to arrange for a headstone for the pauper's grave. The simple inscription, which includes four lines by Burns, reads:

Here lies Robert Fergusson, poet
Born September 5th 1750

Died October 16th 1774
No sculptured Marble here nor pompous lay
No storied Urn nor animated Bust
This simple Stone directs Pale Scotia's way
To pour her Sorrows o'er her Poet's Dust

For Burns, Fergusson was 'My elder brother in Misfortune/By far my elder brother in the muse'. R. L. Stevenson, who was born exactly a hundred years after Fergusson, also felt a deep attachment to the poet:

Ah! What bonds we have – born in the same city; both
sickly, both pestered, one nearly to madness, one to the
madhouse, with a damnatory creed; both seeing the stars
and the dawn, and wearing shoe-leather on the same ancient
stones, under the same pends, down the same closes . . . You
will never know, nor will any man, how deep this feeling is:
I believe Fergusson lives in me.[28]

Robert Fergusson's grave continues to provide inspiration to new generations of writers. Robert Garioch unites Edinburgh's past and present in his 'At Robert Fergusson's Grave, October 1962':

Canongait kirkyaird in the failing year
is auld and grey, the wee roseirs are bare,
five gulls leam white agin the dirty air:
Why are they here? There's naething for them here.

Why are we oursels? We gaiter near
The grave. Fergussons mainly, quite a fair
Turn-out, respectful, ill at ease, we stare
At daith – there's an address – I canna hear.

Aweill, we staund bareheidit in the haar,
Mourning a man that gaed back til the pool
Twa-hunner year afore our time. The glaur
That haps his banes glowers back. Strang, present dool

Rugs at my hairt. Lichlie this gin ye daur:
Here Robert Burns knelt and kissed the mool.

In 2004 a statue to Fergusson, located immediately outside the Kirk, was unveiled at a ceremony marked by a specially written poem by the Edinburgh Makar, Stewart Conn.

WHITEFOORD HOUSE AND QUEENSBERRY HOUSE

Further down the Canongate is Whitefoord House. This was the town house of an early patron of Burns, Sir John Whitefoord, as well as being the home of the influential philosopher and biographer Dugald Stewart (1753–1828) between 1806 and 1812, before he moved to 7 Moray Place in the New Town. Stewart was a crucial figure in the Scottish Enlightenment for, though not an original thinker, he was a brilliant teacher who passed to his students the idea of a liberal culture. He was not without his faults, not least his failure to return books. Confessing to being weak at arithmetic an Edinburgh wit retorted that might be true but he was very good at book-keeping. It was Stewart who, after returning from a holiday in Ayrshire where he had met Burns, passed a copy of the Kilmarnock edition of the poems to the critic Henry Mackenzie. The result was the influential review in the *Lounger* which did so much to establish Burn's reputation.[29]

Directly opposite is Queensberry House, now part of the Scottish Parliament complex. Built in 1681 it remained in the Queensberry family between 1686 and 1801. John Gay (1685–1732), author of *The Beggar's Opera*, stayed there, while private secretary to the Duchess of Queensberry (Catherine, the wife of the 3rd Duke), after his sequel *Polly* was prohibited in 1729, because members of the government had been satirised in it. A plaque records that Jenny Ha's Change House, a tavern frequented by Gay and Allan Ramsay, was situated in front of Queensberry House from 1600 to 1857. The house is associated with a macabre tale. The eldest son of the second Duke, who, according to Robert Chambers in his *Traditions of Edinburgh* (1824), was 'an idiot of the most unhappy sort – rabid and gluttonous, and who grew early to an immense height', was left alone with a kitchen-hand on the day the Act of Union was confirmed in 1707. When his family returned from the celebrations they found he had killed the young boy, placed the body on the spit and eaten him. The story has inspired several writers, most recently Ian Rankin whose novel *Set in Darkness* (2000) begins with the discovery of a skeleton in Queensberry House.

Next door is the new Scottish Parliament Building. In Paul Johnston's futuristic political satire about an Edinburgh inflicted by drought, *Water of Death* (1999), the Council chamber for the new city administration is located at:

> what used to be the Scottish Parliament – as if that ever
> had much to do with open government, with its carefully
> selected party lists and craven protection of vested
> interests . . . No expense had been spared when the place
> was built on a site previously occupied by a brewery.
> Fluids of various kinds were apparently a major interest
> of the architect – it did rain a lot more then, I suppose.
> In addition to the boat design, there were pools of water
> placed inside and outside the structures to reflect the
> walls and sky . . . The Parliament chamber itself was
> decorated with as many native Scottish materials as the
> designers could think of – granite slabs, red sandstone
> facings, tapestries spun in the Outer Hebrides,
> chandeliers of Cairngorm quartz and the like.[30]

JAMES ROBERTSON

The Parliament's first writer-in-residence was the poet, novelist and short story writer James Robertson (1958–). Robertson's Edinburgh University doctorate was on Walter Scott and his knowledge of the writer and Scottish history has informed both of his historical novels.

The Fanatic (2000) cuts between seventeenth century and contemporary Scotland, where a central character Andrew Carlin plays the ghost of Major Weir in a 'haunted Edinburgh' tour, to explore a world of witchcraft, corrupt government and religious bigotry as well as the theme of the divided self. As Carlin puts it, "The last thing we need's anither split fuckin personality . . . we don't need mair doubles, oor haill fuckin culture's littered wi them.'

Much of *Joseph Knight* (2003),which won both the Saltire Society Book of the Year Award that year and the Scottish Arts Council Book of the Year Award in 2004, is set in Enlightenment Edinburgh. The book tells the story of a black slave brought to Scotland from the West Indies and his original master's quest to find out what happened to him.

During his residency Robertson gave three master classes examining the historic relationships between Scottish writers and politicians and between Edinburgh and writers. In one of them he looks at the memorable scenes in Scottish literature set in and around the High Street and Canongate and asks:

> What sustains the tension between tradition and
> innovation, between dream and reality, that seems such a
> part of the Old Town's character? Is it the presence of a
> half-wild mountain so close to the city centre? Is it the
> area's ability to absorb the Festival, the Fringe, ghost tours,
> street artists, and tens of thousands of visitors while still
> having an indigenous population going about their daily
> lives? Perhaps it is simply that so much history has
> occurred in this ancient core of Edinburgh that nothing
> any more surprises it, while it continues to surprise us, its
> temporary residents and custodians.

Near the foot of the Canongate on the north side is White Horse Close which contains the now reconstructed White Horse Inn, the starting point for the coaches to London. It was also where Prince Charles Edward's army had their Edinburgh headquarters and figures in Scott's *Waverley*.[31]

HOLYROOD

The Abbey of Holyrood was founded in 1128 by David I who, according to legend, had a miraculous escape from death here. While out riding he was attacked by a stag. As the king was about to be gored the stag vanished, leaving a cross in his hands – the Holy Rood. In thanksgiving the king founded an abbey on the spot, although all that remains today is the roofless nave of the church.

Adjacent is the Palace of Holyroodhouse, the royal seat of the Kings of Scotland and one of the sights of Edinburgh with its distinctive baronial architecture and fairy-tale setting against the rugged splendour of Arthur's Seat. The present palace was begun by King James IV at the beginning of the sixteenth century and, after his death at the Battle of Flodden in 1513, completed by his son James V.

Many of Edinburgh's earliest writers were attached to the palace as court poets, such as William Dunbar (c. 1460–c. 1513), perhaps the most talented and wide-ranging of the Scottish medieval makars who served James IV. While much of his poetry is ceremonial and relates to court life, Dunbar was a harsh commentator on the Edinburgh of his time, criticising the city for its materialism, lack of spiritual values, corruption, poverty and filthiness. Two of his best-known poems are 'Tydingis fra the Sessioun', in which he mocks the legal establishment, and 'To the Merchants of Edinburgh', which castigates the city authorities for putting profit before the needs of the city.

Another writer attached to the court of James IV and critical of the corruption of power was David Lyndsay (c. 1486–1555) who later as Lyon King of Arms was one of the most important figures at the court of James V. His literary reputation rests on *Ane Pleasant Satyre of the Thrie Estaitis in Commendation of Vertew and Vituperatioun of Vyce*, widely regarded as the first great play in Scottish drama. A contemporary satire on the vices of spiritual and secular society, it was first performed in 1540 and then again in 1554. It was not performed again until it was triumphantly staged by Tyrone Guthrie at the 1948 and 1949 Edinburgh Festivals, in an adaptation by Robert Kemp, at the Assembly Hall of the Church of Scotland on the Mound.

Damaged during the English occupation of 1543, and again by fire during Cromwell's occupation in 1650, the palace was restored to its present state under the direction of Charles II at the end of the seventeenth century. When John Wesley (1703–91) paid a visit in the 1770s it was but a shadow of its former self. He noted in his journal:

I took one more walk through Holyroodhouse, the mansion
of ancient kings: but how melancholy an appearance does it
make now! The stately rooms are dirty as stables: the colours
of the tapestry are quite faded; several of the pictures are cut
and defaced. The roof of the royal chapel is fallen in; and the
bones of James the Fifth, and the once beautiful Lord
Darnley, are scattered about like those of sheep or oxen. Such
is human greatness![32]

Little seems to have changed by the 1870s when Stevenson was to write
in his *Picturesque Notes*:

The Palace of Holyrood has been left aside in the growth of
Edinburgh and stands grey and silent in a workman's quarter
among breweries and gas works. It is a house of many
memories. Great people of yore, kings and queens, buffoons
and grave ambassadors, played their stately farce for centuries
in Holyrood. Wars have been plotted, dancing has lasted deep
into the night, murder has been done in its chambers. There
Prince Charlie held his phantom levees, and in a very gallant
manner.[33]

It was at Holyroodhouse that one of the best-known episodes in Scottish
history took place – the murder in March 1566 of Mary, Queen of Scots'
secretary David Rizzio on the orders of her husband Lord Darnley. The
bloodstained spot, where the terrified Italian was stabbed over fifty times,
can still be seen in Mary's apartments. The tragic event has inspired
countless novels and plays, including Rafael Sabatini's *The Night of
Holyrood*, Algernon Swinburne's *Bothwell* and even an opera *Rizzio* by
Charles Dibdin, performed at the Theatre Royal, Drury Lane in 1820.

In his story 'The Silver Mirror', Conan Doyle describes a recurring
vision of the murder of Rizzio:

But I saw more to-night. The crouching man was as visible as
the lady whose gown he clutched. He is a little swarthy fellow,
with a black pointed beard. He has a loose gown of damask

trimmed with fur. The prevailing tints of his dress are red.
What a fright the fellow is in, to be sure! He cowers and
shivers and glares back over his shoulder. There is a small knife
in his other hand, but he is far too tremulous and cowed to use
it. Fierce faces, bearded and dark, shape themselves out of the
mist. There is one terrible creature, a skeleton of a man, with
hollow cheeks and eyes sunk in his head. He also has a knife in
his hand. On the right of the woman stands a tall man, very
young with flaxen hair, his face sullen and dour. The beautiful
woman looks up at him in appeal. So does the man on the
ground. This youth seems to be the arbiter of their fate. The
crouching man draws closer and hides himself in the woman's
skirts. The tall youth bends and tries to drag her away from
him. So much I saw last night before the mirror cleared. Shall I
never know what it leads to and whence it comes? It is not a
mere imagination, of that I am very sure. Somewhere, some
time this scene has been acted, and this old mirror has reflected
it. But when – where?[34]

To the north of the palace is a weird little garden pavilion with pyramidal
roof, dormer windows and lofty chimneys, known as Queen Mary's
Bath-House. It is said that Mary used to come here to bathe in white
wine, in the hope of making herself more attractive. Lewis Spence reflects
on the scene in his poem 'The Queen's Bath-House, Holyrood':

> Time that has dinged down Castels and his toures,
> And cast great crowns like tinsel in the fire,
> That halds his hand for palace nor for byre,
> Stands sweir at this, the oe of Venus' boures.
> Not time himself can dwell withouten flowers,
> Though aiks main fa' the rose sall bide entire;
> So sall this diamant of a queen's desire
> Outflourish all the staines that Time devours.
> Many a strength his turrey-heid sall tine
> Ere this sall fa' whare a queen lay in wine,
> Whose lamp was her ain lily flesh and star,

The walls of luve the mair triumphant are
Gif luve were waesome habiting that place;
Luve has maist years that has a murming face.

THE COWGATE

Running parallel and to the south of the Canongate is Holyrood Road,
now a busy road taking traffic to the south of the city and the site of both
The Scotsman newspaper's headquarters and BBC Scotland.

The Cowgate or Soo-Gate (South Gate) begins just beyond St
Mary's Street and burrows under the South and George IV Bridges. It is
a dank, dark gorge where on both sides the windowless buildings rise to
several storeys. Though there has been some refurbishment, and a few
bars and clubs have opened in the area, it still exudes a sinister feeling.

It is difficult to imagine that during the reign of James III the
Cowgate was an aristocratic quarter. Writing in the 1860s the travel
writer, Alexander Smith, noted that if one stood on the South Bridge and
looked down:

> instead of a stream, you see the Cowgate, the dirtiest,
> narrowest, most densely peopled of Edinburgh streets.
> Admired once by a French ambassador at the court of one of
> the James, and yet with certain traces of departed splendour,
> the Cowgate has fallen into the sere and yellow leaf of
> furniture brokers, second-hand jewellers, and vendors of
> deleterious alcohol. These second-hand jewellers' shops, the
> trinkets seen by bleared gaslight, are the most melancholy
> sights I know. Watches hang there that once ticked
> comfortably in the fobs of prosperous men, rings that were
> once placed by happy bridegrooms on the fingers of happy
> brides, jewels in which lives the sacredness of death-beds.
> What tragedies, what disruptions of households, what fell
> pressure of poverty brought them here! Looking in through
> the foul windows, the trinkets remind one of shipwrecked
> gold embedded in the ooze of ocean – gold that speaks of
> unknown, yet certain, storm and disaster, of the yielding of

planks, of the cry of drowning men. Who has the heart to
buy them, I wonder? The Cowgate is the Irish portion of the
city. Edinburgh leaps over it with bridges; its inhabitants are
morally and geographically the lower orders. They keep to
their own quarters, and seldom come up to the light of day.
Many an Edinburgh man has never set his foot in the street;
the condition of the inhabitants is as little known to
respectable Edinburgh as are the habits of moles, earth-
worms, and the mining population.[35]

Even now, in spite of restoration, the Cowgate, at least at night, retains
that air of danger. Ian Rankin's contemporary detective John Rebus looks
down into the Cowgate while walking home one night:

There were clubs still open down there, teenagers spilling on
to the road. The police had names for the Cowgate when it
got like this: Little Saigon; the blood bank; hell on earth.
Even the patrol cars went in twos.[36]

Though the poet William McGonagall (1825–1902), best-known for his
poem on the Tay Bridge rail disaster, spent most of his life in Dundee, he
was born and died in the Cowgate. He is thought to have inspired the
name Minerva McGonagall, a character in J. K. Rowling's *Harry Potter*.

THE GRASSMARKET

The Cowgate becomes the Grassmarket where Candlemaker Row and
Victoria Street converge. With its restored medieval houses and original
cobbles, it makes an attractive scene in contrast to the Cowgate. Above
to one's right the Castle dramatically hovers, the steep sides of the Castle
Rock glistening like smoked glass, and while some of the doss-houses of
yesterday remain many have been replaced by antiques shops, bistros and
boutiques.

At the most easterly end is the West Bow, the site of the Traverse
Theatre from 1969 until its removal to purpose-built premises in
Cambridge Street in 1992. The Traverse was founded during the 1962

Edinburgh Festival when the Cambridge Footlights, then including Graham Chapman, John Cleese, Ian Lang and Trevor Nunn, persuaded a local landlord to lease Kelly's Paradise, a former doss-house and brothel in James Court. It opened officially the following January and since its foundation the Traverse has pioneered many new Scottish plays, by among others Stanley Eveling and Stewart Conn, as well as acting as a focus for experimental theatre in Edinburgh.

THOMAS WEIR

The West Bow, now Victoria Street, was home to Major Thomas Weir, a man of impeccable reputation and commander of the Edinburgh Town Guard. who had escorted the Marquis of Montrose to his execution. Weir, a strict Presbyterian, lived with his sister Grizel, possibly in an incestuous relationship, and in a fit of delirium confessed in 1670 to witchcraft. Both he and his sister were executed in the Grassmarket and their home, long left empty, was subsequently believed to be haunted. Weir has inspired numerous novels about the divided self, not least James Hogg's *The Private Memoirs and Confessions of a Justified Sinner* and R. L. Stevenson's *Dr Jekyll and Mr Hyde*. Sir Robert Redgauntlet, one of the persecutors of the godly, in Sir Walter Scott's *Redgauntlet* has an ape called Major Weir.[37]

At the White Hart Inn, an eighteenth-century coaching stop, a plaque states 'in the White Hart Inn Robert Burns stayed during his last visit to Edinburgh 1791'. William Wordsworth (1770–1850) was also supposed to have stayed there on his Edinburgh visit, with his sister Dorothy, in September 1803, during which time they visited Sir Walter Scott at Lasswade.

A small enclosed garden in the centre of the Grassmarket marks the site on which the city's public gallows stood until 1784. Here, too, was the scene of the famous Porteous riot in September 1736. Earlier that year two smugglers, Wilson and Robertson, were sentenced to death for a petty crime. Many people felt the sentence was too severe and when Wilson was cut down from the gallows the crowd threw stones at the guard. The Captain of the Guard, John Porteous, responded by firing on the crowd, killing eight. He was put on trial, found guilty but then reprieved. The Edinburgh mob, incensed by what they saw as an affront to the city and Scots Law, stormed the Tolbooth and dragged Porteous out to be hanged. The story forms the background to Sir Walter Scott's *The Heart of Midlothian*.[38]

BURKE AND HARE

Violence is also to be found at the junction of Lady Lawson Street and West Port. Here stood Tanner's Close, where the infamous murderers Burke and Hare lived. When in November 1827 an old man died, owing his landlord William Hare £4 in rent, Hare persuaded his lodger William Burke to take the old man's body to Robert Knox (1791–1862), the leading anatomy lecturer at the University. They were paid £7 and promised the same rate for further bodies. Realising that a good living could be made in this way the two men selected their victims largely from among the elderly and sick, plied them with drink and then suffocated them.

Burke and Hare might have carried on indefinitely but on Hallowe'en 1828 they were caught. According to one story, one of Dr Knox's students recognised the corpse as that of a lady he had been drinking with only the night before but it is more likely that the victim was reported missing and traced back to the two men. They were arrested and tried for murder but Hare turned King's Evidence and saved himself at the expense of Burke who was hanged near St Giles in front of some 25,000 spectators. His body followed that of his victims, being publicly dissected and a wallet was made from his skin.

Knox was vilified for his 'no questions asked' policy, his house attacked and his effigy burnt. A macabre doggerel was coined:

> Down the Close and up the Stair,
> But and ben wi' Burke and Hare.
> Burke's the butcher, Hare's the thief,
> Knox the man who buys the beef.

Shunned by Edinburgh society, including Walter Scott who accused him of 'trading deep in human flesh', unable to secure a University professorship and distraught by the deaths of his wife in childbirth and then his four-year-old son from scarlet fever, he moved south. In 1856 he obtained a job at the Brompton Cancer Hospital, dying six years later.

His memory lives on in the plays by James Bridie, himself a doctor and lecturer in medicine, *The Anatomist* (1931), and Owen Dudley Edwards's *Hare and Burke* (1994) and Dylan Thomas's film treatment *The Doctor and the Devil*; R. L. Stevenson's 'The Body Snatchers' is also based on the story;[39] and in Iain Banks's *Complicity* a body is found cut up on a slab in a fishmongers in High Riggs, off West Port.

PART II

The University Quarter

B y the middle of the eighteenth century the city was beginning to expand outside the original city walls, first towards the south, and then to the north and the New Town of James Craig and Robert Adam. This expansion was accompanied by a corresponding development in Scottish life and letters which would come to be called the Scottish Enlightenment.

One of its most important figures neatly straddles the period and indeed the geographical development, growing up in the first expansion on the south side but spending most of his life in the New Town. Walter Scott (1771–1832) was born, the ninth of twelve children, in College Wynd, now Guthrie Street; a plaque at 8 Chambers Street notes his birthplace 'near this spot'. His father was a lawyer and his mother, Anne Rutherford, the daughter of a former Professor of Medicine at the University. Anne Rutherford had lost her first six children in infancy and this, combined with the fact that young Walter was stricken by poliomyelitis, an illness which left him with a permanent limp in his right leg, persuaded the family to move to the nearby George Square, which was regarded as healthier than the closely packed houses of College Wynd.

George Square was the first development of size outside the old city wall, pre-dating the New Town by some twenty years, and attracted the cream of Edinburgh society. Walter Scott's parents moved to No. 25, on the west side in 1772 where their neighbours included the writer Henry Mackenzie and the 'hanging judge' Lord Braxfield, who was to become the model for R. L. Stevenson's Weir of Hermiston. Though part of his childhood was spent with his paternal grandparents in the Borders, it was from George Square that Scott went to the High School and Edinburgh University, was apprenticed to his father's law firm and from where he married in 1797.[1]

Yet another writer associated with George Square is Rebecca West (1892–1983). Born Cicily Isabel Fairfield, she lived at Hope Park Square and then 24 Buccleuch Place, attending George Watson's Ladies College then at 5 George Square, which she called John Thompson's Ladies College in her novel The Judge (1922). West felt trapped in Edinburgh and the book satirises the provincial nature of the place:

They were passing down the Meadow Walk now, between
trees that were like shapes drawn on blotting-paper and lamps
that had the smallest scope.
    'Edinburgh's a fine place,' he said. 'It can handle even an
asphalt track with dignity.'
    'Oh, a fine place,' she answered pettishly, 'if you could
get away from it.'[2]

West left the city of her youth as a young woman, never to return, and
her reputation is based largely on books such as *The Return of the Soldier*
(1918) and *The Meaning of Treason* (1949).

The University of Edinburgh now dominates George Square.
Against much opposition, most of the square was pulled down in the
1960s to build the huge David Hume and William Robertson towers on
the east side and the library, designed by Basil Spence, on the south side.
Only the west side and the gardens have survived.

Robert Garioch (1909–81), a graduate of the university and later
writer-in-residence 1971–73, in his poem 'A Wee Local Scandal' gives
some indication of the passions unleashed over the episode:

> The University has got a wee
> skyscraper at the corner of George Square,
> fowerteen storeys, the day I wes there;
> it's maybe sunk; I've no been back to see
>
> the Hume Toure – it hits ye in the ee,
> yon muckly black rectangle in the air,
> a graund sicht frae the Meedies, man; it fair
> obliterates Arthur's Seat, nae word of a lee.
>
> But whit a scandal! That's the Dauvit Hume
> plewed in the professorial election;
> hou can the outwail'd candidate presume
> to name sic architectural perfection?

Dauvit Hume Toure, indeed! Whit a let-doun!
It shuid hae been the Will Cleghorn Erection.

Garioch was a schoolmaster in the city all his life apart from the Second
World War, much of which he spent in Italian and German POW camps,
an experience from which he never properly recovered. Edinburgh has
provided much of the inspiration for his work, much as it did for his hero
Robert Fergusson, though he was by no means uncritical of the city of
his birth. In 'To Robert Fergusson' he looks back with some regret to the
Edinburgh of the eighteenth century:

> Auld Reekie's bigger, nou, what's mair,
> and folk hae the greater share
> of warldlie gear may take the air
>   in Morningside,
> and needna sclim the turnpike stair
>   whar ye wad byde.

> But truth it is, our couthie city
> has cruddit in twa pairs a bittie
> and speaks twa tongues, ane coorse and grittie,
>   heard in the Cougait
> the tither copied, mair's the pitie,
>   frae Wast of Newgate.

> Whilk is the crudd and whilk the whey
> I wad be kinna sweirt to say,
> but this I ken, that of the twae
>   the corrupt twang
> of Cougait is the nearer tae
>   the leid ye sang.

Garioch's *Collected Poems* was published in 1977 and, after slow
recognition, he has come to be regarded as one of Scotland's finest
twentieth-century poets. His writing on Edinburgh includes the twenty-
four poems that make up 'The Edinburgh Sonnets', his irreverent look at
the Festival 'Embro to the Ploy' and a short play about Edinburgh, *The
Masque of Edinburgh* (1954). He is commemorated by a plaque, placed in
1983 by the Saltire Society, at 4 Nelson Street in the New Town.[3]

Buccleuch Place, a wide street of tall but rather stony-faced houses built in the 1780s, now occupied by university departments, lies immediately behind the David Hume Tower. Francis Jeffrey (1773–1850) lived at No. 18 in a house that has now entered Edinburgh literary history. It was there in a third-floor flat in March 1802 that he, a fellow advocate Francis Horner (1778–1817) and the famous wit Sydney Smith (1771–1845), founded *The Edinburgh Review*.

Over the next twenty years the Whig magazine would become so influential that it drew writers from all over Britain, turning Edinburgh into the literary capital of the land, and became perhaps the most important magazine in Europe. The first issue of 750 copies quickly sold out and within five years the circulation was 7,000, rising to a peak in 1818 of monthly sales of over 14,000 copies. Part of its success was due to Jeffrey, who remained editor until 1829, and part due to the support of its publisher Archibald Constable, who paid the contributors very generously.

Contributors included Thomas Carlyle, Thomas Macaulay (1800–59), MP for Edinburgh 1839–47 and 1852–57, and William Hazlitt, who spent four days in the city in 1822 securing a divorce under Scots law which he describes in *Libor Amoris or the New Pygmalion* (1823). The magazine's touch on literary matters was, however, not always sure. It rejected the work of the Lakeland Poets and Byron's response to its harsh reviews of his early poems was the satirical poem *English Bards and Scotch Reviewers*. Sir Walter Scott, although a Tory, was a frequent contributor until 1808 when Jeffrey published a critical thirty-five page review of *Marmion*.

At his various addresses in the New Town, 62 Queen Street and 92 George Street, and his country house on Corstorphine Hill Jeffrey held salons that made him one of the most notable literary figures of the period. He combined this literary career with politics and in 1830 was appointed Lord Advocate in the reforming Whig administration of the 1832 Reform Bills, a government which included fellow *Edinburgh Review* contributors Henry Brougham as Lord Chancellor and Henry Cockburn (1779–1854) as Solicitor-General. He was raised to the Bench as Lord Jeffrey in 1834 and died at his home in 24 Moray Place in 1850. His sarcophagus stands near the west wall of the Dean cemetery.

By 2025 and Paul Johnston's *Water of Death* the street had changed:

> In the old days the street had been filled with university departments. I could remember coming to some interesting sessions on the social anthropology of the criminal here. Now it was in a state of advanced disrepair, a lot of the four-storey buildings boarded up. Nasmyth Barracks extension took up three houses halfway down. They had a delightful north-facing view over the blown-out remains of the David Hume Tower and other architectural monstrosities of the 1960s which had been devastated during the drugs wars.[4]

THOMAS DE QUINCEY

Towards the end of his life Thomas De Quincey (1785–1859) lodged at 42 Lothian Street, now swept away by the Edinburgh University Student Centre. He had come to Edinburgh from the Lake District where he had been friendly with the Lakeland Poets, and was to spend some forty years at a series of addresses around the city – 9 Great King Street, 1 Forres Street, 29 Ann Street, 113 Princes Street and 71 Clerk Street. The demands of a large family and restrictions of a limited income meant that for much of that time he seemed to be dodging creditors even though the publication of *Confessions of an English Opium Eater* (1821) immediately established him in the top rank of writers.

De Quincey lived most of the last ten years of his life at his cottage in Lasswade, to the south-east of Edinburgh, and it was there that the American writer Ralph Waldo Emerson visited him in 1848. He is buried in St Cuthbert's churchyard at the west end of Princes Street, but his best memorial remains his portrait as Mr Wastle in Lockhart's series of satirical portraits *Peter's Letters to his Kinsfolk*. Christopher Wallace's novel *The Resurrection Club* (1999), which draws on various episodes in Edinburgh history, most notably Deacon Brodie and Burke and Hare, ends at De Quincey's grave.

Another lodger in Lothian Street was Charles Darwin (1809–82) who spent two years at Edinburgh University from 1825. He complained of finding the lectures dull and spent much of his time collecting specimens to study from the Forth.

'SYLVANDER' AND 'CLARINDA'

Lothian Street runs into Potterrow in which Robert Burns's great love 'Clarinda' lived; there is a plaque to her just south of the site of her home. Burns had met Agnes McLehose (1759–1841) in 1787 during his second visit to Edinburgh. At the time she was in her late twenties with several small children, her husband having fled to Jamaica to escape his debtors. Attracted perhaps as much by Burns's reputation as a lover as his talents as a poet, she invited him to have tea with her. Though unable to attend, Burns wrote to her and so began the correspondence between 'Sylvander' and 'Clarinda'. The affair between the 'ploughman poet' and the 'lady of fashion', though probably chaste, soon became public knowledge and only ended when Burns left Edinburgh. It has left us with one of his finest poems *Ae Fond Kiss*:

> Fare-thee-weel, thou first and fairest!
> Fare-thee-weel, thou best and dearest!
> Thine be ilka joy and treasure,
> Peace, Enjoyment, Love and Pleasure!
>
> Ae fond kiss, and then we sever!
> Ae fareweel, Alas for ever!
> Deep in heart-wrung tears I'll pledge thee,
> Warring sighs and groans I'll wage thee.

They did, in fact, meet once more, just before she left for Jamaica in the hope of affecting a reconciliation with her husband. A poignant entry in her diary shows she loved Burns 'till the shadow fell': 'This day I can never forget. Parted with Robert Burns in the year 1791 never more to meet in this world. Oh may we meet in heaven.' She died aged eighty-two in a tenement flat at 14 Calton Hill, now demolished, having survived Burns by forty-five years. Their relationship has been the subject of many works of fiction, such as Robert Kemp's play *The Other Dear*

Charmer and Alistair Campsie's novel *The Clarinda Conspiracy* (1989), which revolves around an establishment plot against Burns.

Across the Meadows is Sciennes Hill House, a two-storey house of rough stone that now forms part of Sciennes House Place. It was there during Burns's 1787 visit that he met the sixteen-year-old Walter Scott at the home of the Professor of Moral Philosophy, Adam Ferguson. A vivid account of the meeting and description of Burns is given in Lockhart's *Life of Sir Walter Scott*:

> His person was strong and robust; his manners rustic, not clownish; a sort of dignified plainess and simplicity, which received part of its effect perhaps from one's knowledge of his extraordinary talents . . . There was a strong expression of sense and shrewdness in all his lineaments; the eye alone, I think, indicated the poetical character and temperament. It was large and of a dark cast, and glowed (I say literally glowed) when he spoke with feeling or interest.[5]

SANDY BELL'S

Sandy Bell's Bar in 25 Forrest Road is the local for the University's School of Scottish Studies and was the unofficial headquarters of the Edinburgh University Folksong Society, one of whose guiding spirits was the writer Stuart MacGregor (1935–73). His photograph and copies of his love song 'The Sandy Bell's Man' hang near the fireplace.

After training as a doctor at the University, MacGregor spent four years in the Royal Army Medical Corps before returning to Edinburgh as a lecturer in Social Medicine based at the Usher Institute in Warrender Park Road. His novels are largely set against the backdrop of university and medical life, especially his largely autobiographical first book *The Myrtle and the Ivy* (1967) which centres on the denizens of Sandy Bell's.

His second, more complex, novel *The Sinner* (1973), is about the ideals of an Edinburgh folk singer, contemptuous of mid-Atlantic commercialised art and the gutlessness of Scottish politicians. His tragic death in a car accident in Jamaica at the age of thirty-seven robbed literature of a promising talent.[6]

Another frequenter of the bar was Hamish Henderson (1919–2002), who lived nearby. Now largely known as a folklorist and the founder of the School of Scottish Studies at Edinburgh University, Henderson first made his reputation as a poet with *Elegies for the dead in Cyrenaica* (1948), based on his experiences during the Desert War. His poem *Floret silva undique* from the sequence *Auld Reekie's Roses* gives a picture of an Edinburgh freed from its Calvinist tradition. Henderson was instrumental in creating the first Edinburgh People's Festival in 1951 as 'the Scottish underbelly' to the official Festival. It lasted until 1954 when it transformed itself into the Festival Fringe.

GREYFRIARS

One of Edinburgh's best-known churches is Greyfriars Kirk at the top of Candlemaker Row. Originally a convent established by Dutch friars in the thirteenth century, the kirk was opened in 1620, the first new church to be built in Edinburgh since the Reformation. Stevenson described it as:

> One of our famous Edinburgh points of view: and strangers
> are led thither to see, by yet another instance, how strangely
> the city lies upon her hills. The enclosure is of an irregular
> shape; the double church of Old and New Greyfriars stands
> on the level at the top; a few thorns are dotted here and
> there, and the ground falls by terrace and step slope towards
> the north. The open shows many slabs and table tombstones;
> and all around the margin the place is girt by an array of
> aristocratic mausoleums appallingly adorned.[7]

Little seems to have changed in the century since he wrote those lines. There is a sense of calm about the place, a feeling that the quiet graves are watching one and have some tales to tell.

The church is best known for its associations with the Covenanters, a movement that grew up in opposition to Charles I's proclamation that the Episcopal faith would be Scotland's religion. It was in the southern annexe of the churchyard that 1200 Covenanting prisoners were held because the prisons were full and here that the Covenant was signed in

1638 on the through-stane or horizontal gravestone on the south side of the church. Near the steps leading to the northern entrance is the Martyrs' Monument.

The graveyard has been called the Westminster Abbey of Edinburgh. Among the most important literary figures buried in the churchyard are the unfortunate Captain Porteous; the bookseller William Creech; the poet Allan Ramsay; the printer William Smellie; Clement Little, founder of the University Library and Sir George Mackenzie of Rosehaugh, founder of the Advocates Library; George Buchanan (1506–82), tutor to Mary, Queen of Scots and her son James, as well as the author of an important twenty-volume history of Scotland; and the widely derided poet William McGonagall (c. 1825–1902).

A plain mural tablet on the north side of the terrace commemorates Henry Mackenzie (1745–1831), an important linking figure between the Scottish Enlightenment and the age of Walter Scott. Born on the day Bonnie Prince Charlie landed in 1745, Mackenzie had several addresses in the city, most notably George Square where he was a neighbour of Walter Scott and 6 Heriot Row where he died. At one stage he was the most popular British novelist of his generation, though his most famous book *A Man of Feeling* (1771) now seems weak and sentimental. Scott dedicated *Waverley* to 'Our Scottish Addison, Henry Mackenzie' and during his lifetime he was highly thought of as an essayist but his posthumous reputation rests principally on his championing of Byron, Burns and Scott especially as editor of two influential magazines, *The Mirror* and *The Lounger*.[8]

Also buried at Greyfriars is the Gaelic poet Duncan Ban MacIntyre (1724–1812), best known for his long poem 'Moladh Beinn Dobhrainn' ('The Praise of Ben Dorain'), later translated into English by Hugh MacDiarmid and Iain Crichton Smith. Originally a Perthshire gamekeeper, MacIntyre spent over half his life in Edinburgh, where he served in the City Guard. Though principally a nature poet he was also a shrewd commentator on the growing divisions between the social classes in Edinburgh.

The church, which figures in *Guy Mannering* (1815) has many associations with Walter Scott. His father is buried there and it was while coming out of the church that the teenage Walter first met a fifteen-year-old girl, who many think to have been the love of his life. She was the daughter of Sir John and Lady Jane Stuart-Belsches and was not only well-born but an heiress. His attentions came to nothing and a few years later she married a friend of his called William Forbes. Scott was heartbroken and even thirty years later wondered why it 'should still agitate my heart'. Williamina Stuart-Belsches is often thought to have been the model for Greenmantle in *Redgauntlet* (1824) and Margaret in *The Lay of the Last Minstrel* (1805). She died in 1810 at the age of thirty-five.[9]

In 1797, while in the Lake District, Scott met a French émigré Charlotte Carpentier to whom he immediately proposed marriage. There is some suggestion he could have been on the rebound from Williamina, who had married shortly before, and certainly he was to later write:

> Mrs Scott's match and mine was of our own making and proceeded from the most sincere affection on both sides, which has rather increased than diminished during twelve years' marriage. But it was something short of love in all its forms, which I suspect people only feel once in all their lives; folk who have been nearly drowned in bathing rarely venturing a second time out of their depth.[10]

Outside the church is a small red granite tombstone to Greyfriars Bobby, a Skye terrier who was the faithful companion of a shepherd Jock Gray, who died in 1858. The dog refused to leave his graveside until its death fourteen years later and became such a legend it was granted the freedom of the city. At the suggestion of Queen Victoria the loyal terrier was buried close to his master in the churchyard. Eleanor Atkinson's book *Greyfriars Bobby* (1912) commemorates the dog and his devotion.

GEORGE HERIOT'S

The imposing George Heriot's School with its turreted corner towers is next door to Greyfriars. Founded by George Heriot (1563–1623) ('Jingling Geordie' in Scott's novel *The Fortunes of Nigel*), jeweller to King James IV in the seventeenth century, it has educated many eminent writers including, in this century, the historical novelist Nigel Tranter

(1909–2000). Edward Topham on his visit to Edinburgh in 1774, thought that it was 'a large and magnificent edifice, and has infinitely more the look of a palace than Holyroodhouse', a characteristic it shares with many of Edinburgh's schools. The novel *Walter Crighton or Reminiscences of George Heriot's Hospital* (1898) by Jamieson Baillie gives a good idea of the nineteenth-century schoolboy's experiences there.

Almost opposite stood the Royal Infirmary for over a hundred and thirty years, from 1870 until its move to the south of the city. Many of the medical novels of Colin Douglas (Colin Currie 1945–), a consultant at Edinburgh's City Hospital, are set there and it figures in William Paul's *Sleeping Pretty* (1995).

THE UNIVERSITY OF EDINBURGH

Education has always been highly valued in the city and nowhere more so than the University of Edinburgh, the original part of which is situated at the eastern end of Chambers Street. Founded in 1582 as the 'Tounis College', the university buildings stood on the site of Kirk o' Field, the house which was blown up in 1567 causing the death of Mary, Queen of Scots' husband, Lord Darnley. A number of novels have commemorated this well-known episode in Scottish history.

The University flourished and was at the forefront of the Scottish Enlightenment. Matthew Bramble in *The Expedition of Humphrey Clinker* noted that:

> Edinburgh is a hot-bed of genius. I have had the good
> fortune to be made acquainted with many authors of the first
> distinction: such as the two Humes, Robertson, Smith,
> Wallace, Blair, Fergusson, Wilkie etc and I have found them
> all as agreeable in conversation as they are instructive and
> entertaining in their writings.[11]

Of the above names almost all had either been educated or taught at the University. They included David Hume, the historian and philosopher; John Home, the dramatist; William Robertson, the historian and Principal of the University; Adam Smith, author of *The Wealth of Nations*

(1776) and Adam Ferguson, who with his *Essay on the History of Civil Society* (1766) founded the modern discipline of sociology. These men created an 'Athens of the North' and in turn attracted writers and scholars to the city.

THOMAS CARLYLE

Thomas Carlyle (1795–1881) arrived at the University in November 1809, after a three-day walk from his birthplace of Ecclefechan in Dumfries. His first lodgings were in Simon Square and later in Bristo Street. He threw himself into his studies for a general arts degree, distinguishing himself in both Latin and Mathematics. In 1817, after teaching in Annan and Kirkcaldy, he returned to Edinburgh to start his theological training and also began to write. It was a time of great personal unhappiness, partly because of his dislike of his subject and teachers, and partly because of loneliness. He was to remain in Edinburgh for another eleven years, lodging in the New Town, off Leith Walk and at 21 Comely Bank, then with views over green fields. In 1828 he left to seek his fame and fortune in London, having failed in his application for the Chair of English Literature.

However, Edinburgh remained dear to his heart and he returned as Rector of the University in 1866, an honour he regarded as the greatest of his life. Now eminent as a historian, social writer and thinker, his speech, in which he reviewed his time at the University, was a success but his joy was mitigated by the death of his wife three weeks later. Inheriting her estate of Craigenputtock he donated it, together with ten bursaries, to the University. Herr Teufelsdröckh's university in the autobiographical *Sartor Resartus* (1836) is based on Edinburgh.

STEVENSON, BARRIE
AND CONAN DOYLE

It is extraordinary that three of Britain's best known authors – Robert Louis Stevenson (1850–94), J. M. Barrie (1860–1937) and Arthur Conan Doyle (1859–1930) – attended the University within the space of a few years and were influenced by each other.

Stevenson greatly admired Barrie's work and repeatedly invited him to Vailima. He wrote to Henry James in December 1892: 'You and Barrie and Kipling are my Muses Three,' while to Barrie he went further:

> I am proud to think you are a Scotchman . . . and please do
> not think when I thus seem to bracket myself with you, that I
> am wholly blinded with vanity . . . I am a capable artist; but
> it begins to look to me as if you are a man of genius.[12]

Stevenson seems to have been drawn by the fact that 'both made our stages in the metropolis of the minds: our Virgil's "grey metropolis" and I count that a lasting bond'. Barrie includes a portrait of Stevenson in his reminiscences of the University, *An Edinburgh Eleven* (1889), and on Stevenson's death wrote an elegiac poem 'Scotland's Lament'.

Conan Doyle also had a great deal of respect for Stevenson. He was asked to finish *St Ives* but 'did not feel equal to the task' and it was done by Arthur Quiller-Couch instead. Towards the end of his life Stevenson began a correspondence with Conan Doyle in which he professed his admiration for the Sherlock Holmes stories.

In turn, Barrie and Conan Doyle were friends. In 1893 they collaborated on an English comic opera *Jane Annie* but it was not a success. Conan Doyle in his autobiography claimed it 'was a bitter thought for both of us' but it does not seem to have affected their friendship. A few days after it was withdrawn, after only a few performances, Barrie sent Conan Doyle a parody of Sherlock Holmes entitled 'The Adventures of the Two Collaborators', which Doyle thought the best of the Sherlock Holmes parodies.

R. L. STEVENSON

Stevenson spent several unhappy years at the University between 1867 and 1875, where he cared little for his studies. He rarely attended his engineering classes, preferring to spend his time walking, talking and drinking. His time there was mitigated only by the chance to edit the University magazine and by his membership of the Speculative Society.

'The Spec', which continues to meet on Tuesday evenings in

ground-floor rooms in the north-east corner of the Old Quad, was the
University's literary and debating society. Founded in 1764 by, among
others, William Creech, it has traditionally been dominated by lawyers
and writers. Members have included Francis Jeffrey, Henry Cockburn,
John Gibson Lockhart, Walter Scott and, more recently, Hugh
MacDiarmid, Alexander McCall Smith and Ross Leckie. Stevenson was
twice President of the Society and wrote several papers for it. In 'A
College Magazine' he describes where they met in Old College:

> a hall, turkey-carpeted, hung with pictures, looking when
> lighted up at night with fire and candle, like some godly dining-
> room; a passage-like library, walled with books in their wire
> cages and a corridor with a fireplace, benches, a table, many
> prints of famous members and a mural tablet to the virtues of a
> former secretary. Here a member can warm himself and loaf and
> read: here, in defiance of Senatus-consults, he can smoke.[13]

The weekly meetings in Stevenson's time were from eight to midnight,
but were broken at nine when some of the members would leave 'to buy
pencils'. This ruse meant in fact a drink at Rutherford's Bar in nearby
Drummond Street. Twenty years after his visits Stevenson was to write to
his old friend, Charles Baxter:

> Last night as I lay under my blanket . . . all of a sudden I had
> a vision of Drummond Street. It came on me like a flash of
> lightning: I simply returned thither, and into the past. And
> when I remember all I hoped and feared as I pickled about
> Rutherford's in the rain and the east wind; how I feared I
> should make a mere shipwreck, and yet timidly hoped not;
> how I feared I should never have a friend, far less a wife, and
> yet passionately hoped I might; how I hoped (if I did not
> take to drink) I should possibly write one little book etc, etc.
> And then now – what a change! I feel somehow as if I should
> like the incident set upon a brass plate at the corner of that
> dreary thoroughfare for all students to read, poor devils, when
> their hearts are down.[14]

The one-storey 'howf', with its wooden façade, is still there, over a hundred and fifty years after it first opened. Inside, the regulars, intent on their dominoes and pints, are oblivious to its famous literary visitors, which have included Conan Doyle and Hugh MacDiarmid.

Elizabeth Gaskell's parents lived in Drummond Street between 1801 and 1804 before moving to London. Mrs Gaskell (1810–65) visited Edinburgh at least twice in 1831 and 1864, and gives a portrait of mid-nineteenth-century Edinburgh in 'Round the Sofa', an introduction to *My Lady Ludlow and Other Tales* (1859).

J. M. BARRIE

J. M. Barrie matriculated in 1878 at the age of eighteen. His intention after leaving Dumfries Academy had been to become a writer immediately, but his mother persuaded him that he should first obtain a university education. While at the University he began to review theatre for the *Edinburgh Courant* and books for *The Scotsman* and tried to form a literary club at a coffee house opposite St Giles. A fellow student later remembered Barrie as:

> A sallow-faced, round-shouldered, slight, somewhat delicate-
> looking figure, who went quietly in and out amongst us,
> attracting but little observation, but himself observing all and
> measuring up men and treasuring up impressions.[15]

Barrie lodged first in a top-floor flat at 14 Cumberland Street and then at 20 Shandwick Place. He later published a poem called 'The Old Lecture Room: Edinburgh University Revisited' in which he imagined himself as an old man looking back on his university career and leaves a picture of his teachers and contemporaries in *An Edinburgh Eleven* (1889).

On graduating he took lodgings at 3 Great King Street, with a Mrs Edwards who was to provide the inspiration for his story 'The Old Lady Shows Her Medals'. Shortly afterwards he was offered a job as a leader writer on the *Nottingham Journal* and never again lived in Edinburgh. However, he did return to receive an honorary LL.D in 1909 and became Chancellor of the University in 1930, when he succeeded Lord Balfour who had then been Chancellor for forty years. Perhaps this later recognition persuaded him to look upon his Alma Mater rather more generously for he left £5,000 to it in his will.

S. R. CROCKETT

Samuel Rutherford Crocket (1859–1914), whose name was to be so commonly linked with Barrie as a member of the Kailyard School, was in the last year of his Arts course at the University when Barrie matriculated, though they do not seem to have met. He later returned to study theology at the New Theological College but after Barrie had left.

Crockett, a Free Church minister until able to become a full-time author, wrote over forty novels, of which the best known, *The Stickit Minister* (1893), is dedicated to R. L. Stevenson. Stevenson dedicated his 'Hills of Home' poem to Crockett. In his novel *Cleg Kelly, Arab of the City* (1896) Crockett drew from his experiences as a missionary in the Edinburgh slums and the book has many scenes around the St Leonards area of the city where he lodged as a student.

ARTHUR CONAN DOYLE

Arthur Conan Doyle began his medical studies in 1876, graduating as a Bachelor of Medicine in 1881 and going on to take his doctorate on aspects of syphilis in 1885. As a student he lodged in Howe Street in the New Town. In his semi-autobiographical and largely forgotten early novel *The Firm of Girdlestone* (1890) he leaves a bitter picture of the university:

> Edinburgh University may call herself, with grim jocoseness,
> the 'alma mater' of her students, but if she be a mother at all,
> she is one of a very stoic and spartan cast, who conceals her
> maternal affections with remarkable success. The only signs of
> interest she ever deigns to evince towards her alumni are
> upon those not infrequent occasions when guineas are to be
> demanded from them . . . The University is a great unsympa-
> thetic machine, taking in a stream of raw-boned cartilaginous

youths at one end, and turning them out at the other as learned divines, astute lawyers and skilful medical men. Of every thousand of the raw material about six hundred emerge at the other side. The remainder are broken in the process.[16]

Conan Doyle was perhaps being rather unfair. The university was cosmopolitan with a large intake from England and the colonies. It may have been rather remote but then he did not spend all his time there. For seven months, for example, from March to October 1880 he abandoned his medical studies to join a whaling trip to Greenland. It was while he was at Edinburgh that his first story was published. 'The Mystery of Sasassa Valley', a light-hearted thriller set in South Africa about a demon who turned out to be a diamond, appeared in *Chambers' Edinburgh Journal* in September 1879. Conan Doyle's literary career had begun. He was subsequently to write several stories using Edinburgh as a background.[17]

At the University Conan Doyle met a man who was to change his life: Joseph Bell (1837–1911), a lecturer and surgeon at the Royal Infirmary of Edinburgh:

Bell was a very remarkable man in body and mind. He was thin, wiry, dark, with a high-nosed acute face, penetrating grey eyes, angular shoulders, and a jerky way of walking. His voice was high and discordant. He was a very skilful surgeon, but his strong point was diagnosis, not only of disease, but of occupation and character.[18]

Conan Doyle became his clerk, responsible for preparing case notes and showing patients into the large room in which Bell sat in state surrounded by his dressers and students. This position allowed him to observe the doctor's extraordinary powers of deduction. It was on Bell that Conan Doyle later modelled his detective Sherlock Holmes. Pupil and master stayed in touch and Bell took a keen interest in the Sherlock Holmes stories and 'even made suggestions which were not', Doyle noted, 'very practical'. Bell cleverly managed to profit from the association by contributing a preface to *A Study in Scarlet* (1887). The irascible zoologist Professor George Challenger in *The Lost World* (1912) was reputedly based on another Edinburgh professor William Rutherford (1839–99).

Hunter Steele's *The Wishdoctor's Song* (2005) is a campus novel satirising the fictional city of Deenburgh set in the early 1970s but which in its study of fractured identity lies in the tradition of Hogg and Stevenson.

THE OLD HIGH SCHOOL

Almost opposite the Old Buildings of the University is Infirmary Street, and at the foot of High School Yards is the old High School of Edinburgh. Though the peripatetic school is thought to be over eight hundred years old, it is not until the sixteenth century that much is known about it. Its former pupils include the founder of the New Town, George Drummond, Robert Fergusson, James Boswell, William Smellie, Francis Jeffrey, Henry Cockburn who writes about it in *Memorials of His Time*, Henry Mackenzie and, more recently, Sydney Goodsir Smith, Robert Garioch and Norman MacCaig.

Walter Scott began his schooling there in 1779, two years after it opened, in the new building, recollecting that he 'glanced like a meteor from one end of the class to the other, and commonly disgusted my kind master as much by negligence and frivolity as I occasionally pleased him by flashes of intellect and talent'. George Borrow, there some thirty years later, writes about the school in *Lavengro*:

> High School! Called so, I scarcely know why; neither lofty in thyself nor by position, being situated in a flat bottom; oblong structure of tawny stone, with many windows fenced with iron netting – with thy long hall below, and thy five chambers above, for the reception of the five classes, into which the eight hundred urchins who styled thee instructress were divided.
>
> Thy learned rector and his four subordinate domines; thy strange old porter of the tall form and grizzled hair, hight Boee, and doubtless of Norse ancestry, as his name declares; . . .
> Yes, I remember all about thee, and how at eight of every morn

we were all gathered together with one accord in the long hall, from which, after the litanies had been read (for so I call them, being an Episcopalian), the five classes from the five sets of benches trotted off in long files, one boy after the other, up the five spiral staircases of stone, each class to its destination.[19]

THE NORTH BRIDGE

If one travels down the South Bridge and crosses the High Street one comes, after the original *Scotsman* office, which is now a hotel, to the North Bridge. Iain Banks's *Complicity* is set in the offices of a Scottish broadsheet, *The Caledonian,* and one of the murdered bodies in the book is found adorning an empty plinth on the west side of the bridge. The bridge is also the scene of a mysterious death in Rankin's *Set in Darkness* (2000).

The present North Bridge dates from the end of the last century, though its predecessor, built in the 1760s, was the first part of the New Town expansion.

Edward Topham, visiting Edinburgh fourteen years later, was immediately struck by the strong winds on the bridge, a situation which remains unchanged. If one can withstand the wind the North Bridge is a marvellous vantage point to look out on Edinburgh. S. R. Crockett has a powerful description in his novel *Kit Kennedy* of the view from the bridge with Waverley Station 'sunk in a pale, luminous, silver mist through which burnt a thousand lights, warm, yellow and kindly', while Stevenson used to lean on the parapet of the bridge and watch the trains departing:

On a voyage to brighter skies. Happy the passengers who shake off the dust of Edinburgh, and have heard for the last time the cry of the east wind among her chimney tops! And yet the place establishes an interest in people's hearts; go where they will, they take a pride in their old home.[20]

PART III

The New Town

'. . . 'New Town': everywhere else in Scotland, it
meant the likes of Glenrothes and Livingston,
places built from nothing in the fifties and sixties.
But in Edinburgh, the New Town dated back to the
eighteenth century. That was about as new as
the city liked things.

IAN RANKIN, *Dead Souls* (1999)[1]

The Old Town had become so overcrowded by the mid-eighteenth century that expansion was required. Some 25,000 people were crammed into 138 acres. It was George Drummond, six times Lord Provost, whose ideas were embodied in the 1752 *Proposals*. Seven years later the Nor' Loch was drained and between 1763 and 1772 the North Bridge was built across it to link up with Edinburgh's port of Leith. Finally in 1766 a competition was announced for designs for a New Town.

A twenty-seven-year-old architect, James Craig, won the competition using one of the oldest of town planning patterns: the chequerboard or gridiron. His scheme involved a wide central street on the crest of the hill which he named after the ruling monarch George. This was balanced by two open-sided terraces: Princes Street and Queen Street. Between them ran two smaller streets, Thistle Street and Rose Street, designed to accommodate coach houses, shops and tradesmen's homes. At each end of George Street there was to be a church: St Andrew's at the east and St George's at the west; the Act of Union still within living memory, the intention was to show the partnership of Scotland and England. Soon the wealthy flocked north to the healthier and less crowded climes of this new development and the New Town was born.

PRINCES STREET

There has, however, always been an awkward division between the Old Edinburgh and the New Town. It is Princes Street that marks the dividing line between the medieval town with its buildings etched haphazardly against the skyline and the ordered symmetry of the New Town. To the south the turrets, crow-stepped gables, chimneys and spires of the High Street, to the north the fanlights, delicately scrolled lampholders and brass doorplates of George Street and Heriot Row.

Eric Linklater well recognised this demarcation line when he described Princes Street as 'a sort of schizophrenia in stone', although now it is a clutter of different architectural styles ranging from highly ornate Victorian Gothic to chromium, black marble, neon and plate glass. It is a street in search of an identity – the main thoroughfare linking east and west, the city's principal shopping precinct or a street of important buildings and monuments built to impress? It has certainly always been the preserve of the commercial world and is now dominated by the household names to be found in most high streets in the country. Khalid, the central character of Joan Lingard's *The Prevailing Wind*, is scathing about it:

> Let us contemplate the street of the Princes, the home of
> the shortbread kings and the Baronets of Bombazine. It is
> a fine street, is it not, despite its vulgar moments? It has
> width and colour, gardens and a bandstand, a gallery of art
> with another tucked behind, and a big ugly hotel at either
> end. What more could a street want.[2]

The two hotels he refers to are the Balmoral (formerly the North British), at the east end, and the Caledonian at the west end. Muriel Spark stayed for several weeks at the North British during her father's final illness:

> I spent most of my time in my room waiting for the hours of
> visiting my father to come round. I think at such times in
> one's life one tends to look out of the window oftener and
> longer than usual. I left my work and my books and spent my
> time at the window. It was a high, wide window, with an
> inside ledge, broad and long enough for me to sit comfortably
> with my legs stretched out. The days before Easter were
> suddenly warm and sunny. From where I sat propped in the
> open window frame, I could look straight onto Arthur's Seat
> and the Salisbury Crags, its girdle. When I sat the other way
> round I could see part of the Old City, the east corner of
> Princes Street Gardens, and the black Castle Rock. In those
> days I experienced an inpouring of love for the place of my
> birth, which I am aware was psychologically connected with
> my love for my father and with the exiled sensation of
> occupying a hotel room which was really meant for strangers.[3]

ARCHIBALD CONSTABLE
AND WILLIAM BLACKWOOD

The first house to be built in Princes Street was in 1769 at No. 10, on the site now opposite the Balmoral Hotel. Here, Archibald Constable (1774–1827), already the publisher of *The Edinburgh Review* and *Encyclopaedia Britannica*, set up his publishing firm in 1822 and here his authors Scott, Lockhart, Jeffrey and Cockburn would meet. Constable was an important catalyst in the establishment of Edinburgh as a literary centre. Cockburn was to write of his publisher:

> Abandoning the old timid and grudging system, Constable
> stood out as the general patron of all promising publications,
> and confounded not merely his rivals in trade, but his very
> authors, by his unheard-of prices. Ten, even twenty, guineas
> for a sheet of review, £2,000 or £3,000 for a single poem, and
> £1,000 each for two philosophical dissertations, drew authors
> from dens where they would otherwise have starved, and
> made Edinburgh a literary mart, famous with strangers, and
> the pride of its own citizens.[4]

A few doors west at No. 17 another bookseller, William Blackwood (1776–1834) had been established for some six years, after moving from his premises at 64 South Bridge. Blackwood had entered the bookselling trade in 1790, had become the Scottish agent for Byron's publisher John Murray and by the time he was established in Princes Street was a wealthy man. For example, just before moving he had published Walter Scott's *Tales of my Landlord,* which had sold 6000 copies in a week.[5]

BLACKWOOD'S MAGAZINE

In 1817 Blackwood founded the magazine that was to take his name, determined to provide a Tory rival to the Whig *Edinburgh Review.* After a false start he appointed two young men who with their high spirits, combative natures and strong views quickly established the reputation of the magazine. John Wilson (1785–1854), who used the pseudonym 'Christopher North', had won the Newdigate Prize for Poetry at Oxford and had come to Edinburgh in 1815 to complete his law studies after seven years in the Lake District, where he had been friendly with De Quincey and Wordsworth, after he lost most of his inheritance due to mismanagement of his estate by an uncle.

The second editor, John Gibson Lockhart (1794–1854), was another Oxford-educated advocate, and at the time *Blackwood's* was launched, he was only twenty-three. A striking man with piercing eyes, he was also rather deaf, which led people to assume he was aloof. Between 1837 and 1838 he published a seven-volume life of his father-in-law, Walter Scott. He died at Abbotsford and is buried at Scott's feet in Dryburgh Abbey.

It was an article that appeared in the October 1817 issue that overnight was to put *Blackwood's* firmly on the literary map. The Chaldee Manuscript was a satirical portrait of the literary and political figures of the day, written in the language of the Old Testament. The Whigs and their supporters were lampooned, the Tories praised, and though now the contents look dated and parochial, at the time it attracted attention all over the country. Suddenly the magazine had found a voice, which increasingly became vituperative.

In 1819 Blackwood published *Peter's Letters to his Kinsfolk*, a series of social and biographical sketches of Edinburgh written by Lockhart which give one of the best accounts of intellectual Edinburgh life at the time and has good character portraits of among others Henry Cockburn, Francis Jeffrey, Henry Mackenzie and Walter Scott.

The magazine's reputation and sales were consolidated by the success of the satirical 'Noctes Ambrosianae', which appeared between 1822 and 1835. Written by James Hogg and John Wilson they were a series of topical, critical, political and convivial dialogues that were supposed to have taken place in Ambrose's tavern near the site now occupied by the Café Royal, and described the activities of, among others, the 'Ettrick Shepherd', 'Christopher North' and the 'Opium Eater', characters based respectively on James Hogg, John Wilson and Thomas De Quincey.

JAMES HOGG

James Hogg (1770–1835) was born in and worked as a shepherd in the Borders but through his employer, he met Walter Scott, who took him on as an assistant in his search for Border ballads. Hogg came to Edinburgh in 1810 where he contributed to various magazines such as *Blackwood's* and edited a weekly literary magazine, *The Spy*, consolidating his reputation with a series of poems, *The Queen's Wake* (1813).

Hogg had a number of Edinburgh addresses: Anne Street (subsequently demolished when Waverley Bridge was built), Harrow Inn in the Grassmarket (now 46–54 Candlemaker Row) and Deanhaugh Street. To a certain extent Hogg was an anachronism in a city that was increasingly more genteel and snobbish. He was never quite taken seriously by literary society and in 1815 he returned to farm and write in the Borders.

Though Hogg published several novels, he is now remembered for *The Private Memoirs and Confessions of a Justified Sinner* (1824), one of the classic novels of Scottish literature. The book tells the story through the multiple narrative of two brothers, George Colwan and Robert Wringhim; the latter confesses to his brother's murder at the instigation of a stranger Gil-Martin after stalking him 'in the galley of the Parliament House, in the boxes of the play-house, in the church, in the assembly, in the streets, suburbs and the fields' until their confrontation on the top of Arthur's Seat. It has numerous scenes around the city and its themes of the concept of a dual personality and Calvinist belief in the Elect would later be explored in Stevenson's *The Strange Case of Dr Jekyll and Mr Hyde* (1886) and Spark's *The Prime of Miss Jean Brodie* (1961). A champion of the book was André Gide, who wrote an introduction when it was republished in 1947.

THE SCOTT MONUMENT

It is Scott who in more ways than one dominates Edinburgh. Towering over Princes Street is perhaps the most famous literary building, and certainly the largest memorial in the city. Reaction to it has been mixed, with some hailing it as a fitting monument to Scotland's greatest writer, others being less complimentary. Ruskin thought it a 'small, vulgar Gothic steeple' while Dickens, looking across at it from his hotel bedroom, likened it to 'the spire of a Gothic church taken off and stuck in the ground'. Completed in 1844 at a cost of some £15,000 the Scott Monument, intended originally to be sited in Charlotte Square, was the work of a young self-taught architect George Meikle Kemp, who accidentally drowned in the Union Canal, necessitating the work to be completed by his brother-in-law, William Bonnar.

The monument takes the form of an open Gothic cross surmounted by an ornately detailed spire rising to 200 feet. The statue in grey Carrara marble, cut by John Steell, depicts the seated Scott wrapped in a shepherd's plaid with his deerhound Maida at his feet. The exterior is decorated by eighty-four statuettes of characters from his novels and figures from Scottish history; the four most prominent, above the main arches, being Prince Charles Edward, the Lady of the Lake, Meg Merrilees and the Last Minstrel.

THE MOUND

The Mound was formed from the earth thrown up when digging the foundations of the streets in the New Town. Begun in 1781, it had by 1830 assumed its present dimensions. When work was at its height more than 1800 cartloads of rubble were being deposited each day. At the time, Henry Cockburn described it as an 'abominable incumbrance' but it forms a useful link between the Old and New Towns and is now a distinctive landmark in Edinburgh.

Some of the best views of Princes Street are from the top of the Mound. Alexander Cross in James Allan Ford's novel *A Statue for a Public Place* looks down to:

> The bottom of the Mound, the National Gallery of Scotland with its Ionic columns and the gallery of the Royal Scottish Academy with its Doric columns, and on either side of them the valley with trees in cold-burnt leaf and flower-beds in cinderglow, and along the opposite brink of the valley the mile-straight stretch of Princes Street, concealing behind its architectural confusion the eighteenth-century classical grace of the New Town. He saw it all with disturbing clarity, the familiar revealed as unfamiliar. He saw it all and was excited by it and felt obliged to explain his excitement. There was no magic in the unfamiliarity, nothing that had dropped out of God's sleeve. It was caused by the slant of the sun and by the unusual stillness and dryness of the air: this October light, making a long thrust from the south-east, had a cold-tempered point that whittled every outline against the sky, laid bare every

sunward surface, sliced off clean shadows and cut out a deep perspective; this northern air had its own power of refraction and, indeed, its own power of heady stimulation.[6]

Ford (1920–) was educated at the High School and Edinburgh University. During the Second World War he served with the Royal Scots, winning a Military Cross in Hong Kong in 1941 and, together with his brother who died in one, spent the rest of the war in Japanese prisoner-of-war camps. His war experiences have provided the background to his novels *The Brave White Flag* (1961) and *Season of Escape* (1965), and several of his short stories, while *A Statue for a Public Place* (1965), *A Judge of Men* (1968) and short stories such as 'A Kind of Possession' offer a wry view of Edinburgh middle-class life.

JOYCE CARY

Joyce Cary (1888–1957) used to have classes in the Royal Scottish Academy, then the Royal Institute Building, while studying at the Board of Manufacturers School of Art, now the Edinburgh College of Art, between 1907 and 1909. While in the city Cary lodged at 16 St Bernards Crescent. It was in Edinburgh that Cary abandoned painting for writing and where his first book, a collection of poetry, was published. He was to look back fondly to his time in Edinburgh and would later receive an honorary Doctorate of Laws from the University. It was while returning on the train from giving a lecture in Edinburgh in 1942 that Cary began his best-known novel, *The Horse's Mouth*.

Edinburgh is famous for its bitter wind and nowhere is it more apparent than Princes Street. Magnus in Eric Linklater's *Magnus Merriman* suffers its full force:

The wind hurried him along Princes Street. It blew with a bellow and a buffet on his stern and half-lifted his feet from the pavement. It beat his ears with a fistful of snow, and clasped his ribs with icy fingers. It tore the clouds from the sky, and laid bare, as if beyond the darkness, the cold grey envelope of outer space. Heads bent and shoulders thrusting like Rugby forwards in a scrum, east-bound pedestrians struggled against it, and westward travellers flew before it with prodigious strides. To the left, towering blackly, like iron upon the indomitable rock, was the Castle. To it also the storm seemed to have given movement, for as the clouds fled behind its walls the bulk of its ancient towers and battlements appeared to ride slowly in the wind's eye, as though meditating a journey down the cavernous channel of the High Street to Holyroodhouse, its deserted sister.[7]

It seems strange, therefore, that the Princes Street Promenade should be an Edinburgh tradition. It was something that both Thomas Carlyle, at the beginning of the nineteenth century, and Edwin Muir, in his book *Scottish Journey* (1935) a century later, particularly noticed. Its particular characteristic Muir noted was 'not only to observe, but also to be observed, and if you omit one of these duties you strike at its *amour-propre* and perhaps at its existence'.[8]

THE NEW CLUB

The New Club, opposite the Mound on Princes Street, with its commanding views over Princes Street Gardens to the Castle is the premier gentleman's club in the city. Both internally and externally it has changed, with the William Burns palace-fronted building of 1834 being replaced in 1966 with a more modern one of dark grey granite. Eric Linklater, in *The Merry Muse* (1959), describes a club which bears a similarity to the old building:

> The United Universities Club was a massive building that looked across Princes Street, over the gardens and the ravine beyond them, at the Castle on its towering height. But the social level of the United Universities was such as to let it regard the eminence of its royal neighbour without any consciousness of inferiority. In the matter of comfort, or splendour of decoration, the castle on the Rock had never come within a hundred leagues of the club in Princes Street, and very few of the courtiers who attended the Stuart kings

would have passed the scrutiny of its Election Committee. Its two principal rooms, on the ground floor and the first floor, could have accommodated a durbar for the King-Emperor, in the spacious days when the Crown enclosed an Empire, and the main staircase was broad enough not only for maharajahs but for their elephants.[9]

PRINCES STREET GARDENS

Princes Street Gardens occupy the bed of the Nor' Loch, once famed for its mammoth eels and innumerable waterfowl. They were landscaped at the beginning of the nineteenth century by the Princes Street proprietors at the cost of some £7000. Walter Scott, who was given a key to the gardens and used to cross them each day on his way from Castle Street to the Law Courts, recorded in his journal how his journey was 'through a scene of grandeur and beauty perhaps unequalled, whether the foreground or distant view is considered'.

Little has changed to this day. Dramatically the south side of Princes Street veers into an abyss and one is in a quiet and grassy oasis. Here are sheltered walkways, rows of inscribed benches, statues and neatly laid-out flowerbeds. In summer, musical bands play and ice-cream men peddle their wares. Something of the atmosphere is captured in Robert Garioch's poem 'In Princes Street Gardens':

> Doun by the baundstaund, by the ice-cream barrie,
> there is a sait that says, Wilma is Fab.
> Sit doun aside me and gieze your gab,
> jist you and me, a dou, and a wee cock-sparrie.

In contrast, it was in an air-raid shelter in the Gardens that the Labour politician and journalist, Tom Driberg, picked up a Norwegian sailor during the Second World War and had 'the narrowest shave of my life'. Driberg recalled how:

> The stillness of the shelter was broken by a terrifying sound –
> the crunching very near at hand of boots on the gravelled

floor. Instantly the blinding light of a torch shone full on us, and a deep Scottish voice was baying, in a tone of angry disgust: 'Och, ye bastards – ye dirty pair o' whores'.[10]

The two were taken to the local police station where, on learning Driberg was the columnist William Hickey, the sergeant, who read his column every morning, let him off. Compton Mackenzie used the episode in his novel *Thin Ice* (1956) about the precarious life of a homosexual politician.

At the western edge of the Gardens, in a hollow dell, is St Cuthbert's Church. It is the graveyard, however, where, among others, Thomas De Quincey is buried, that immediately grabs the attention. Steep steps lead past austere carved figures to walled gardens lined with huge mausoleums. Above, the Castle throws eerie shadows through the trees on the ground, while at the foot of the graveyard the trains hurtle past.

The Gardens have several literary memorials including one to R. L. Stevenson – a grove of birch trees designed by Ian Hamilton Finlay – and monuments to Allan Ramsay, John Wilson and the publisher and Lord Provost Adam Black (1784–1874), whose son James Tait Black endowed the annual fiction and biography prizes that bear his name.

The last memorial in Princes Street is a large granite Celtic cross in memory of Dean Ramsay (1793–1872), the minister of the adjacent St John's Episcopal Church. His *Reminiscences of Scottish Life and Character* was one of the bestsellers of the day, going through twenty editions. Built in 1817, St John's has a splendid interior modelled on St George's Chapel, Windsor. Among those buried here are Walter Scott's mother and the novelist Catherine Sinclair.

CATHERINE SINCLAIR

Catherine Sinclair (1800–64) was one of the most popular novelists of her day, best known now for *Holiday House* (1839), the first book to show children behaving much as they do today and with adults treating them with sympathy. It is said that her novel *Beatrice* (1852) sold over 10,000 copies in a few months in the United States alone. It was Sinclair who first guessed the identity of the anonymous author of the Waverley novels. There is a monument to her at the west end of Queen Street though she lived first at 6 Charlotte Square and then 133 George Street.

Her father, Sir John Sinclair of Ulbster (1754–1835), was the compiler of the twenty-nine volume *Statistical Account of Scotland*, the forerunner of the modern census. He was over six feet tall, as were all his fifteen children by two wives, which led to the pavement outside his home in George Street becoming known as the Giant's Causeway.[11]

JOYCE HOLMS

Leading into Charlotte Square from Princes Street is Hope Street and at No. 27 are the offices of Buchanan Stewart, the fictional law firm for which Joyce Holms's detective pair Fizz Fitzgerald and Tam Buchanan work. Holms, a former private investigator, presents a more genteel Edinburgh than that found in the novels of her crime-writing contemporaries, such as Ian Rankin, Quintin Jardine and Chistopher Brookmyre, though she is not afraid of dealing with issues such as child abuse, murder and drug barons.

The series is marked by its humour and the tensions between the middle-aged staid lawyer and his more bohemian student legal assistant and makes extensive use of Edinburgh locations. *Payment Deferred* (1996) opens with a murder in a lane behind Royal Crescent, the eponymous drug dealer in *Mr Big* (2000) is hung from the North Bridge and *Hot Potato* (2004) includes scenes in Corstorphine.

CHARLOTTE SQUARE

Charlotte Square, with its classical Corinthian pillars, balustrades, circular panels and windows, is perhaps the crowning achievement of Robert Adam and one of the most beautiful of European squares. It has, however, few literary connections, save the diarist Elizabeth Grant of Rothiemurchus (1797–1885), whose *Memoirs of a Highland Lady* (1898) paints a vivid portrait of Edinburgh life at the beginning of the nineteenth century, being born at No. 5.

Most of the buildings are now occupied by offices, while No. 6 is the official residence of the Secretary of State for Scotland. Next door, No. 7 has been restored to its original splendour and is now a museum, known as the Georgian House, in the care of the National Trust for Scotland. Distinguished former residents include the pioneer of antiseptic surgery, Joseph Lister, at No. 9; Sir William Fettes, the founder of the school that bears his name, at No. 13; and Lord Cockburn at No. 14.

Henry Cockburn (1779–1854) provides in *Memorials of His Time* (1856) a fascinating picture of Edinburgh at the beginning of the nineteenth century. In his duality of outlook he perhaps also stands as a representative Edinburgh figure. He looked back with fond regret at the expansion of the city and yet realised the need for social change. He was part of the Establishment, yet had a hankering for the low life. He felt Scottish but had closer affinities with the English.

WALTER SCOTT AND NORTH CASTLE STREET

Walter Scott, Cockburn's almost direct contemporary and neighbour, was able to articulate many of these conflicts in his numerous novels. Scott took lodgings on the second floor of No. 108 George Street for a few weeks after his marriage in 1797, before moving with his wife Charlotte to 10 South Castle Street and eventually to 39 North Castle Street, which was to remain his town house for the next twenty-eight years.

The house, now offices, is clearly identifiable with an inscription at the front, above the bow window, and a bust of Scott visible through a fanlight above the door. It was from this house that Scott left each morning to discharge his official duties at Parliament House and from here many of his books were written. There are numerous descriptions of the house and in particular his study which had:

A single Venetian window opening on a patch of turf not
much larger than itself and the aspect of the place was
sombrous. The walls were entirely clothed with books, most of
them folios and quartos . . . A dozen volumes or so, needful
for immediate purposes of reference, were placed close by him
on a small moveable frame . . . All the rest were in their proper
niches, and wherever a volume had been lent, its room was
occupied by a wooden block of the same size, having a card
with the name of the borrower and date of the loan, tacked on

its front . . . The only table was a massive piece of furniture which he had constructed on the model of one at Rokeby, with a desk and all its appurtenances on either side that an amanuensis might work opposite to him when he chose . . . His own writing apparatus was a very handsome old box richly carved, and lined with crimson velvet, and containing ink-bottles, taper-stand, etc in silver . . . The room had no place for pictures, except one, an original portrait of Claverhouse, which hung over the chimney-piece with a Highland target on either side, and broadswords and dirks (each having its own story) dispersed star fashion round them.[12]

It was here Scott lived while at the peak of his success. When he had to leave it after his financial problems in 1826 he was heartbroken as he noted in his journal:

> March 15 – This morning I leave No. 39 Castle Street, for the last time . . . In all my former changes of residence it was from good to better; this is retrograding. I leave this house for sale, and I cease to be an Edinburgh citizen, in the sense of being a proprietor, which my father and I have been for sixty years at least. So farewell, poor 39.[13]

Some thirty years later another writer was to live almost opposite. The author of *The Wind in the Willows* (1908), Kenneth Grahame (1859–1932), was born at 32 North Castle Street. His father was a lawyer and used to make the same journey as Scott to the Law Courts each day. In 1860 Grahame senior was made a sheriff in Argyll and the family left Edinburgh never to return.[14]

The poet and dramatist Albert Mackie (1904–85) was living at 34 North Castle Street when he published his first book *Poems in Two Tongues* (1928), which was much admired for its colloquial use of Scots. Mackie, editor of the *Edinburgh Evening Dispatch*, immediately after the Second World War, was in fact a Leith man; born in Brunswick Road, he had been brought up in Shaw's Street and Gayfield Street, and educated at Broughton Secondary School.

The Oxford Bar at No. 8 Young Street has been a favoured watering-hole for writers since the nineteenth century. Many of the Scottish Renaissance writers drank there and one of them, Sydney Goodsir Smith, immortalised it in *Carotid Cornucopius*.[15]

It has achieved recent popularity as the regular haunt of the critically acclaimed crime writer Ian Rankin (1960–) and his best-known character, the maverick Detective Inspector John Rebus, christened 'Morse of the North' after being televised with John Hannah in the central role. The proprietor of the bar – called the Sutherland Bar in the early novels – John Gates has lent his name to the pathologist Professor Gates in the series.

Based first in St Leonards, then briefly exiled to Craigmillar police station – nicknamed Fort Apache – and, from *Fleshmarket Close* (2004), in Gayfield Square, Rebus's investigations have taken him all over the city, laying bare the various murky sides of the capital, from protection rackets in Leith to corruption in high places. Rankin's great skill with the series has been to write intelligent thrillers dealing with important contemporary issues ranging from child abuse to the Scottish Parliament and to make the changing city a central feature of the story. As the series has progressed, the novels have grown in complexity and literary quality, demonstrating that, through his mouthpiece Rebus, Rankin has much to say about modern Edinburgh and the nature of Scottish identity.

Like many Edinburgh novelists his inspiration has been drawn from the city's literary history, most notably in *Hide and Seek* (1990), where he admits he 'tried to update Jekyll and Hyde, make him a policeman and bring it up to date'. He has also acknowledged the influence of Hogg's *Confessions of a Justified Sinner*. Interviewed by another Edinburgh novelist, Peter Gutteridge, Rankin stated:

> I hope the series as a whole will stand as a commentary on
> and investigation of Scotland at the end of the twentieth and
> beginning of the twenty-first century. Crime novels shouldn't
> be written in aspic. Edinburgh itself is the perfect setting for
> crime writing. It has a split personality – it's a city of history
> and museums and royalty, but at the same time there is this

feeling that behind the thick walls of those Georgian townhouses there are all sorts of terrible things happening.[16]

Rankin was born in Fife and grew up in Cardenden, which figures in a number of his novels. It was while studying at Edinburgh University for a PhD on Muriel Spark that he began writing and his first Rebus novel *Knots and Crosses* was published in 1987. However, it was not until he won the Crime Writers Gold Dagger for the ninth in the series, *Black and Blue* (1997), that the series took off, selling over 100,000 copies per title. By the beginning of 1999 his titles filled half the top twenty slots in the Scottish bestseller lists.

GEORGE STREET AND THE ASSEMBLY ROOMS

George Street has a distinguished population of statues – the theologian Dr Chalmers, King George IV, William Pitt – which strangely all face south, for the best views are to be had to the north, down the steep slopes towards the Firth of Forth. It was these views across to Fife which Alexander Smith especially noted:

> From George Street, which crowns the ridge, the eye is led
> down sweeping streets of stately architecture to the villas and
> woods that fill the lower ground, and fringe the shore; to the
> bright azure belt of the Forth with its smoking steamer or its
> creeping sail, and beyond, to the shores of Fife, soft blue, and
> flecked with fleeting shadows in the keen clear light of spring,
> dark purple in the summer heat, tarnished gold in the
> autumn haze; and farther away still, just distinguishable on
> the paler sky, the crest of some distant peak, carrying the
> imagination into the illimitable world.[17]

Halfway along George Street are the Assembly Rooms built in 1787 and extended at various times in the next century. A focus at one time of the social life of the New Town, with its regular dancing assemblies, it has entered literary history, for it was here at a dinner of the Edinburgh Theatrical Association in February 1827 that Scott first publicly admitted he was the author of the Waverley novels.

Scott had started work on his novel about the 1745 Jacobite Rising in 1805. Both his publisher James Ballantyne and a close friend Lord Kinedder disliked the book and Scott abandoned it for several years. After moving to Abbotsford, he revised it and in 1814 Constable published the book with considerable success. By the end of the year it had sold 5,000 copies and made Scott £2,000. Its author, however, remained the 'Great Unknown'.

A number of explanations have been advanced for why Scott should wish to remain anonymous. As a clerk to the Court of Session, he may have felt it rather unbecoming also to be a novelist. Equally, he may have simply preferred to keep his public life and private interests quite separate. By 1827 'the author of Waverley' had published twenty-three novels including *Rob Roy* (1817), *Heart of Midlothian* (1818), *Ivanhoe* (1819) and *Quentin Durward* (1823), and his identity was an open secret. The book had been a considerable financial and critical success and Scott now felt no embarrassment in confessing to them.

CHARLES DICKENS

Charles Dickens (1812–70) gave several readings at the Assembly Rooms in the 1840s and 1850s and, after reading his *A Tale of a Christmas Carol* to a packed audience in the Music Hall in 1858, he remarked:

> I never have forgotten, and I can never forget, that I have the
> honour to be a burgess and guild-brother of the Corporation
> of Edinburgh. As long as sixteen or seventeen years ago, the
> first great public recognition and encouragement I ever
> received was bestowed on me in this generous and
> magnificent city – in this city so distinguished in literature
> and so distinguished in the arts. You will readily believe that
> I have carried into the various countries I have since
> traversed and through all my subsequent career, the proud
> and affectionate remembrance of that eventful epoch in my
> life; and that coming back to Edinburgh is to me like
> coming home.[18]

Such affection for Edinburgh from a Londoner may owe much to the fact that his wife's family came from the city. Dickens's father-in-law, George Hogarth, had been a friend of Scott and had married one of the daughters of George Thomson, the poet and friend of Burns; Hogarth's brother-in-law was Scott's printer James Ballantyne.

Dickens had first come to Edinburgh in 1834, sent by the *Morning Chronicle* to report on the granting of the freedom of the city to Earl Grey, the force behind the Great Reform Bill. His genius was early recognised by both Cockburn and Jeffrey, the latter of whom arranged for the granting of the City's Freedom and a public dinner in Dickens's honour in 1841.

In 1848 he took the part of Slender in an amateur charity production of *The Merry Wives of Windsor* at the Theatre Royal, situated where the main post office stood near Waterloo Place. His 'Story of the Bagman's Uncle', a chapter within *The Pickwick Papers* set in Edinburgh, demonstrates his knowledge of the city's topography. The name of Ebenezer Scrooge was supposedly taken from a gravestone in Canongate Kirk.

Dickens's contemporary, William Makepeace Thackeray (1811–63), also delivered several lectures at the Assembly Rooms in the 1850s , but was less popular, being hissed in 1858 for making disparaging remarks about Mary, Queen of Scots. Each man, however, had his own following in the city and each was asked to represent the city in Parliament.

From 1947 to 1980 the Assembly Rooms were the home of the Edinburgh Festival Club. In his poem 'Embro to the Ploy' Robert Garioch speculates on the divided nature of the city and the consequences of the underworld and respectable society meeting at the Festival Club:

> The auld Assembly-rooms, whaur Scott
> foregethert wi his fiers,
> nou see a gey kenspeckle lot
> ablow the chandeliers.
> Til Embro drouths the Festival Club
> a richt godsend appears;
> it's something new to find a pub
> that gaes on sairvan beers

eftir hours
in Embro to the ploy.

Jist pitten-out, the drucken mobs
frae howffs in Potteraw,
fleean, to hob-nob wi the Nobs,
ran to this Music Haa,
Register Rachel, Cougait Kate,
Nae-neb Nellie and aa
stauchert about amang the Great,
what fun! I never saw
the like,
in Embro to the ploy.

Since its inauguration in 1947 the Edinburgh International Festival has done much to promote Scottish writing and writers, as well as to introduce music, drama and art from around the world. There have been adaptations of Hogg's *The Confessions of a Justified Sinner* and revivals of Home's *Douglas,* as well as new plays by James Bridie, Eric Linklater and Sydney Goodsir Smith, and tributes to Walter Scott, Hugh MacDiarmid and John Buchan.[19]

PERCY BYSSHE SHELLEY

Percy Bysshe Shelley (1792–1822) lodged for five weeks in 1811 at 60 George Street in a ground- and first-floor flat after running away with his sixteen-year-old sweetheart Harriet Westbrook. They were married at the home of the Revd Joseph Robertson at 225 Canongate that August. The house in George Street remains little changed except for the conversion of the ground floor into a shop and the addition of another storey. Shelley returned two years later and lodged briefly at 36 Frederick Street with his wife and small child in an attempt to avoid his creditors in the south.

His second wife, Mary Wollstonecraft Godwin (1797–1851), set part of her novel *Frankenstein* (1818) in Edinburgh. In chapter nineteen her narrator passes through Edinburgh:

I visited Edinburgh with languid eyes and mind; and yet that
city might have interested the most unfortunate being. Clerval

did not like it so well as Oxford, for the antiquity of the latter city was more pleasing to him. But the beauty and regularity of the new town of Edinburgh, its romantic castle and its environs, the most delightful in the world, Arthur's Seat, St. Bernard's Well, and the Pentland Hills compensated him for the change and filled him with cheerfulness and admiration.

There is a Frankenstein pub at 24 George IV Bridge.

BLACKWOOD'S MAGAZINE

The offices of *Blackwood's Magazine* were, from 1830 until 1972, opposite the Assembly Rooms at 45 George Street, before moving to Thistle Street where it ceased publication in 1980. Its contributors during this period included John Galt, Bulwer Lytton, Anthony Trollope, R. D. Blackmore, Henry James, Oscar Wilde, John Buchan (with *The Thirty-Nine Steps*), Walter de la Mare, J. B. Priestley, Ian Hay, Nevil Shute and Neil Munro.

Blackwood's published all but one of George Eliot's novels. Her lover G. H. Lewes submitted *Scenes from a Clerical Life* in 1856 and it was immediately accepted; *Adam Bede*, *The Mill on the Floss* and *Silas Marner* followed. In 1862 she moved to the *Cornhill Magazine* with *Romola* for an advance of £10,000, an extraordinary sum for the time, but returned to *Blackwood's* four years later with *Felix Holt*.

Some authors, despite many attempts, never became *Blackwood's* authors. In 1835 and 1836 a fifteen-year-old boy wrote a number of times asking for his work to be considered. He even pressed for an interview declaring 'a journey of three hundred miles shall not deter me'. His entreaties went unanswered, perhaps, as one subsequent commentator noted, because of 'the faint but authentic undertones of madness' in the letters. The young boy was Branwell Brontë.

Later *Blackwood's* turned down a book by H. G. Wells, sending to Wells's agent a letter that has a modern ring to it:

Though very well written, I am sorry to say I am not impressed by it. The price he demands for the serial issue seems to me quite prohibitive: likewise the advance on account of royalties on publication. The sum mentioned seems to me excessive for the work after it has appeared in serial form.[20]

Conan Doyle offered the magazine several stories and in 1888, after *Micah Clarke* had been turned down, wrote:

> Your note about Micah Clarke is so very kind that I cannot
> help thinking that you must have debated in your own
> mind whether you should or should not bring it out. If by
> meeting you in any way I could alter your decision I should
> be quite ready to trust to the success of the work for my
> own review, allowing the expences (sic) of publication to be
> defrayed out of the sale first, and then the profits to be
> divided in such a way as to its success myself. As an
> Edinburgh man I should be very glad if my first solid book
> should appear through you.[21]

In the event Blackwood failed to recognise Conan Doyle's promise and published only one of his stories, 'A Physiologist's Wife'; even then they kept it for fifteen months.

Another difficult relationship was with Joseph Conrad, who wrote to William Blackwood in February 1899 from Hythe:

> When I sit down to write for you as if in a friendly
> atmosphere, untrammelled like one is with people that
> understand, of whom one is perfectly sure. It is a special
> mood, and a most enjoyable one. Well, I must get on with
> the wretched novel which seems to have no end and whose
> beginning I declare I've forgotten. It is a weird sensation; the
> African nightmare feeling I've tried to put into Heart of
> Darkness is a mere trifle to it.[22]

In October that year Blackwood's published the opening chapters of *Lord Jim*. The magazine exercised great patience with the novelist, lending him money and paying for stories that were sometimes never delivered. By 1903 that patience was exhausted and the association ended.

In many ways it marked the end of an era and *Blackwood's* was never as influential in the twentieth century as it had been in the previous one.

MILNE'S BAR

On the corner of Hanover Street and Rose Street stands Milne's Bar, one of the most famous literary bars in Edinburgh. There is little now to belie its heritage, except some framed photographs of Sydney Goodsir Smith, Robert Garioch, Norman MacCaig, Sorley Maclean and Hugh MacDiarmid with, below, respectively, their poems 'Never Nae Mair', 'An Alabaster Box', 'November Night', 'Springtide' and 'In an Edinburgh Pub'.

Milne's Bar, throughout the 1950s and 1960s, was the meeting place of a whole generation of poets and acolytes dedicated to writing in the Scots tongue and therefore can be said to be almost the centre of the Scots Literary Renaissance. Other writers frequently to be found there included George Mackay Brown (1921–96), Donald Campbell (1940–), George Campbell Hay (1915–84) and Tom Scott (1918–1995).

Alasdair Gray, in his novel *1982, Janine*, has a scene in the bar, the unholy trinity of which were MacDiarmid, MacCaig and Smith:

> The bar was crowded except where three men stood in a small
> open space created by the attention of the other customers. One
> had a sombre pouchy face and upstanding hair which seemed
> too like thistledown to be natural, one looked like a tall sarcastic
> lizard, one like a small sly shy bear. 'Our three best since Burns,'
> a bystander informed me, 'barring Sorley, of course.'[23]

Norman MacCaig (1910–96), as *The Poems of Norman MacCaig* (2005) shows, has written widely about Edinburgh and is a sharp observer of its foibles. Born in London Street his family moved shortly afterwards to Dundas Street where his father ran a chemist's shop. He was educated at the Royal High School and then read classics at Edinburgh University. From 1934 to 1970 he was a schoolteacher, his final job as headmaster of Juniper Green Primary School, and he subsequently taught at the University of Stirling and was writer-in-residence at Edinburgh University. Among those to visit him at his home at 7 Leamington Terrace in Bruntsfield was Hugh MacDiarmid.[24]

Sydney Goodsir Smith (1915–75) came to Edinburgh at the age of twelve. Like MacCaig and Robert Garioch he was educated at the Royal High School and Edinburgh University and spent his entire life in the city, where for a time he was the art critic of *The Scotsman*. For many years he lived at 50 Craigmillar Park, the 'Schloss Schmidt', which he shared for a time with Sorley Maclean and his wife, and there is a plaque to him at 25 Drummond Place, his home towards the end of his life.

Smith's poetry in its vibrant depiction of low life harks back to the work of Ramsay and Fergusson. MacDiarmid thought his linguistic romp *Carotid Cornucopious* (1947) did 'for Edinburgh no less successfully what Joyce did for Dublin in *Ulysses*' . . . the awareness of James Joyce and most other avante-garde writers, and above all of Jarry's *Ubu Roi* has clearly been superadded to the recaptured spirit of Dunbar, Sir Thomas Urquhart, and Burns'.[25] Its flavour and authenticity is apparent in the names of some of the bars that the central character visits – the Abbotsfork and the Haw-Haw Hures at Quaenisfanny. The city also figures in three long conversational poems *The Vision of the Prodigal Son* (1960), *Kynd Kittock's Land* (1965) – the title is taken from a ballad by William Dunbar – and *Gowdspink in Reekie* (1974).

Sorley Maclean (1911–96), who wrote as Somhairle MacGill-Eain, is now regarded as one of Scotland's greatest Gaelic poets and largely responsible for the revival of the Gaelic poetic tradition in the twentieth century. Born on the island of Raasay he came to Edinburgh in 1929 to study English at the University. It was while training to be a schoolmaster that he met Christopher Murray Grieve (Hugh MacDiarmid) (1892–1978) in Rutherford's. The two immediately struck up a friendship that lasted until MacDiarmid's death.

Maclean first appeared with Garioch in *Seventeen Poems for Sixpence* (1940) and his first solo work, the first published collection of Gaelic verse in a modern idiom, was published in November 1943 under the title *Dain do Eimhir agus Dain Eile*. It was not, however, until his inclusion in *Four Points of a Saltire* in 1970 that he became known to a general audience. MacLean taught at Boroughmuir High School between 1939 and 1940, and then from 1943 to 1956, before becoming headmaster of

Plockton Secondary School until his retirement in 1972.[26]

Among the distinguished visitors to Milne's Bar were Stevie Smith, Dylan Thomas and W. H. Auden. So famous did the gatherings there become that 'the Rose Street poets' were forced to decamp a few yards east to the much more elegant establishment, the Abbotsford. With its ornate plaster work, island bar and wooden panelling the Abbotsford remains much as it was when it was patronised in the 1960s.

The writer Alan Bold (1943–98), who knew the circle, has recalled:

> MacDiarmid alternating between affability and intensity, MacCaig delivering swift sarcastic verbal thrusts, Smith with a monocle in his eye and a glass in his hand and sometimes an inhaler at his throat to ward off attacks of asthma. All three poets were incessant smokers as well as heavy drinkers so their presence was surrounded by a tobacco cloud of unknowing.[27]

Bold was one of the most prolific of recent Edinburgh writers. Born and brought up at the top of Leith Walk he was educated at Broughton High School, like his great hero MacDiarmid, and at Edinburgh University. For many years he worked as a journalist before taking up writing full-time. In addition to his award-winning biography of MacDiarmid and his poetry, he compiled countless anthologies and wrote books about, among others, Muriel Spark and modern Scottish literature.

ST ANDREW SQUARE

St Andrew Square was, until recent dispersal to purpose-built offices, the financial centre of the capital. No. 35, then Douglas's Hotel, was where the dying Walter Scott spent his last two nights in Edinburgh on his return from Italy in July 1832. He knew the area well, for after his bankruptcy and the death of his wife he had spent two months in the lodging house of a Mrs Browne round the corner at 6 North St David Street.

Three doors away at No. 9 lived Sir David Brewster (1781–1868), the inventor of the kaleidoscope and later Principal of Edinburgh University, who while editor of the *Edinburgh Encyclopaedia* between 1808 and 1830 provided work for the young Thomas Carlyle. Another resident was

David Hume at 8 South St David Street, where he was visited by Benjamin Franklin in 1771.

QUEEN STREET

St Andrew Square leads into Queen Street, one of the New Town's finest residential streets. Sydney Smith, one of the founders of *The Edinburgh Review*, lived for a time at No. 19 before moving after his marriage to 46 George Street and 24 Moray Place. He had first come to Edinburgh in 1798 to act as a private tutor, lodging at 38 Hanover Street, and remained in the city until 1804.

John Wilson, 'Christopher North', resided with his mother at No. 53, even after his marriage, before moving to 29 Ann Street in 1819 and his final home, 6 Gloucester Place, in 1826. Next door at 52 Queen Street chloroform was discovered at the home of Dr James Young Simpson.

It was at the Philosophical Institution in Queen Street that John Ruskin (1819–1900), whose family originally came from Edinburgh, delivered his famous series of lectures on architecture in November 1853.

Just over thirty years later Oscar Wilde (1854–1900) gave two lectures in the Queen Street Hall. *The Portrait of Dorian Gray* is supposed to have been based on Father John Gray (1866–1934), a priest at St Peter's Church, Falcon Avenue, whom Wilde had met in London in 1889. Gray's first collection of poems *Silverpoints* (1893) were paid for by Wilde.

Eric Linklater's Magnus Merriman lived in Queen Street in:

A row of tall flat-fronted houses whose residential dignity had been somewhat impaired by the invasion of offices and a few shops of a superior kind. His flat was at the top of the house and its windows looked north across gardens and a descending terrace of intersecting streets to a mistiness that in fine weather dissolved and revealed the steely brightness of the Forth. Beyond that were the ancient kingdom of Fife, soberly coloured, and the rising blue shadow of the Ochil hills, that outpost of the Highlands and a promise of farther heights.[28]

Linklater knew this area well; during the early 1930s he shared a flat at 11

Above. Edinburgh Castle. The most dominant building in the city, the Castle figures in numerous Edinburgh novels.

Left. Canongate Kirk. Amongst those buried here are Robert Fergusson, Burns's 'Clarinda', Adam Smith and the founder of the New Town, George Drummond.

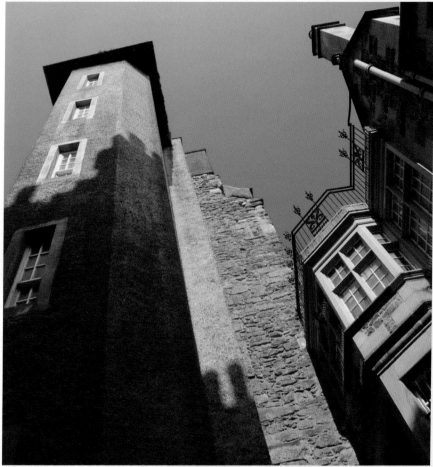

Above. James Court. Philosopher David Hume lived here.

Right. Lady Stair's Close. Robert Burns stayed here during his first visit to Edinburgh. The site of the Writers' Museum.

LADY STAIR'S CLOSE

Above. Royal Exchange. The scene of murders in Iain Banks's *Complicity* and Ian Rankin's *Mortal Causes*.

Left. The Tolbooth. Features in the novels *The Heart of Midlothian* and *Ringan Gilhaize*. When the gaol there was demolished in 1817 Walter Scott was presented with the heavy wooden door: it remains in Abbotsford to this day.

Above. Grassmarket. Burns and Wordsworth, amongst other writers, have stayed at the White Hart Inn and the infamous Porteous riot took place here in 1736.

Left. Greyfriars Kirk. Strong Walter Scott associations and burial place of Captain Porteous, Allan Ramsay, poet William McGonagall and George Buchanan, tutor to Mary, Queen of Scots.

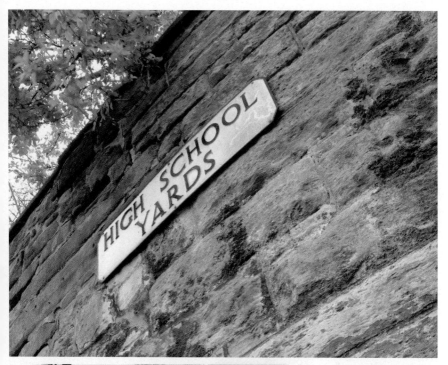

Above. High School Yards. Site of Royal High School whose former pupils include James Boswell, Walter Scott, George Borrow, Robert Fergusson and Norman MacCaig.

Left. 25 Forrest Road. Sandy Bell's Bar is a renowned gathering place for the literary and folk worlds, and is particularly associated with the late Hamish Henderson and the School of Scottish Studies.

Right. 11 Picardy Place. A colony of Picardy silk weavers lived on this site in the seventeenth century. A statue marks the site of Conan Doyle's birthplace in 1859.

Below. 39 North Castle Street. Walter Scott's home from 1798 to 1826, and where he lived while at the peak of his success.

Left. 17 Heriot Row. The childhood home of Robert Louis Stevenson, a verse from 'Leerie the Lamplighter' is inscribed on the railings by the front door.

Below. 5 Young Street. The Oxford Bar features in Ian Rankin's Rebus stories.

Overleaf. A view of the city centre from Calton Hill.

Top. Assembly Rooms. Dickens and Thackeray are among the many to have performed here and it was here that Walter Scott publicly admitted that he was the author of the Waverley novels.

Above. Scotland Street. The fictional setting for Alexander McCall Smith's novel *44 Scotland Street.*

Left. The Scott Monument. Built to commemorate Walter Scott between 1840 and 1844, the 200-ft monument was designed by a joiner, George Kemp, who drowned in the Union Canal before the work was completed.

Below. 19 Hazelbank Terrace. J K Rowling's home after the success of the Harry Potter novels allowed her to give up teaching in 1998 and move from Leith.

Top. Braid Hills Hotel. Features in several novels including *The Prime of Miss Jean Brodie* and *44 Scotland Street.*

Above. Craiglockhart. Now an extension of Napier University, it was here, in 1916, when it was a military hospital, that Wilfred Owen and Siegfried Sassoon met.

Above. Fettes College. The purported school of James Bond. Blown up in Old Fettesian Paul Johnston's novel *Body Politic*.

Left. James Gillespie's School. Model for Marcia Blaine School in *The Prime of Miss Jean Brodie*.

Top. Warriston Cemetery.
Scenes in Jules Vernes's
Backwards to Britain.

Right. Dean Village.
Mentioned in Eric
Linklater's *The Merry Muse.*

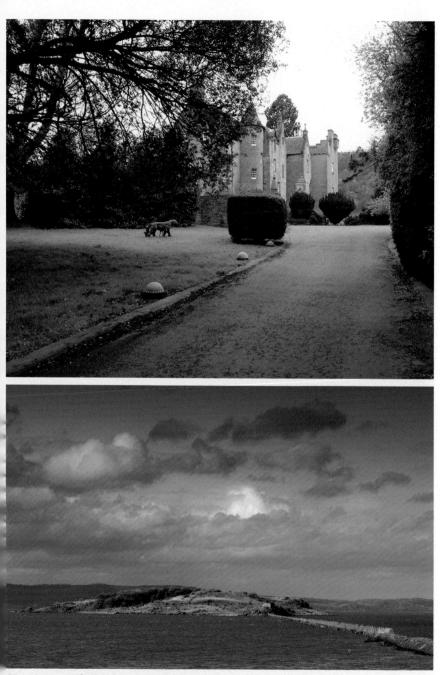

Top. Craigcrook Castle. Amongst the visitors to Francis Jeffrey's home were Hans Christian Andersen, Alfred Tennyson, Charles Dickens and George Eliot.

Above. Cramond Island. Supposedly the inspiration for Stevenson's *Treasure Island* and where Miss Jean Brodie spent her weekends.

Top. Salisbury Crags. A popular murder site and suicide spot in Edinburgh novels.

Above. Silverknowes Beach. A location in Irvine Welsh's *Marabou Stork Nightmares*.

York Place. The portrait painter, Henry Raeburn (1756–1823), whose sitters included Henry Mackenzie, David Hume, James Boswell, William Creech and Walter Scott, had his studios in York Place.

ARTHUR CONAN DOYLE

York Place runs into Picardy Place, which takes its name from a colony of Picardy silk weavers established here in the seventeenth century, and it was here Arthur Ignatius Conan Doyle (1859–1930) was born at No. 11. His father Charles worked for the Scottish Office of Works and had designed the small statues of historical figures for the fountain of Holyroodhouse; his mother was distantly related to Walter Scott.

While his father Charles supplemented his income by sketching for magazines and books, money was scarce and he failed to exercise his parental responsibilities. An epileptic, he eventually took to drink and was committed to Crichton Royal Institution, a mental hospital near Dumfries, where he died in 1893. The Conan Doyle birthplace was pulled down in the 1960s to make room for the huge roundabout at the top of Leith Walk. The mysteries of Paolozzi's sculptures outside St Mary's Roman Catholic Cathedral are pondered by a statue of Sherlock Holmes. A plaque opposite, on the surviving side of the street, marks the house.[29]

At the age of seven Conan Doyle was sent to live at the eighteenth-century Liberton Bank House, which stands beside the Braid Burn at the north end of Gilmerton Road. At the time it was owned by the sister of John Hill Burton, the Historiographer Royal for Scotland and a friend of the family. Conan Doyle dedicated his novel *The Firm of Girdlestone* to Burton's son William. Nowadays the house sits back from one of the principal roads into Edinburgh and it is hard to imagine it as ever being in the country but in the 1860s it was felt the country air would benefit the young child.

The young Conan Doyle was sent to a local school, most probably Newington Academy in Salisbury Place. He did not enjoy his time there, partly because he was separated from his mother and partly because of the school's tough regime. The school became a hospital for incurables in 1879 and is now the headquarters of Historic Scotland. When the Doyles moved to 3 Sciennes Hill Place, close to the school, the young Conan Doyle returned to live at home.

Between 1875 and 1877 the family rented a house in Argyle Park Terrace. It was larger and the more expensive rent was covered by taking in a young medical student, Bryan Waller. Later as a medical student at the University Conan Doyle, together with his family, lived for a short time at 23 George Square, which had been inherited by Waller. Waller, besides providing financial support, was to be an important influence on Conan Doyle's decision to take up a literary career. A descendant of the poet Edmund Waller and nephew of the writer Barry Cornwall, he had published a collection of poems at the age of twenty-two. It was Waller who it has been suggested was an inspiration for Sherlock Holmes and was the suitor of Conan Doyle's sister Annette.

The final Conan Doyle address in the city was 15 Lonsdale Terrace where the family are listed for 1881 and 1882. Running into Lonsdale Terrace is Lauriston Gardens where in his first published book *A Study in Scarlet* (1887) the body of Enoch Drebber is discovered. It seems Conan Doyle's knowledge of London was so hazy he was forced to use Edinburgh place names. His Edinburgh connections, however, continued for he fought an Edinburgh seat as a Liberal Unionist in the 1900 election.

SHERLOCK HOLMES AND EDINBURGH

Edinburgh also claimed Sherlock Holmes as her own – his rationalism one of city's best known traits – with several adventures taking place in the city. Caleb Carr's *The Italian Secretary* (2005) has Holmes and Watson investigating the death of David Rizzio. David Pirie's Murder Rooms series – *The Patient's Eyes* (2002) and *The Night Calls* (2003)- takes as its starting point the fact that Doyle studied under Joseph Bell and puts them together. In *The Patient's Eyes* they look into the case of a young heiress traumatised by an attacker who killed her parents while in *The Night Calls* they investigate a series of bizarre assaults on women in the brothels of 1878 Edinburgh. Howard Engel's *Mr Doyle and Dr Bell* (1997), set in 1879, has Joseph Bell enlisting the help of his student Conan Doyle to try and right a miscarriage of justice case, their adventures including meeting Disraeli and R. L. Stevenson. In Val Andrews's *Sherlock Holmes and the Theatre of Death* (1997) Holmes investigates the real-life death of the illusionist 'The Great Lafayette' in a fire at Edinburgh's Empire Palace Theatre, now the Festival Theatre in Nicolson Street, on 9 May, 1911. Anthony O'Neill's Gothic novel *The Lamplighter* (2003), about grave-robbing and murder in 1886, is not explicitly a Sherlock Holmes novel but the amateur detectives are a retired Edinburgh Professor of Logic and Metaphysics Thomas McKnight and his sidekick Canavan.

THE SECOND NEW TOWN

To the north of Queen Street lies the first extension of the New Town begun at the turn of the nineteenth century and largely completed by 1823. Dundas Street provided the north/south axis with Heriot Row, Northumberland Street and Abercromby Place the cross-bars. Finally, on land originally belonging to the Earl of Moray, a series of beautiful crescents and streets were built, now among the best addresses in Edinburgh – Randolph Crescent, Ainslie Place and the octagonal Moray Place.

The Scottish Institution for the Education of the Daughters of Gentlefolk, which the heroine of Iona MacGregor's lesbian detective novel *Death Wore a Diadem* (1989) attends, is based on the Scottish Institution for Young Ladies which was based in Moray Place between 1834 and 1870.

During the 1970s a generation of Scottish writers calling themselves the Heretics, such as Stuart MacGregor, Donald Campbell, Norman MacCaig, Sorley Maclean, Robert Garioch, Liz Lochhead and Tom Leonard, met monthly on the first Thursday of each month in the basement bar of the New Town Hotel in Darnaway Street mixing readings of poetry and prose with folk music. Darnaway Street also figures in Ian Rankin's *The Falls* (2001)[30]

QUEEN STREET GARDENS

Elizabeth Grant of Rothiemurchus noted when she took lodgings at the beginning of the nineteenth century:

> There were no prettily laid out gardens then between Heriot
> Row and Queen Street, only a long strip of unsightly grass, a

green, fenced by an untidy wall and abandoned to the use of
the washer-women. It was an ugly prospect, and we were
daily indulged with it, the cleanliness of the inhabitants being
so excessive that, except on Sundays and 'Saturdays at e'en'
squares of bleaching linens and lines of drying ditto were ever
before our eyes.[31]

Fifty years later all that had changed and the gardens are amongst the
prettiest sights in Edinburgh. Moray McLaren has written 'Edinburgh is
a city of autumn. It is her best and loveliest season. Sunset transfigures
her as it does few other places.' McLaren's novel *The Pursuit* captures
beautifully this particular quality of the city:

> The town was bathed in that luminous silver and pale gold
> glow which the northern autumn alone can produce. There are
> always one or two days of this exquisitely peaceful benevolence
> even after the great storms break and before the purgatory of
> an Edinburgh winter begins. The trees in the Heriot Row
> gardens that had of late been bending beneath the wind stood
> motionless and delicate as filgree. Their discarded leaves lay
> heaped in brown, yellow, and here and there crimson on the
> grass of the gardens and in the streets. The sky was of the
> palest most flawless blue. Even the grey Georgian houses facing
> uphill and into the south had lost their severity and had, in the
> deep, silver interstices of their stones, caught something of the
> sunlight in which they had been bathed all day long.[32]

HERIOT ROW

Heriot Row is a dignified street of huge houses with neat front doors and
brass plaques that advertise this street of advocates. One of the central
characters of McLaren's *The Pursuit*, Fleming-Stewart, lives in Heriot
Row and is well aware of its history. He leads a visitor to the window.

> 'Out there in those gardens about ninety years ago a small
> boy played by himself and made up dreams, some of them

pleasantly adventurous, some of them evil. Later on when he was about thirty, he wrote what he called "A Shilling Shocker" entirely concerned with the problems of evil. It has plenty of absurdities and betises in it – and some fine phrases. It's fantastic and incredible, but it took the English-reading world by storm and is still a favourite plot.'

'I know,' said Jim, 'R. L. Stevenson's Dr Jekyll and Mr Hyde. He lived here in Heriot Row.'

'Precisely. But he couldn't have written it if he hadn't known Edinburgh in his bones. This aristocratic, respectable old city of ours has a tradition of subterranean evil which it has not yet shaken off.'[33]

That boy was Robert Louis Stevenson who moved from Inverleith Terrace to live at 17 Heriot Row in 1856. Each night his faithful nurse Cummy would carry him to the nursery window and point out the lights in the Queen Street houses where perhaps also 'there might be sick little boys and their nurses, waiting like us for the morning'. He would look out of the window for Leerie the Lamplighter 'for we are very lucky, with a lamp before the door'. A verse from 'Leerie the Lamplighter' is inscribed on the railings by the front door. The four-storey Georgian terraced house bears a close resemblance to that 'citadel of the proprieties', the house in Stevenson's highly autobiographical novel *The Misadventures of John Nicholson* (1888).

EDINBURGH ACADEMY

It was from Heriot Row that Stevenson made his way to school, first to Mr Henderson's School round the corner at 36 India Street, then to Edinburgh Academy in Henderson Row. The school had been founded in the early 1820s by Henry Cockburn and another advocate Leonard Horner who felt that the Greek instruction at the High School was not of sufficiently high a standard to compete with the growing number of English public schools. As a result many parents had begun to send their sons south to school.

Both men were Whigs and realised that if their plans were to succeed they had to enlist the support of the Tories, which is how Walter Scott became involved in the enterprise. Scott, then at the height of his fame, served as a Director until 1832 and made the principal speech at the opening ceremony. The school rapidly established itself as one of the leading educational establishments in the city. One of the earliest applicants for a teaching post was supposedly Thomas De Quincey but, in spite of the support of Samuel Coleridge, his application was turned down.

Stevenson started at the school in the autumn of 1861 aged eleven. He seems to have kept very much to himself and made little impression. Two years later he left to join his mother whose poor health meant she had to spent the winter in France. However, he remained fond of the school and often attended and wrote verses for the annual dinner. There is a portrait of him in the School Hall together with that of R. M. Ballantyne, who had been at the school twenty years before Stevenson. There can be few schools that boast the authors of two children's classics such as *Coral Island* and *Treasure Island.*

Other writers to have been educated there include Bruce Marshall (1899–1987), whose satirical novel *George Brown's Schooldays* (1946) may be based on the school and the academic J. I. M. Stewart (1906–94) who, as Michael Innes, wrote donnish detective stories featuring Inspector John Appleby as well as a number of short stories set in Edinburgh.

Stevenson's final school was kept by a Robert Thompson on the west side of Frederick Street. There he was able to develop his individuality so that by the time he left in 1867 he was regarded as quite a non-conformist. A contemporary leaves this picture of the young Stevenson:

At that time Louis Stevenson was the queerest looking object you could conceive. To begin with he was badly put together, a slithering, loose flail of a fellow, all joints, elbows, and exposed spindle-shanks, his trousers being generally a foot too short in the leg. He was so like a scarecrow that one almost expected him to creak in the wind. And what struck us all was that he seemed to take a pride in aggravating the oddities of nature. When the weather happened to be fine – and I don't remember seeing him when it wasn't – he came in a battered

straw hat that his grandfather must have worn and laid aside
because it was out-of-date. Under that antiquated headgear his
long, lank hair fell straggling to his shoulders, giving him the
look of a quack or gypsy. He wore duck trousers and a black
shirt, with loose collar and a tie that might be a strip torn
from a cast-away carpet. His jacket was of black velvet and it
was noticeable that it never seemed good or new. We
remarked among ourselves that there must be a family trunk
full of old clothes which he was wearing out.[34]

As a child, Stevenson often went ice-skating at Cox's Gymnasium, which
was situated between Royal Crescent and Dundas Street, and while at
Edinburgh University he took minor roles in a number of private
theatricals at the home of his engineering professor Fleeming Jenkin, first
at 5 Forres Street and then from 1874 at 3 Great Stuart Street.

DRUMMOND PLACE

A short walk away is Drummond Place where a plaque at No. 25
commemorates Sydney Goodsir Smith who lived there towards the end
of his life. A few doors away at No. 28 was the home of Charles
Kirkpatrick Sharpe (1791–1851), a friend of Walter Scott. An eccentric
Edinburgh figure, whose visiting card bore only the musical notation C
sharp, his letters give a good picture of the city during the first part of the
nineteenth century. The house was filled with such a vast collection of
books and memorabilia, including supposedly part of Robert Bruce's
shroud and a tea-caddy used by Mrs McLehose, that on his death the
auction of the contents lasted six days.

Another writer who lived in Drummond Place was Compton
Mackenzie (1883–1972), the author of over a hundred books including
Sinister Street and *Whisky Galore!*. Mackenzie moved to No. 31 in the
spring of 1953, where he was visited by James Thurber and Thornton
Wilder. Thurber's short story 'The Catbird Seat' was relocated in Edin-
burgh when it was filmed as *The Battle of the Sexes* with Peter Sellers.

The house stands on the shoulder of a small rise and on one side
looks over its own gardens to the Firth of Forth and on the other across

public gardens. Mackenzie lived there with his second wife Chrissie and, after she died, with her sister Lily. Here Mackenzie completed his multi-volume autobiography and here he died on St Andrew's Day 1972, seven weeks short of his ninetieth birthday. He was buried on the Island of Barra where he had lived during the Second World War. At his burial the eighty-two-year-old piper collapsed during the last lament and died a few minutes later.

Just below Drummond Place is Fettes Row where the writer Margaret Oliphant (1828–97), regarded as Edinburgh's first full-time woman of letters, lived for many years. In her time she was a highly successful and prodigious writer of novels, many of them for *Blackwood's Magazine*, whose history she wrote.

SCOTLAND STREET

Leading north off Drummond Place is Scotland Street, described by Alexander McCall Smith in his novel *44 Scotland Street* (2005) as lying 'on the edge of the Bohemian part of the Edinburgh New Town, the part where lawyers and accountants were outnumbered – just – by others'.[35]

Inspired by Armistead Maupin's *Tales of the City* and originally a serial novel in *The Scotsman*, *44 Scotland Street* centres on the lives of a range of characters living at this fictional address. There are numerous episodes set around the New Town, most particularly in the Cumberland Bar in nearby Cumberland Street, and in various Edinburgh institutions such as Valvona & Crolla (an Italian delicatessen at the top of Leith Walk), Jenners tea-room, Sandy Bell's bar and the Braid Hills Hotel – a favourite of Miss Jean Brodie – with walk on-parts given to a number of well-known Edinburgh residents such as Ian Rankin.

McCall Smith pokes gentle fun at the eccentricities and aspirations of middle-class life in Edinburgh – the chartered surveyor and stalwart of the Conservative Association who dreams of membership to Muirfield golf club, the mother whose precocious five-year-old is already learning Italian and the saxophone – but his lightness of touch does not obscure some more serious underlying themes about the character of the city and its citizens. As one character observes, 'Of course, Edinburgh's full of double standards, isn't it? Hypocrisy is built into the stonework here.'[36]

PART IV

The Villa Quarters

One of the most enduring images of the city is Calton Hill. Numerous postcards immortalise its cluster of monuments, and photographers seek to capture it from every possible angle. From it can be had some of the best views of Edinburgh. It is therefore appropriate in seeking to satirise Edinburgh's pretensions that Norman MacCaig should begin his long poem about Edinburgh 'Inward Bound' with one of its most prominent symbols:

> On Calton Hill
> The twelve pillars
> Of this failed Parthenon
> Made more Greek by the Cargo boat
> Sailing between them
> On the cobwebby waters of the Firth
> Should marry nicely with the Observatory
> In the way complements do
> Each observing the heavens
> In its different way.

MacCaig is referring to the National Monument, sometimes called 'Edinburgh's Disgrace', modelled on the Parthenon, and designed to commemorate the Scottish soldiers and sailors who had fought in the Napoleonic Wars. Its foundation stone was laid by George IV during his visit in 1822, but owing to lack of funds the work was never completed. Subsequently, there were plans to finish the monument and dedicate it to Burns, Queen Victoria or turn it into a National Gallery.

Other buildings on Calton Hill include the Old City Observatory and the Nelson Monument, built in 1807–8 to mark the victory at Trafalgar. Below on Regent Road is the old Royal High School – described by Sir John Summerson as 'the noblest monument of the Scottish Greek Revival' – which moved here from High School Yards in 1829 and was adapted in the late 1970s to take the Scottish Assembly.

On the south side of Regent Road is the Burns Monument. This was where Alexander Smith thought the best views in Edinburgh were to be had, especially at night:

It is more astonishing than an Eastern dream. A city rises up before you painted by fire on night. High in air a bridge of lights leap the chasm; a few emerald lamps, like glow-worms, are moving silently about in the railway station below; a solitary crimson one is at rest. That ridged and chimneyed bulk of blackness, with splendour bursting out of every pore, is the wonderful Old Town, where Scottish history mainly transacted itself; while, opposite the modern Princes Street is blazing throughout its length.[1]

R. L. STEVENSON

Stevenson's parents and grandparents are buried in the New Calton Burying Ground, situated through some black iron gates, beside the monument. The burial ground, which grips the side of the hill, has commanding views across to Salisbury Crags. The Stevenson family grave is a flat-roofed calaboose by the eastern wall, the gates rusty, the walls covered in graffiti. A marble slab in the middle of the floor commemorates Thomas Stevenson and his son:

Robert Louis Stevenson
Essayist, Poet and Novelist
Born at Edinburgh 13th November 1850
Died in Samoa 3rd December 1894
And buried on VAEA Mountain

The Old Calton Burying Ground is little more than a patch of grass at the foot of Calton Hill, just off Waterloo Place. Among those buried here are David Hume, in a tomb designed by Robert Adam, and the rival publishers, united in death, William Blackwood and Archibald Constable. The Calton Jail, at one time Scotland's largest prison, was situated on Regent Road between 1817 and 1925.

This part of Edinburgh has many associations with Stevenson. He devotes a chapter to it in *Picturesque Notes* and set a number of scenes from his novel *The Misadventures of John Nicholson* around the Calton Hill. His uncle Alan, builder of the Skerrymore lighthouse, lived at 25

Regent Terrace, while Greenside Parish Church at the foot of Royal Terrace was for a time the Stevenson family church. Stevenson often worshipped here and has described the church in *Random Memories*.

Stevenson's paternal grandfather lived in a large rambling house with a paddock, 1 Baxter Place, at the top of Leith Walk. The paddock is now a car park and the house, now called Robert Stevenson House, is occupied by a group of publishers. A brass plaque in the hall reads:

In this building Robert Stevenson, Engineer, lived and
worked. From No. 1 he designed and supervised many works
including bridges, harbours, prisons and lighthouses, the
most famous of these being the Bell Lighthouses. He was the
grandfather of Robert Louis Stevenson, Author.

At the corner of nearby Antigua Street is the stationer's shop, celebrated in *A Penny Plain and Twopence Coloured*.[2]

HOWARD PLACE

Stevenson knew the area well, having been born at 8 Howard Place, a rather sombre Georgian terrace to the north of Canonmills on the Water of Leith. The two-storey house was small and suffered damp; it was far from healthy, given the amount of effluent from the mills and tanneries, as well as sewage, that was poured into the river, so in 1853 the Stevensons moved to the corner of Inverleith Terrace (now No. 9) which was on higher ground and had previously been occupied by the writer William Edmondstoun Aytoun (1813–65), best known for his 'Lays of the Scottish Cavaliers', a ballad romance in the style of Walter Scott. The house in Howard Place was between 1926 and 1963 a museum and the head-quarters of the Robert Louis Stevenson Club.

The poet W. E. Henley (1849–1903), a friend and collaborator of Stevenson, lived at 11 Howard Place while editor of the *Scots Observer* in Thistle Street. Stevenson based some of Long John Silver on his rumbustious friend, who had lost part of his left leg at sixteen following a tubercular infection, and they wrote four plays together in the 1880s, including *Deacon Brodie or The Double Life* (1880). J. M. Barrie was a friend and took a particular interest in the Henleys' child Margaret, who used to call him 'Friendy-Wendy', the name he was later to immortalise in *Peter Pan*; she died of cerebral meningitis aged five in 1894.

Later, another important Edinburgh writer, Lewis Spence (1874–1955), lived at 34 Howard Place. Though born in Dundee, Spence came to Edinburgh as a young man to study dentistry at the University. He spent most of his life in the city, where he worked for a time on *The Scotsman* and where he was a familiar figure in his bowler hat and spats. Spence was a founding figure with Hugh MacDiarmid of the Scottish Literary Renaissance which aimed to 'bring Scottish literature into closer touch with current European tendencies in technique and ideation' and also of the Scottish National Party.

Round the corner is Warriston Crescent, an attractive cul-de-sac whose houses have gardens running down to the Water of Leith. Frederick Chopin stayed at No. 10 when he gave a recital in Queen Street in 1848. Further along at No. 25 lived the poet and critic George Bruce (1909–2002), the author of a book on the Edinburgh International Festival, and a BBC producer for over twenty years.

Moray McLaren (1901–71), the BBC's first Programme Director for Scotland, lived for many years nearby in Inverleith Row. Born at 14 Walker Street and educated at Merchiston and Cambridge, McLaren served in the Foreign Office during the Second World War before returning to Edinburgh in 1945. The author of several novels, volumes of short stories and biographies of Boswell and Stevenson, his study of Edinburgh in the twentieth century, *The Capital of Scotland* (1950) is one of the most perceptive accounts of the city.

JULES VERNE

Edinburgh is not obviously associated with the French author Jules Verne (1828–1905), best known for *Journey to the Centre of the Earth* (1864), *20,000 Leagues Under the Sea* (1870) and *Around the World in 80 Days* (1873), but his novel *Backwards to Britain,* only published in 1989, is a lightly fictionalised account of his trip to Scotland in 1859.

The two central characters stay in a hotel in Princes Street and the book abounds with descriptions of Edinburgh sights as they visit the

Scott Monument, the National Gallery, the Grassmarket, St Giles, Parliament House, Holyrood, Arthur's Seat, Portobello, Calton Hill, the High School and the Castle. Verne, who had Scottish ancestry, shows himself to be very knowledgeable about both Scottish history and literature. The characters have particular friends in Inverleith Row who take them to visit the newly laid-out Warriston Cemetery:

> as if it was a pleasure ground and the most natural place on
> earth to visit. It was indeed a lovely garden, with lawns and
> box shrub borders along the paths. The tombs were a pleasure
> to contemplate and in that cool shaded place they made one
> yearn to lie down there in eternal peace. In such a cemetery,
> death does not take on the funereal gloom of France's
> mausoleums and truncated columns: the tombs are like
> charming cottages where life flows past, leisurely and pleasant.[3]

The cemetery plays a more sinister role in Ian Rankin's *The Hanging Garden* (1998).

ROYAL BOTANIC GARDEN

The Royal Botanic Garden in Inverleith Place was formed in 1824 when the old 'Physic Gardens' at the foot of the Calton Hill were abolished and now covers over seventy acres. Norman MacCaig has written several poems set there including 'Botanic Gardens' and 'Reclining figure by Henry Moore'. The garden plays a crucial role in Christina Kooning's novel *A Mild Suicide* (1992) and provides the climax to Quintin Jardine's police thriller *Skinner's Trail* (1994).

From the gardens, particularly just in front of Inverleith House, there are wonderful views to the Castle and Salisbury Crags.

> South of the Rhododendron Walk, from a small eminence in
> the Garden, there is a good broad view of the city, reaching
> from the unfinished Acropolis on the Calton Hill to the
> distant slopes of the Pentlands. The Castle on its Rock rises
> in the midst of the view, and far to the left of it Edinburgh's

private and domestic mountain, Arthur's Seat, is elevated
above the Salisbury Crags that loom, from here, as if they
impended upon the rough North Sea. Spires and pinnacles
advertise the innumerable churches of the city: the two St
Georges, the solid burden of Playfair's St Stephen's in front of
the towering steeple of the High Church, St Andrew's and the
Tron and the crown of St Giles. There is woodland in the
foreground, such charming woodland, with pine-needles on
its little paths and blue Tibetan poppies, or yellow primulas,
to enliven the shadow of the conifers; and always a new
prospect of trees and flowers as the visitor more deeply
invades the climbing pattern of the wood.[4]

FETTES COLLEGE

At the west end of Inverleith Place stands the imposing, if slightly
ridiculous, Fettes College. Built by David Bryce in 1870, in what has been
called Franco-Scottish Gothic style, to provide an English public school
education north of the border, the school has produced an extraordinary
number of writers given its reputation as a rugby school. In Ian Miller's
novel *School Tie* (1935) Fettes becomes Sinclair College:

A monument to the commercial ability and public spirit of
the late Sir James Sinclair, an early nineteenth-century
merchant prince. The heir to his princedom died young, and
Sir James left a substantial portion of his worldly goods for
the establishment of a school for the sons of poor but worthy
citizens. His trustees, with admirable forethought, invested
the money and allowed the interest to accumulate. The result
was that thirty years later their successors were able to enlarge
considerably on Sir James's original idea.[5]

This is an exact copy of the life of its founder Sir William Fettes and such
Fettes slang as New Man, Big Side and House Belows figures in the book.
Ian Hay, the pen name of J. H. Beith (1876–1952), who wrote about
Edinburgh in his novel *The Right Stuff*, was there for five years from 1890

while W. C. Sellar (1899–1951), the part-author of the comic masterpiece *1066 and All That* and a theatre collaborator with P. G. Wodehouse, was Head Boy during the First World War. Both later returned to teach at the school. Robert Bruce Lockhart (1887–1970), best known for *Memoirs of a British Agent,* based on his experiences in Russia during the First World War, is another Old Fettesian and, according to popular tradition, Ian Fleming's character James Bond was sent to Fettes after an indiscretion with a ladies' maid at Eton.

Norman Cameron (1905–53) went from Fettes to Oxford in the early 1920s where he became a friend of Robert Graves. After a posting to Nigeria as an educational officer in 1932, he went to live in Mallorca with Graves and Laura Riding. Cameron was known as a translator of Rimbaud and Villon, as well as a poet in his own right. Graves wrote the introduction to his *Collected Poems* (1957).

Ruthven Todd (1914–78) spent several unhappy years there from 1928 where his contemporaries included the poet George Campbell Hay. Todd went on to the Edinburgh College of Art and then worked briefly as a journalist in the city. Though he wrote several books of art history, edited the works of William Blake and was the author of half a dozen adventure novels it is as a poet he is best remembered. Most of his life was spent in the United States but he does leave a bitter picture in the auto-biographical poem 'In Edinburgh' (1940):

> I was born in this city of grey stone and bitter wind
> Of tenements sooted up with lying history:
> This place where dry mounds grow crusts of hate, as rocks
> Grow lichens. I went to school over the high bridge
> Fringed with spikes which curiously, repel the suicides;
> And I slept opposite the rock garden where the survivors,
> Who had left Irving and Mallory under the sheet of snow,
> Planted the incaruillia and Saxifrages of the Himalayas.

The son of the novelist John MacDougall Hay, George Campbell Hay (1915–84) studied modern languages at Oxford and then worked in the Department of Printed Books in the National Library of Scotland. His first collection of poems *Fuaran Sleibh* was published in 1947 and with

Sorley Maclean, William Neil and Stuart MacGregor he contributed to *Four Points of a Saltire* (1970). Although Gaelic was not his mother tongue and he has written in both Scots and English, Hay is now recognised as one of the most important Gaelic poets of the century.

Other Fettes poets include Will Ogilvie (1869–1963), often described as the 'Border Kipling', W. L. Lorimer (1885–1967), known for his translation of the New Testament into Scots, Hal Summers (1911–) and Christopher Salvesen (1935–). Their work is collected in *A Nest of Singing Birds* (1995), edited by Gordon Jarvie.

Though his reputation is based on his three historical crime novels set in Germany in the 1930s, collected together as *Berlin Noir* (1993), and subsequently on futuristic thrillers such as *Gridiron* (1996), Philip Kerr (1956–) was brought up in Edinburgh. He satirises Fettes and Edinburgh in his short story 'The Unnatural History Museum'. The school is blown up by drugs dealers in Old Fettesian Paul Johnston's *Body Politic*.[6]

PAUL JOHNSTON

Johnston (1957–) read Greek at Oxford and his classical education is apparent in his futuristic satirical political crime novels which give a new slant to Edinburgh's description as 'The Athens of the North' and which present a questioning vision of an independent future Edinburgh – *Body Politic* (1997), which won the Crime Writers Association Award for the best first crime novel, *The Bone Yard* (1998), *Water of Death* (1999), *The Blood Tree* (2000) and *The House of Dust* (2001), all of which feature subversive blues-loving investigator Quintilian Dalrymple.

The series begins in 2020 after another Scottish Enlightenment, with Edinburgh an independent city state based on the principles of Plato's republic, crime-free and entirely devoted to tourism. In this new Edinburgh, an historical theme park, there is a 10 p.m. curfew, food and clothing are rationed by coupon, suicide and cars are banned and the High Street is off limits unless one works there. The National Library of Scotland has become the Edinburgh Heritage Centre, Parliament House is called the Halls of the Republic, Holyrood Park is Enlightenment Park and Holyrood Palace has been destroyed in rioting. Princes Street Gardens is a race-track, Queen Street Gardens is an all-weather running track, the Tolbooth Church on Castle Hill is a strip joint frequented by Thai tourists, George Heriot's is a hotel for rich Chinese tourists and there are gaming tents in Charlotte Square.

Citizens meet for compulsory weekly sex sessions with designated partners at the Pleasance Building, executions are held on Fridays on the gallows in the Lawnmarket and tourists are able to buy soft drugs. 'The Marijuana Club on Hanover Street that the Tourism Directorate in its wisdom named "The Grass Kilt" was doing good business.'[7]

Edinburgh's past is always present. The Usher Hall has been renamed Stevenson Hall after R. L. Stevenson and the series of barracks around the city bear the name of famous former residents: Bell, Hume, Knox, Scott and Watt. All place names with suspect cultural connotations have been changed so Eton Terrace is now Academy Place.

Johnston says he was influenced by Jekyll and Hyde – there are several references to the book in the series – and that he is:

> interested in playing with the continuum that runs from Edinburgh's past. It stretches from the philosopher Hume, Robert Louis Stevenson, the city's architecture, through the present-day gap between Edinburgh's aspirations and its social problems, and into the future. But the legacy of the past is always there . . . Glasgow is much more open and in your face – violent and hedonistic, and proud of it – but Edinburgh provides more fertile ground for writers, and crime writers in particular, because of its dual nature . . . It's the physical nature of the city that has influenced me most . . . a series of sharp perpendiculars that suggest lofty ambitions and philosophies at the top and dirty physicality in the festering cellars.[8]

In the first book Dalrymple is called in by the Council of the City Guardians to find a serial killer, the ENT (the Ear, Nose and Throat man) and the second, set the following year, revolves around a series of murders where the victims are found with music tapes in their bodies. By 2025 and *Water of Death*, global warming has rendered the city an arid desert with the Meadows completely parched. When a body is discovered in the Water of Leith beside the Colonies Dalrymple is called in to find out who is trying to hold the city to ransom. In *The Blood Tree*, set in 2026, Dalrymple is tasked with finding out why some of Edinburgh's brightest teenagers are being abducted to the much-feared democratic city-state of Glasgow, while in *The House of Dust*, set in 2028, he goes to a business-orientated New Oxford to seek advice on Edinburgh's mounting crime wave.

QUINTIN JARDINE

Bob Skinner, another anti-establishment cop and the hero of Quintin Jardine's series of Skinner crime novels, is based at police headquarters in Fettes Avenue. Like Rankin and other Edinburgh writers, he is interested in the duality of Edinburgh and indeed the first in the series, *Skinner's Rules* (1993), begins:

> As a city, Edinburgh is a two-faced bitch. There is the face on
> the picture postcards, sunny, bright and shining, prosperous
> and smiling at the world like a toothpaste ad. But on the
> other side of the looking glass lies the other face: the real
> world where all too often the wind blows cold, the rain lashes
> down and the poverty shows on the outside.[9]

His books abound with references to Edinburgh locations – Parliament Square, New Assembly Close, Redford Barracks, the Secretary of State's official residence in Charlotte Square, the George Hotel, the Pleasance theatre complex to name a few. In *Skinner's Rules*, Skinner, head of Edinburgh's CID, is drawn into a series of murder investigations after the body of a young lawyer is found in an alleyway close to Advocates Close. In *Skinner's Festival* (1994) an explosion rocks Waverley Market in Princes Street in the midst of the Festival, with a group demanding political separation from Britain claiming responsibility. *Fallen Gods* (2003) has an incendiary device destroying a valuable painting in the Royal Scottish Academy while *Lethal Intent* (2005) has the son of a police officer found dead in the shadow of Edinburgh Castle as Albanian gangsters infiltrate the Edinburgh underworld. Edinburgh also figures in several of Jardine's Oz Blackstone private investigator series.

To the south is Comely Bank where Thomas Carlyle began his married life at No. 21 in 1826. This leads into Raeburn Place and then Deanhaugh Street, where James Hogg lodged in 1813 while writing *The Queen's Wake*.

If one climbs Dean Terrace, the Water of Leith running alongside to the left, one comes to Danube Street. Until it was closed in the mid-1970s, 17 Danube Street was the site of Edinburgh's best-known brothel. Its madame, Dora Noyce, who ran it from 1943 until her death in 1977, bears more than a passing resemblance to Ma Blinkbonnie and her salon in Bruce Marshall's novel *The Black Oxen*. Hector Macmillan's 'play with music', *Capital Offence*, staged at the Royal Lyceum in 1981, is also based on the brothel.

ANN STREET

As with so much in Edinburgh the dubious and the respectable are in close proximity. Above Danube Street is Ann Street, described by John Betjeman as 'the most attractive street in Britain' and reputedly the model for J. M. Barrie's play *Quality Street*. Built between 1816 and 1823, the street was named after the wife of the portrait painter Sir Henry Raeburn, who owned the land. The street stands in contrast to the stern and somewhat forbidding beauty of the surrounding eighteenth-century streets. The two rows of what look like dolls' houses, with their brightly coloured doors and landscaped gardens, combine to make this one of the prettiest and most exclusive residential streets in Edinburgh.

John Wilson moved to 29 Ann Street in 1819 and there De Quincey lodged for a year after coming in one night to shelter from the rain. R. M. Ballantyne (1825–94) was born two doors down at No. 25. His family had moved to Edinburgh the year before on the appointment of his father as editor of the *Edinburgh Weekly Journal*, first staying for a few months at 25 Comely Bank. After Edinburgh Academy Robert Ballantyne joined the Hudson's Bay Company, his experiences in northern Canada later being used in his adventure stories.

Coral Island (1858), the adventures of three castaways on a South Pacific Island, was a favourite of the young R. L. Stevenson and there are certain similarities to *Treasure Island* (1883). The two writers much admired each other but met only once. One morning in 1866, after the morning service at St Cuthbert's Church in Princes Street, Ballantyne was approached by a boy in his teens and asked if he would join the boy's family for dinner but Ballantyne was unable to accept because of another engagement. On Ballantyne's death, Stevenson, who was to die later that year, helped to raise money to provide a fund to support his wife and children. Another admirer was J. M. Barrie who wrote a preface to an edition of *Coral Island*.

The other side of the street also has several literary associations. The two daughters of the critic David Masson, Flora (1856–1937) and Rosaline (1867–1949), both authors in their own right, lived at No. 11, while Robert Chambers (1802–71), the publisher and author of *Traditions of Edinburgh* (1824) lived at No. 28 between 1834 and 1838. Chambers edited the *Chambers Encyclopaedia* (1859–68) and the monthly magazine *Chambers Journal*, which would later in the century publish among others Thomas Hardy, Arthur Conan Doyle, John Buchan and Neil Gunn.

Helen Bannerman (1862–1946), the author of *Little Black Sambo* (1899), left her four children with her sister Mary at 50 Ann Street to complete their education while she stayed in India with her doctor husband. Born at 35 Royal Terrace and educated in Edinburgh, Bannerman left for India on her marriage in 1889, retiring to Edinburgh in 1918, where she remained until her death.[10]

DEAN BRIDGE AND VILLAGE

Dean Park Crescent, which runs parallel to Oxford Terrace where Rebus's girlfriend Patience Aitken lives, leads on to the Dean Bridge, which towers one hundred feet above the Water of Leith. When it was built in 1832 it was one of the highest in the world and as the poet Robert McCandless noted fifty-five years later a place:

> Where many a man
> Alas has ran
> There in an evil hour
> And cast away

His life that day
Beyond all human pow'r.

So serious was the problem of suicide becoming that eventually the stone parapet was heightened. Even this does not seem to have solved the problem. In Eric Linklater's *The Merry Muse* the central character reflects on how he might kill himself before settling on the Dean Bridge.

Telford built it – in 1830? About then – and how nobly its four arches spanned the broad, high-wooded gorge down which the little Water of Leith so modestly chattered on its journey to the sea! It was a gorge that looked as if it had been carved from the rock by the insistent current of a mountainfed, tempestuous stream, but darkly twinkling a hundred feet below the bridge there was only a little piddle of water in which small boys occasionally caught a trout or two. An ideal site for the termination of a life which, in earlier years, had had its views of grandeur, but now was only a runnel talking itself out of existence: talking quietly and in good temper, but with a settled purpose.[11]

Bell's Brae, once the main road to the north, descends steeply into the gorge to the picturesque Dean Village below. Here Stevenson's Catriona lived with Lady Allardyce 'in a decentlike small house in a garden of lawns and appletrees'. The weavers' cottages on Damside were pulled down by the proprietor of *The Scotsman*, John Ritchie Findlay, because they spoiled the view from his house in Rothesay Terrace. They have now been replaced by Well Court which, with its gables and large tower, makes a pleasant contrast with the surrounding village.

From the village one can walk along the Water of Leith west in the direction of the Scottish National Gallery of Modern Art, or east towards Stockbridge. A few hundred yards towards the latter is St Bernard's Well, refurbished at the beginning of the nineteenth century by the publisher, William Nelson, who used to walk three miles a day to drink the dark sulphurous waters.

James King (J. K.) Annand (1908–93) was born next door to St

Bernard's Well at 11 Mackenzie Place, now known as St Bernard's Cottages, and lived there until his marriage in 1936. Annand's reputation rests largely on his Scots verse for children *Sing it Aince for Pleasure* (1965), *Thrice for Joy* (1973) and *Twice to Show Ye* (1979), but he also edited *Lallans*, the magazine of the Scots Language Society, and the literary magazine *Lines Review*.[12]

From the Dean Village, Dean Path climbs the other side of the valley until it returns to Queensferry Road at the Dean Cemetery. Among those buried there are Henry Cockburn, Francis Jeffrey, John Wilson and his son-in-law William Aytoun and Joseph Bell. Dean House, which was demolished to make way for the construction of the cemetery in 1845, was the scene of the novel *Miller of Deanhaugh* by James Ballantine (1808–77).

THE WESTERN NEW TOWN

South of the Dean Village is the Western New Town. Drumsheugh House in Drumsheugh Gardens was the setting for one of the most sensational scandals of the nineteenth century. In the early 1800s two young teachers, Jane Pirie and Marianne Woods, founded a boarding school for girls. At first it was very successful but, after one of the girls told her mother she had seen the two teachers in bed together, many of the parents withdrew their daughters and the school was forced to close. Pirie and Woods successfully sued for damages and their story inspired the successful Broadway play of the 1930s, Lillian Hellman's *The Children's Hour*, a factual account of the story is given in Lillian Faderman's *Scotch Verdict* (1985).

No doubt Eric Linklater was thinking of this area when he created Rothesay Crescent in *Magnus Merriman* for there is a Rothesay Place and Terrace nearby. This was the 'west-endy' part of Edinburgh *par excellence* as he makes perfectly clear describing the crescent as:

A semi-lune of tall houses, solemn in mien, dignified, wealthy in fact and implication. Here was respectability achieved in such perfection as to be magnificent indeed. Here was dignity wrought by endeavour and most zealously preserved. Here

were roofs that covered success, and though that success
might seem incomplete to an impartial observer – like a wall-
pear that may grow no higher than its wall, nor stretch its
branches north and south to contemplate its shadow at
afternoon, but must be content to live in two dimensions
only – yet the occupants of the houses showed in their
bearing no trace of doubt, and obviously had made of their
rich circumscription a cosmos that contented them.[13]

In Palmerston Place is St Mary's Episcopal Cathedral, the only church in
Scotland to have its own choir school. Walpole Hall was erected in
memory of G. H. S. Walpole, Bishop of Edinburgh from 1910 to 1929.
His son, the novelist Hugh Walpole (1884–1941), often visited his parents
at their home in 1 Eglinton Crescent and from his visit at the end of 1910
began his habit of starting all his novels on Christmas Eve. Nineteen
novels were to follow this way. Walpole never cared for the Edinburgh
climate so he never stayed long but because of family associations he held
the city in some affection and often stayed with his sister Dorothy who
lived in Corstorphine.

The novelist and short story writer Fred Urquhart (1912–95) was
born at No. 8. In 1919 the family moved to 37 West Cottages, Granton,
which figures in his novel *Time Will Knit* (1938). The cottages, which
were between the middle and west piers, were demolished before the
Second World War. Urquhart later lived at 1 and then 10 Fraser Grove,
off Granton Road.

Leaving Broughton High School at fifteen, Urquhart worked for
seven years in Cairns Bookshop in Teviot Place and for a firm of tailors
in George Street, an experience which he used in his story 'Sweet',
collected in *I Fell for a Sailor* (1940). Subsequently, he had a series of jobs
in publishing working as a literary agent in London, a reader for MGM
and a scout for Walt Disney before returning to Edinburgh in 1989.

WALTER SCOTT

Scott lived at 6 Shandwick Place from November 1827 until his retirement from the Clerkship of the Court of Session in July 1830 when he

moved to Abbotsford permanently. On the day he moved into Shandwick Place he renewed contact with the mother of Williamina Stuart-Belsches, who lived close by at 12 Maitland Street. The visits continued until the old lady's death in 1829.

Scott also lived for a period at 3 Walker Street and 16 Atholl Crescent, the home of his publisher Robert Cadell. Cadell had formerly been a partner in his father-in-law's firm Constable but after the failure of the firm Cadell purchased the copyright of the Scott novels from *Waverley* to *Quentin Durward* for £8,500 and then published an 'Author's edition', which was highly successful. Scott wrote in his journal at the time of the break:

> Constable without Cadell is like getting the clock without the pendulum; the one having the ingenuity, the other the caution of the business.[14]

Coming out of Atholl Crescent, through Rutland Square, is Rutland Street, at one time regarded as the 'Harley Street' of Edinburgh. From 1850 until his death the essayist Dr John Brown (1810–82), the 'Scottish Charles Lamb', lived at No. 23. His collection *Rab and his Friends* (1959), essays on the human nature of dogs, was highly regarded at the time, selling over 50,000 copies. Brown, though by profession a doctor, was well-known among the literary figures of the day and among his close friends were Oliver Wendell Holmes, John Ruskin, Mark Twain, William Thackeray and Thomas Carlyle.

TOLLCROSS AND FOUNTAINBRIDGE

The area to the north and west of Lothian Road is a mixture of neighbourhoods. Along Lothian Road itself are situated various cinemas and theatres. In Grindlay Street is the Royal Lyceum theatre where T. S. Eliot's *The Cocktail Party* had its world premiere while round the corner in Cambridge Street is the Traverse Theatre. Edinburgh resident Kate Atkinson (1951–), best known for *Behind the Scenes at the Museum* (1995), has written two plays for the latter – *Nice* (1996) and *Abandonment* which premiered as part of the Edinburgh International Festival in 2000.

Squeezed between them is Edinburgh's principal concert venue, the Usher Hall. Named after the head of a brewing family who gave £100,000 in 1896 to 'promote and extend the cultivation of, and taste for, music, not only in Edinburgh, but throughout the country', it was completed in 1911. In his poem 'Choral Symphony' Stewart Conn casts a witty look at the sort of audience the Usher Hall sometimes attracts:

> The customary conversation
> Gives way to applause
> For the Orchestra. Then
> A roar, as Karajan
> Takes the stand. He raises
> His baton; the strings sweep in.
>
> During the interval, we remain
> Seated. Two Edinburgh ladies
> Behind us complain:
> 'Such Teutonic discipline
> Breeds perfection,
> Not Art.' Their companion agrees.
>
> At the end they join in,
> As the ovation goes on
> And on. What has changed their tune?
> We overhear 'Weren't the Chorus
> Superb!' 'As one voice.'
> 'And that lace, on Muriel's dress.'

In Paul Johnston's *Body Politic* a woman is strangled and her liver cut out in the lavatories of the Usher Hall and the venue provides the dramatic opening scene of Alexander McCall Smith's *The Sunday Philosophy Club* (2004). Violence is also to be found at Tollcross fire station, in Ian Rankin's *Mortal Causes* a fictional nightclub where a woman has acid poured down her throat.

The dual sides to the Edinburgh character are never better expressed than in Muriel Spark's novel *The Prime of Miss Jean Brodie*. One theme in the book is the huge disparity in wealth within the city and how the more fortunate view the unemployed. In the following passage the girls are out walking in Tollcross:

> They had come to the end of Lauriston Place, past the fire
> station, where they were to get on a tram-car to go to tea
> with Miss Brodie in her flat at Church Hill. A very long
> queue of men lined this part of the street. They were without
> collars, in shabby suits. They were talking and spitting and
> smoking little bits of cigarette held between middle finger
> and thumb.
>
> 'We shall cross here,' said Miss Brodie and herded the
> set across the road.
>
> Monica Douglas whispered, 'They are the Idle.'
>
> 'In England they are called the Unemployed. They are
> waiting to get their dole from the labour bureau,' said Miss
> Brodie. 'You must all pray for the unemployed and their
> families, I will write you out the special prayer for them . . .
> Sometimes they go and spend their dole on drink before they
> go home, and their children starve. They are our brothers,
> Sandy, stop staring at once. In Italy the unemployment
> problem has been solved.'[15]

BRUCE MARSHALL

In Bruce Marshall's panoramic novel about three generations of an Edinburgh family in the twentieth century, *The Black Oxen* (1972), this tale of two cities is again made clear. The five male characters go to a 'brightly lit dancing hall in Fountainbridge', most probably the old Palais:

> Inside, the orchestra was playing 'Oh, Oh, My Sweet
> Hortense' and on the dance floor a mixed bag of semi-sober
> advocates, Writers to the Signet, solicitors to the Supreme
> Court, chartered accountants, students and keellies
> were revolving with a kaleidoscope of typists, instructresses,
> brickfaced Murray heiresses and lugubrious tarts.[16]

There, one of them, Neil Duncan meets and falls in love with Flora Goodwillie but the path of love does not run smoothly for, as he is told, 'future members of the Edinburgh Stock Exchange don't marry dancing instructresses'. Flora has to point out what is more than a geographical separation: 'You live in Murrayfield and I live at the foot of Leith Walk.'

Though Bruce Marshall (1899–1987) spent much of his life in France, many of his books have an Edinburgh setting. They include three satires on middle-class life: *Teacup Terrace* (1926), *Father Malachy's Miracle* (1931) and *George Brown's Schooldays* (1946). After the First World War, during which he lost a leg, and study at Edinburgh University, he worked as an accountant for fourteen years in Paris. While working for SOE in World War Two he met the Resistance hero 'Tommy' Yeo-Thomas, the subject of Marshall's bestseller *The White Rabbit*.

THE UNION CANAL AND KEN McCLURE

The Union Canal, which joins the Forth and Clyde Canal at Falkirk, was built between 1817 and 1822 to bring coal into Edinburgh. Alexander Trocchi's existential novel *Young Adam* (1954) is set on the canals between Edinburgh and Glasgow, and the Union Canal figures in Ken Begg's *The Anvil Agreement* (1985) and, writing as Ken McClure, in *Trauma* (1995) and *Deception* (2001).

McClure was born and brought up in Edinburgh, close to the Union Canal. He was educated at Craiglockhart Primary School, where he was taught by Norman MacCaig, and Boroughmuir High School where his English teacher was Sorley Maclean. After a year studying marine engineering and a brief period as a musician, he put himself through university, gaining a PhD in molecular genetics and becoming a researcher with the Medical Research Council at the University.

Ken Begg, under his own name or pseudonym Ken McClure, has written six medical thrillers set in Edinburgh. *Fenton's Winter* (1989) is centred on the Royal Hospital for Sick Children, *Resurrection* (1999) takes place at Edinburgh University's Kings Buildings in West Mains Road and Muirhouse, where an outbreak of smallpox breaks out, while *Eye of the Raven* (2005) has scenes at Fettes police station, the Botanic Garden and the Braid Hills Hotel.

Bruntsfield Links has long associations with the game of golf and there have been clubs there for two centuries, though the famous Bruntsfield Links Golfing Society now has a course near Barnton. Smollett writes of Edinburgh golfers in *The Expedition of Humphrey Clinker*:

> Amongst others, I was shown one particular set of golfers, the youngest of whom was turned four score. They were all gentlemen of independent fortunes, who had amused themselves with this pastime for the best part of a century, without having ever felt the least alarm from sickness or disgust, and they never went to bed without having each the best part of a gallon of claret. Such uninterrupted exercise, co-operating with the keen air from the sea, must without all doubt, keep the appetite always on edge, and steel the consti-tution against all the common attacks of distemper.[17]

The claret was no doubt sampled at the Golf Tavern, which for five centuries now has provided the nineteenth hole for those who, in Allan Ramsay's words 'were weary'd at the gowff'. To the east and south lie the residential districts of the Grange and Marchmont, the latter evoked beautifully in Alastair Alpin MacGregor's volume of memoirs *The Golden Lamp*.

MURIEL SPARK

Muriel Spark née Camberg (1918–) was born and brought up at 160 Bruntsfield Place and attended the nearby James Gillespie's School for Girls, which she supposedly took as her model for the Marcia Blaine School in *The Prime of Miss Jean Brodie*. The novel is one of the great Edinburgh novels, filled with allusions to the city's topography, history and literary past, and with an acute ear and eye to the idiom and personality of middle-class Edinburgh.

The schoolmistress, Jean Brodie, like her ancestor Deacon Brodie leads a double life; 'an Edinburgh spinster of the deepest dye', she also stands for freedom from the conventions and prejudices of the Edinburgh *bourgeoisie* with her weekend lover and advanced views. Miss Brodie's 'garls' are the '*crème de la crème*', part of the Calvinist view of the Elect and the Damned, already explored in Hogg's *Confessions of a Justified Sinner*, and Spark draws analogies between the contrasting sides to Edinburgh, Calvinism and Brodie. Sandy, Miss Brodie's star pupil, is conscious:

> . . . that some quality of life peculiar to Edinburgh and
> nowhere else had been going on unbeknown to her all the
> time, and however undesirable it might be she felt deprived of
> it; however undesirable, she desired to know what it was, and
> to cease to be protected from it by enlightened people.
>
> It was then that Miss Brodie looked beautiful and fragile,
> just as dark, heavy Edinburgh itself could suddenly be
> changed into a floating city when the light was a special pearly
> white and fell upon one of the gracefully fashioned streets.[18]

Though most of her life has been spent outside the city and no other book of hers is set in the city, Spark has conceded that 'Edinburgh had an effect on my mind, my prose style and my ways of thought'.[19]

Spark briefly taught at a private day school, The Hill School, at 35 Colinton Road. Another resident of Colinton Road and fellow pupil of Gillespie's was the historical novelist Dorothy Dunnett (1923–2001). Her six-part *Lymond Chronicles* explores the intricacies of sixteenth-century history through the exploits of the Scottish nobleman Francis Crawford of Lymond and was followed by the eight-part *House of Nicccolo* chronicles, set in the banking world of the fifteenth century.[20]

Under her maiden name, Dorothy Halliday, she wrote a series of detective novels based around a boat called Dolly, of which only *Dolly and the Singing Bird* (1968) (subsequently called *The Photogenic Soprano* in the US and *Rum Affair* in Britain) is set in Edinburgh.

JOAN LINGARD

Another contemporary female 'Edinburgh' writer is Joan Lingard (1932–) who uses the city in several of her adult novels and books for older children as a backdrop for her examinations of fragmented family life or what she describes as 'displacement'.

Her adult Edinburgh novels include *The Prevailing Wind* (1964), based on her experiences as a student living in Warrender Park Terrace in the 1950s, *The Headmaster* (1967), about the headmaster of an Edinburgh primary school, whose marriage has broken up and whose world is falling apart and which is set in the neighbouring Grange, *A Sort of Freedom* (1968), *The Second Flowering of Emily Mountjoy* (1979) and *Reasonable Doubts* (1986). In two of her most recent books she has contrasted Scotland and France: *After Colette* (1993), about a woman of mixed French and Scottish parentage, and *The Kiss* (2002) which presents a reworking of Gwen John's love affair with the sculptor Auguste Rodin through a fifteen-year-old's passion for her Edinburgh art teacher.

Lingard, who also lived for a time in Chalmers Crescent, has also set a number of her children's novels in the capital including *The Gooseberry* (1978), a children's novel set in Stockbridge, reissued as *Odd Girl Out* (2000), *Strangers in the House* (1981) and two sets of short stories, *Rags and Riches* (1988) and *Glad Rags* (1990).

Another female writer who sets her novels in the area is the psychological crime writer Carol Anne Davis. One of the murders in her first novel *Shrouded* (1997) takes place in The Meadows, the killer in her second *Safe as Houses* (1999) lives in Marchmont, while *Noise Abatement* (2000), about a couple driven to desperate measures because of a noisy neighbour, is based on her own experiences living in a Marchmont tenement.

Ian Rankin lived for a time in Arden Street at Tollcross, now the home of his fictional detective Rebus.

ST TRINNEAN'S

Few now realise that the girls' school immortalised in the cartoons of Ronald Searle and the films starring Alastair Sim really did exist. Founded at 10 Palmerston Road, off Chalmers Crescent, in 1922, St Trinnean's soon earned a reputation as 'the school where they do what they like'. While liberal in its approach, it was essentially serious-minded and there is no record of teachers being strung up or girls running riot.

Though Searle never met its redoubtable first headmistress Miss C. Fraser Lee, he first learnt of the school while billeted in 1941 with a family in Kirkcudbright, whose two daughters attended St Trinnean's. In July his first cartoon based on the school was published in *Lilliput* but it was not until Searle's return from a Japanese POW camp in 1946 that the school properly entered public consciousness. The school moved to St Leonard's House in Dalkeith Road in 1925 and to Galashiels in 1939. It became a casualty of the war and closed in 1946.[21]

Another school nearby is George Watson's, founded in 1723, which moved to Colinton Road in 1932 after over a hundred years in Lauriston Place. It has produced rather more cabinet ministers than writers but its alumni include the critics William Archer (1856–1924) and David Daiches (1912–). Jessie Saxby's *Ben Hanson* (1884) is set at the school.[22]

CRAIGLOCKHART

Further down Colinton Road is Craiglockhart, now an extension of Napier University of Edinburgh. Built in 1865 as a poorhouse by the City of Edinburgh Parochial Board it became in 1880 the Craiglockhart Hydropathic Institution and then in the summer of 1916 a military hospital under the auspices of the Red Cross.

Wilfred Owen arrived the following summer and threw himself into the activities on offer including editing the *Hydra*, the hospital magazine and teaching at Tynecastle School. The eighth issue lists the arrival of 2nd Lt Siegfried Sassoon of the Royal Welsh Fusiliers. The extraordinary coincidence of two of the First World War's finest poets being sent to the same hospital to recuperate has not been lost on subsequent writers.[23]

Sassoon was to write of Craiglockhart, which he called Slateford war hospital, in his fictional autobiography *Sherston's Progress*:

> Outwardly, War Hospital was . . . elaborately cheerful. Brisk
> amusements were encouraged, entertainments were got up,
> and serious cases were seldom sent downstairs . . . The
> doctors did everything possible to counteract gloom, and the
> wrecked faces were outnumbered by those who were
> emerging from their nervous disorders. But the War Office

had wasted no money on interior decoration: consequently the place had the melancholy atmosphere of a decayed hydro, redeemed only by its healthy situation and pleasant view of the Pentland Hills. By daylight the doctors dealt successfully with these disadvantages, and Slateford, so to speak 'made cheerful conversation'.

But by night they lost control and the hospital became sepulchral and oppressive with saturations of war experience. One lay awake and listened to feet padding along passages which smelt of stale cigarette-smoke; for the nurse couldn't prevent insomnia-ridden officers from smoking half the night in their rooms, though the locks had been removed from all the doors . . . One became conscious that the place was full of men whose slumbers were morbid and terrifying – men muttering uneasily or suddenly crying out in their sleep. Around me was that underworld of dreams haunted by submerged memories of warfare and its intolerable shocks and self-lacerating failures to achieve the impossible.[24]

Sassoon was at Craiglockhart through the intervention of Robert Graves who had made various representations at the War Office. When Graves visited Sassoon in October 1917, Owen was not impressed, writing that he was 'a big, rather plain fellow, the last man on earth apparently capable of the extraordinary, delicate fancies of his books'. Soon after, Sassoon, who found the atmosphere at Craiglockhart oppressive and consequently spent much of his time at the New Club and Scottish Arts Club, returned to England and Owen to the trenches, where he was killed a week before the Armistice. It was at Craiglockhart that Owen wrote several of his best known poems including 'Anthem for Doomed Youth' and Sassoon composed the poems 'The General', 'Base Details' and 'Attack'.

MORNINGSIDE

Morningside was, until the middle of the last century, just a stopping point for farmers on the way to Edinburgh. James Grant in *Old and New Edinburgh* describes how in 1850 'a row of thatched cottages, a line of trees and a blacksmith's forge still slumbered in rural solitude'. It was the coming of the railway in 1872 that changed the district as wealthy citizens rushed to build villas in the sunny or 'morning side', southern part of the city.

Stevenson, in *Picturesque Notes*, noted how:

> The dismallest structures keep springing up like mushrooms; the pleasant hills are loaded with them, each impudently squatted in its garden, each roofed and carrying chimneys like a house. And yet a glance of an eye discovers their true character. They are not houses; for they were not designed with a view to human habitation, and the internal arrangements are, as they tell me, fantastically unsuited to the needs of man. They are not buildings; for you can scarcely say a thing is built where every measurement is in clamant disproportion with its neighbour. They belong to no style of art, only to a form of business much to be regretted.[25]

Morningside has a reputation for staid respectability and shabby gentility. Robert Kemp in his novel *The Maestro* captures something of the area in the following passage:

> In the district where the Urquhart-Innes lived, all the houses resembled little castles and were enclosed by high garden walls topped with broken glass, so that anyone walking through the streets felt himself an outcast from society and hastened back to the pubs and narrow pavements at the east end of the city . . . Not all these stately residences had been able to continue to play their pristine roles. One had a large brass plate to tell that behind these love-discouraging walls lurked St Devenick's School for Girls, another shamefacedly admitted to being the 'Brasenose Hotel, Open to non-residents', a third was Miss Newbattle's Nursing Home and a fourth the regional headquarters of the gas council.[26]

Though old ladies still inhabit huge rambling houses and can be seen shopping in their scarves, hats and bootees, younger families have increasingly been moving in and bigger houses have been divided into flats. In spite of that Morningside, with its manicured hedges, black iron railings and netted windows, remains the heart of old middle-class Edinburgh.

JK ROWLING

The Merchiston area is now home to four of Britains's most successful writers – Joanne K. Rowling (1965–), Ian Rankin (1960–), Kate Atkinson (1951–) and Alexander McCall Smith (1948–).

JK Rowling moved to Edinburgh, where her sister lived at 140 Marchmont Road, from Portugal in 1993 after the break-up of her marriage. With her daughter Jessica, then aged only a few months, Rowling first lived in a flat at 28 Gardner's Crescent, near Princes Street, then rented a one-bedroom unfurnished flat at 7 South Lorne Place in Leith – a ground-floor flat, one of eight spread over four floors, – where she would live for the next three years and complete *Harry Potter and the Philosopher's Stone.*

Unable to write at home, she took to going each day to Nicolson's, a café on the junction of South Bridge and the Royal Mile owned by her brother-in-law and subsequently a restaurant. Nearby is Potterrow and the nearby wynds may well have inspired Diagon Alley, the shopping street for wizards in the Harry Potter stories. She would also write in other cafés such as The Elephant House on George iv Bridge.

She successfully applied to take a PGCE in modern languages at Moray House, now part of the University of Edinburgh, and had placements at St David's Roman Catholic High School in Dalkeith, eight miles south-east of Edinburgh, and Leith Academy close to her home. Qualifying in the summer of 1996, Rowling returned to Leith Academy. *Harry Potter and the Philospher's Stone* was published in June 1997 in an edition of 500 copies but rapidly took off with a $100,000 US deal, selling 70,000 copies in the UK in its first year and winning the Smarties Prize for children's literature.

The success of the book allowed her to give up teaching and in 1998 move from Leith to the more genteel south side of the city and nearer her sister in Marchmont. She found a flat at 19 Hazelbank Terrace, a street of two-storey houses, and Jessica was enrolled in the nearby Craiglockhart Primary School. Within a few years, concerns about security led her to buy an ivy-covered Georgian mansion with eight-feet stone walls in nearby Merchiston.

ALEXANDER McCALL SMITH

Alexander McCall Smith was educated at Edinburgh University and pursued a joint career as academic – becoming Professor of Medical Law at the University in 1995 – and writer of novels and short stories for both adults and children. It was the success of *The No. 1 Ladies Detective Agency* (1998) and his series of detective novels set in Botswana featuring Mma Ramotswe which brought him international success, with translation into over thirty languages. He is now the fastest-selling Scottish writer in America.

Several of his novels and short stories have an Edinburgh background, including *The Sunday Philosophy Club* (2004), the first of a projected four-book series with, as its heroine, the thirty-something Isabel Dalhousie, editor of a review of applied ethics, who lives in Merchiston. According to McCall Smith she is meant to represent a side of Edinburgh less often portrayed in contemporary literature. 'This is the Edinburgh where people attend musical concerts and have dinner parties. Everything is very comfortable and certain; Jean Brodie's Edinburgh brought up to date, in a sense. Morningside fights back!'

Nearby, at 5 Clinton Road, is East Morningside House, the home for many years of Susan Ferrier (1782–1854). Ferrier was born in Lady Stair's Close and had several Edinburgh addresses – her home at 25 George Street is now part of the George Hotel and she died at 38 Albany Street – but this is the house with which she is most often identified. Her first book *Marriage* (1818) earned her the title of 'Scotland's Jane Austen' and she followed it with *The Inheritance* (1824) and *Destiny* (1831). While perhaps too flattering a sobriquet, Ferrier's reputation as a satirist of early nineteenth-century Edinburgh has grown in recent decades. In 1982, to mark the bicentenary of her birth, the National Library of Scotland mounted an exhibition devoted to her life and work.

Another Morningside writer whose work is now being reassessed is Tom MacDonald (1906–75). In an obituary tribute Hugh MacDiarmid, a colleague of his on the Scottish Nationalist magazine *The Free Man,* thought his death a greater loss 'than the deaths of Compton Mackenzie, Neil Gunn, Eric Linklater and George Scott Moncrieff put together'. Though MacDonald, or, as he preferred, Fionn Mac Colla, was born in Montrose, he moved to Edinburgh in 1929, spending many years in Morningside Park. His novels *The Albannach* (1932), *And the Cock Crew* (1945) and *At the Sign of the Clenched Fist* (1967) deal with the repressive influence of Calvinism and the need for the growth of a genuine Scottish culture. George Campbell Hay, a poet with similar nationalist preoccupations, lived at 6 Maxwell Street until his death in 1984.

Further down Morningside Road is Morningside Cemetery which opened as the metropolitan cemetery in 1878. The occupants range from some of the leading Edinburgh figures over the last century to thousands of unknown people who died in the one-time City Poorhouse at Craiglockhart.

One of the best-known people buried in the cemetery is Alison Cunningham, Stevenson's beloved nurse 'Cummy', the subject of his moving poem 'From Her Boy'. In 1893 she took a small flat at 23 Balcarres Street where she lived with a collection of dogs, all of whom died, it was said, from overfeeding, and it was there she was visited by a succession of Stevenson's admirers. Finally, in need of constant care, she moved in with a cousin at 1 Comiston Place, where she died in July 1913 aged ninety-one. She had outlived Stevenson by twenty years.

THE MEADOWS

Returning to the Meadows one comes to Millerfield Place. The street takes its name from the engraver William Miller, who lived for many years in a huge house, Hope Park. Among the books that Miller illustrated were J. G. Lockhart's *Life of Sir Walter Scott* and John Brown's *Rab and His Friends.* R. M. Ballantyne moved to 6 Millerfield Place in July 1866 after his marriage and was a regular attender at the nearby Chalmers Memorial Church before he moved south to Harrow in 1878.

In the first volume of his autobiography, *Two Worlds* (1956), the writer and critic, David Daiches (1912–), paints a portrait of this part of Edinburgh just after the First World War. The Daiches family moved to Millerfield Place in 1919 when Daiches's father became rabbi of the Edinburgh Hebrew Congregation, the two worlds discussed being the Scottish and Jewish.

The twin stone pillars at the east end of Melville Drive were erected by the Nelson publishing family as a gift to the city. Between 1846 and 1878, when it was destroyed by fire, the firm, employing some 600 people, occupied premises at nearby Hope Park. Later they moved to Dalkeith Road, now also demolished.

JOHN BUCHAN

John Buchan (1875–1940) worked for the firm Nelson between 1907 and 1929, brought in as literary adviser by Tommy Nelson, an old Oxford friend to whom he dedicated *The Thirty-Nine Steps*. For several months before his marriage in July 1907 he had made himself familiar with the publishing operation and the Buchans' first home was a Gothic villa at the foot of Arthur's Seat. Susan Buchan has left this description of the house:

> It was enormous even judged by the standards of yesterday,
> but we existed happily in a corner of it with two excellent
> Scots servants. The garden had sweeping green lawns and a
> view of Arthur's Seat which redeemed the gloom of the heavy
> carved woodwork and the sombre curtains which almost
> stood up by themselves from sheer goodness and solidity of
> material. The drawing-room contained armies of sofas and
> well-stuffed armchairs and there were stained-glass windows
> everywhere and all the panoply of the Victorian era.[27]

Later, when the Buchans visited Edinburgh they stayed with friends at 6 Heriot Row.

Buchan's responsibilities included the Nelson Sixpenny Clasics and the Nelson Sevenpenny Library of copyright novels. He himself wrote several books for the firm, including a life of the Marquis of Montrose and a history of the First World War. What, however, gave him most pleasure was his job as editor of a new magazine, the *Scottish Review*. This magazine had been launched in April 1907 and did much, during its two-year existence, to initiate a revival of interest in Scottish writing.

Buchan is now associated with popular thrillers such as *Greenmantle* and *Mr Standfast*, but he was a writer of wide range and had a tremendous interest in Scottish writing. He wrote the preface to Hugh MacDiarmid's *Sangschaw* (1925) and MacDiarmid, not naturally sympathetic to a man like Buchan, some twenty years later was to call him 'Dean of the Faculty of Scottish Letters'.

Though he spent little time in Edinburgh, preferring to stay with relations in the Borders or friends in the Highlands, he had a special regard for the city. In a list of 'Honours Gained and to be Gained', which he compiled while at Oxford, he listed 'Professorship of English in the University of Edinburgh' as his task for 1901–02. Though he never managed it, he was elected Chancellor of the University in 1937. In a lifetime of public service few posts gave him more pleasure than his period as Lord High Commissioner to the General Assembly in 1933 and 1934, which he handled so well he was appointed Governor-General of Canada the following year.

ALANNA KNIGHT

Alanna Knight has written over fifty books, ranging from non-fiction on crime in Edinburgh and R. L. Stevenson to romantic and historical fiction but she is best known for her two crime series set in Victorian Edinburgh – the twelve Inspector Faro mysteries set in the 1870s and the sequel with his daughter, Rose McQuinn, set in the 1890s.

Many of the novels are set in the Newington area where Knight herself lives: Faro lives at 9 Sheridan Place (Dryden Place opposite Pollock Halls) and Rose in Solomon's Tower at Samson's Ribs on Arthur's Seat. Patrick Hymes in *Enter Second Murderer* (1988) kills his victims on Salisbury Crags, the Coffin Lane murders all take place off Dalkeith Road, the Innocent Railway, Duddingston and Prestonfield all feature in *The Evil that Men Do* (1993) while St Anthony's Chapel and Duddingston figure in *Dangerous Pursuits* (2002).

PART V

Edinburgh Villages

E dinburgh is still a city of villages and nowhere is this more true
than Duddingston, nestling on the south side of Arthur's Seat and
a popular spot at weekends, particularly because of its loch:

> In summer a shield of blue, with swans sailing from the reeds;
> in winter, a field of ringing ice. The village church sits above
> it on a green promontory; and the village smoke rises from
> among goodly trees. At the church gates, is the historical
> jougs, a place of penance for the neck of detected sinners, and
> the historical luping-on stane, from which Dutch-built lairds
> and farmers climbed into the saddle. Here Prince Charlie
> slept before the battle of Prestonpans; and here Deacon
> Brodie, or one of his gang, stole a plough coulter before the
> burglary in Chessels Court.[1]

Though it covers some thirty acres the loch is never more than ten feet
deep. Since 1925 it has been a bird sanctuary, the reeds at the southern
edge being especially suitable as breeding grounds for birds. It was at
Duddingston that the sport of curling was invented and one of the most
famous Scottish paintings is Henry Raeburn's picture of the Revd Robert
Walker skating on the loch, although there is controversy about whether
the picture was actually painted by French artist Henri-Pierre Danloux.
Stevenson leaves an evocative picture of a typical skating scene in
Picturesque Notes:

> The surface is thick with people moving easily and swiftly
> and leaning over at a thousand graceful inclinations; the
> crowd opens and closes, and keeps moving through itself
> like water; and the ice rings to half a mile away, with the
> flying steel. As night draws on, the single figures melt into
> the dusk until only an obscure stir, and coming and going
> of black clusters, is visible upon the loch. A little longer,
> and the first torch is kindled and begins to flit rapidly
> across the ice in a ring of yellow reflection, and this is

followed by another and another, until the whole field is
full of skimming lights.[2]

Walter Scott was for a time an elder of the pretty Norman church and
beneath an ash tree in the garden of the manse he allegedly wrote part of
The Heart of Midlothian. The song writer Caroline Oliphant (Lady
Nairne) lived at Caroline Cottage, which for a time she rented to Thomas
De Quincey and his family. The village's quaint charm is sent up in Paul
Johnston's futuristic *Water of Death* where it has become a rehabilitation
centre for second-class citizens:

> Duddingston was the perfect place to put them. It's not too
> far from the city centre but remote enough to keep the
> inmates out of ordinary citizens' view. The fact that the
> village has high stone walls round most of its edges no doubt
> appealed as well. In pre-Enlightenment times there was a
> nature reserve and bird sanctuary by the small loch and the
> smart Victorian houses were priced beyond the range of even
> well-off professional types. These days the place is home to
> deviants instead of rare birds and what used to be a trendy
> pub houses the guard command post.[3]

ARTHUR'S SEAT

Dominating Edinburgh's skyline is Arthur's Seat, which Stevenson called
'a hill for magnitude, a mountain by reason of its bold design'. It is a
popular place to go on those bracing walks the Scots love and many
Edinburgh novels have scenes set on its slopes.[4]

Elspeth Davie (1919–95), in her novel *Coming to Light* (1989),
provides a vivid description:

> The city's ancient volcano could be seen for miles around.
> From such a distance it appeared as a misty, blue hill with a
> few dim, central hollows. Close up it was a fierce, dark-cliffed
> mountain with precipitous streams of red and black rocks
> below which were piled long screes of rusty gravel covered

with patches of grass and wind-bent thorn bushes. Arthur's
Seat was only one of many outbursts of vulcanism in
Scotland. Its dim hollows could now be seen as dark basins
where millions of years ago fires had spurted, where
thundering ash and molten lava had filled the cavities, and
poured out over miles of the surrounding countryside. It
stood high above the city – a dramatic landscape and a lonely
one. Black and red sharp-edged cliffs rose above the path
circling the hill, and beneath it, far below the steep scree
slopes, one looked down upon formal white crescents, over
criss-crossing roads between old houses, over spires and
domes, and across to the stubborn knob of Castle Rock –
that great plug of hard black basalt which had outlived a
whole series of huge, primeval eruptions. Even the moving
ice-sheets had not levelled it.[5]

Dorothy Wordsworth, who climbed it during her Scottish tour in 1803,
remembers sitting on a stone near the ruined St Anthony's Chapel:

> Overlooking a pastoral hollow as wild and solitary as any in
> the heart of the Highland mountains: there, instead of the
> roaring of the torrents, we listened to the noises of the city,
> which were blended in one loud indistinct buzz – a regular
> sound in the air, which in certain moods of feeling, and at
> certain times, might have a more tranquillizing effect upon
> the mind than those which we are accustomed to hear in
> such places. The castle rock looked exceedingly large through
> the misty air: a cloud of black smoke overhung the city,
> which combined with the rain and mist to conceal the shapes
> of the houses – an obscurity which added much to the
> grandeur of the sound that proceeded from it. It was
> impossible to think of anything that was little or mean, the
> goings-on of trade, the strife of men, or every-day city
> business – the impression was one, and it was visionary; like
> the conceptions of our childhood of Bagdad or Balsora when
> we have been reading The Arabian Nights' Entertainments.[6]

The composer Felix Mendelssohn, who spent a week in Edinburgh in July 1829 before going to the Highlands, later wrote of the view from Arthur's Seat: 'Few of my Switzerland reminiscences can compare to this; everything here looks so stern and robust, half enveloped in haze or smoke or fog.' The atmosphere is alleged to have inspired the opening movement of his Third (Scottish) Symphony and Hebrides Overture. So impressed was he with Edinburgh that he later applied, unsuccessfully, for the Professorship of Music.

Encircling Holyrood Park is the Queen's Drive, a broad road about three and a half miles long from which there are some spectacular views of the city. Near the eastern exit from the Park is Muschat's Cairn. The Cairn marks the scene of an infamous crime in 1720 when Nicol Muschat, a surgeon, murdered his wife by cutting her throat after efforts at divorce and poisoning had failed. Originally, the Cairn stood on Hunter's Bog, under Arthur's Seat, but was moved in 1822 so that George IV could see it without getting his feet wet.

The Cairn was also the clandestine meeting place of Jeanie Deans and her lover, the outlaw George Robertson in Scott's *Heart of Midlothian*. In the book Scott gives us an excellent description of Salisbury Crags which, though it refers to 1736, could well apply now:

> If I were to choose a spot from which the rising or setting sun
> could be seen to the greatest possible advantage, it would be
> that wild path winding around the foot of the high belt of
> semicircular rocks, called Salisbury Crags, and marking the
> verge of the steep descent which slopes down into the glen on
> the south-eastern side of Edinburgh. The prospect, in its
> general outline, commands a close-built, high-piled city,
> stretching itself out beneath in a form which, to a romantic
> imagination, may be supposed to represent that of a dragon;
> now, a noble arm of the sea, with its rock, isles, distant
> shores, and boundary of mountains; and now, a fair and
> fertile campaign country, varied with hill, dale and rock, and
> skirted by the picturesque ridge of the Pentland mountains.
> But as the path gently circles around the base of the cliffs, the
> prospect, composed as it is of these enchanting and sublime

objects, changes at every step, and presents them blended
with, or divided from, each other, in every possible variety
which can gratify the eye and the imagination. When a piece
of scenery, so beautiful yet so varied – so exciting by its
intimacy, and yet so sublime – is lighted up by the tints of
morning or of evening, and displays all that variety of
shadowy depth, exchanged with partial brilliancy, which gives
character even to the tamest of landscapes, the effect
approaches near to enchantment.[7]

Conan Doyle's *The Lost World* was supposedly inspired by his daily walk
past Salisbury Crags as a student. The Crags are known as one of
Edinburgh's main suicide spots and a number of novels have murders or
suicides there. Ian Rankin's *Dead Souls* begins at the Crags and a number
of key scenes in *The Falls* are also located there.

The Radical Road underneath Salisbury Crags was built in 1820 at
the instigation of Scott to provide work during a period of high
unemployment and potential political unrest after the Napoleonic Wars.

PORTOBELLO

Portobello was until well into this century Edinburgh's seaside resort,
famous for its salt-water baths, the large open-air swimming pool – the
setting for Fred Urquhart's short story 'The Pool' – and as the birthplace
of the comedian Harry Lauder. Much had changed, however, by the time
Wilhelm de Geer, a Swede, visited it in 1958:

The place looked lovely, fine sand, a gigantic complete
rainbow was arching like an aerial bridge from the shore at
the water's edge right across to the Fifeshire coast. Under it
on the sand, far out, thousands of gulls were shining white in
the dull light. The surface of the water was smooth reflecting
the sun with a silken sheen, in spite of the calm you hear the
ceaseless swishing of the sea. In the north-east Inchkeith gives
the effect of a miniature Mont Saint-Michel, so as long as
you gaze seaward everything appeals to your aesthetic sense.

But turn your glance towards terra firma! Ye gods and little fishes, what a sight! Factories, bathing pool erections that look like unsightly outhouses, a ballroom, a relic from bygone ages. Where there are no buildings there is urban or suburban grass, mangy and dirty, that has grown out of broken-up ground. Now I begin to be suspicious even of the beach . . . [8]

Over the last twenty years attempts have been made to revitalise the area and its appearance is improving. Streets such as the nineteenth-century Brighton Place give some indication of how exclusive the town must once have been.

It was on the sands at Portobello that Walter Scott, the quartermaster of the Royal Edinburgh Volunteer Light Dragoons, used to exercise with his regiment. Scott had been instrumental in forming the Dragoons at the beginning of 1797 after fears of a French invasion. In his full-dress uniform of scarlet coat with blue collar and cuffs and helmet crested with leopardskin and red-and-white hackle he must have been a splendid sight. His poem 'War Song of the Royal Edinburgh Light Dragoons' captures some of his enthusiasm for the cause:

To horse! To horse! The standard flies,
The bugles sound the call;
The Gallic navy stems the seas,
The voice of battle's on the breeze,
Arouse ye, one and all!
From high Dunedin's towers we come,
A band of brothers true;
Our casques the leopard's spoils crown'd
We boast the red and blue.

It was while exercising along the sands that Scott received a kick from his horse that confined him to his lodgings for three days during which time he finished the first canto of *The Lay of the Last Minstrel.*

Scott often stayed during the summer of 1827 at 37 Bellfield Street, a hundred yards from the beach. His son-in-law Lockhart had taken the house for the summer and the writer would come down to see his grandchildren, in particular 'Little Johnnie' for whom Scott was currently writing *Tales of a Grandfather*. The two-storey terraced house, with its neat front garden, is still there, marked by a plaque.

At the top of Bellfield Street, in the High Street next to the Church of St Mark, was situated a detached two-storey villa called Shrub Mount. Here lived the essayist and geologist Hugh Miller (1802–56) for the last four years of his life and here he created a museum for his geological specimens.

Miller had been born near Inverness and came to Edinburgh as a young man to edit *Witness*, the newspaper which became the voice of the Free Church. He wrote over forty books, of which the best known is his autobiography *My Schools and Schoolmasters* (1854).

Two years later, on Christmas Eve, in a fit of depression, he shot himself in the study of his house. He was buried in the Grange Cemetery shortly after the burial of an Edinburgh gunsmith, Thomas Leslie, who had been accidentally killed while inspecting Miller's revolver. An opera based on Miller's life by Reginald Barnet-Ayres and Colin Maclean was performed at the 1974 Festival.

LEITH

Leith has always been Edinburgh's port and until 1920 was a separate town. Alasdair Alpin MacGregor remembered in his autobiography how:

> A trip from Edinburgh to Leith in those days was
> equivalent to a visit to an entirely different town, though
> they were contiguous in the closest sense. The rivalry
> existing between them was considerable, though, to all
> intents and purposes, one scarcely could tell where the
> Scottish Capital ended, and her seaport began. From a
> departmental point of view, however, they were entirely
> separate communities, the one spurning the alleged
> amenities of the other. There were differences too, that no
> schoolboy could fail to notice. The Leith bobbies wore
> dissimilar helmets (less expensive ones, we liked to think!)
> and the Leith bailies' lamps disported a different coat-of-

arms. Leith's tramtrack was of a narrower gauge than ours,
and the vehicles upon it correspondingly smaller. Yet, Leith
was enjoying an electric system when Auld Reekie was still
in the dark ages of traction by cable.[9]

Even now, the divisions, despite the new-found prosperity of the town,
remain. As one character in Isla Dewar's *Women Talking Dirty* (1996) puts
it:

> Edinburgh was style and patter, haircuts and jackets in bars.
> But Leith was full of folk. People spilled from pubs. Of an
> evening the air was boozy. You could get drunk from passive
> drinking. It was a place to live out a recession. And, though it
> was filling with bistros and bars with their names gold
> lettered in Palatino on their windows, low times still suited
> it.[10]

In Elspeth Davie's *Coming to Light* two of the central characters, Steve
and Ben, feel more affinity with Leith than Edinburgh itself:

> Steve simply put the sea itself as his reason. No doubt it was a
> dirty sea, an oily sea down here, but it gave movement, even
> turbulence to the whole scene, unlike the formality of the city
> which could be both beautiful and rather forbidding. Down
> here the sky was fretted with the gesticulating shapes of old
> ships, and near the water were the cracked blocks from an
> ancient harbour wall. Behind new shops stood remains of the
> old – their signboards scoured with half a century of salt. Old
> brass confronted new glitter.[11]

Leith Links, still the main recreation area, have a number of literary
associations. At one time they were notorious for the horse-racing that
took place there, perhaps best observed in Robert Fergusson's poem
about the Leith Races. In *The Expedition of Humphrey Clinker* Matthew
Bramble visits the racecourse where he describes what was then, and still
is, the national sport:

Hard by, in the fields called the Links, the citizens of
Edinburgh divert themselves at a game called golf, in which
they use a curious kind of bat tipped with horn, and small
elastic balls of leather, stuffed with feathers, rather less than
tennis-balls, but of a much harder consistence. This they strike
with such force and dexterity from one hole to another, that
they will fly to an incredible distance. Of this diversion the
Scots are so fond, that when the weather will permit, you may
see a multitude of all ranks, from the senator of justice to the
lowest tradesman, mingled together, in their shirts, and
following the balls with the utmost eagerness.[12]

HUGH MacDIARMID

At the corner of Claremont Road and McDonald Road stands an
imposing building, the former Broughton Junior Student Centre, now
Lothian Regional Council's Property Services department. The poet
Christopher Murray Grieve (1892–1978), known as Hugh MacDiarmid,
came here as a sixteen-year-old student teacher in 1908 from his native
Langholm. He was soon drawn under the sympathetic wing of the
Principal Teacher of English, George Ogilvie. Ogilvie, who became one
of the most influential men in Grieve's life, has left a picture of the young
poet:

> I remember vividly Grieve's arrival among us. I see the little,
> slimly built figure in hodden grey, the small sharp-featured face
> with its piercing eyes, the striking head with its broad brow and
> great mass of flaxen curly hair. He hailed from Langholm, and
> had a Border accent you could have cut with a knife. I am
> afraid some of the city students smiled at first at the newcomer,
> but he very speedily established himself in mine . . . He was
> not, it must be admitted, a model student; in some subjects,
> frankly, he had no interest. As a matter of fact he became the
> despair of most of his teachers. Yet none of them could help
> liking him. He had a most engaging ingenuousness, and I have
> yet to meet the infant who could look as innocent as Grieve.[13]

The atmosphere was a stimulating one, for many of his student-teacher colleagues were also keen to write. These included Mary Baird Aitken, who after returning to Broughton to teach, published a novel, *Soon Bright Day*, about the Scottish radical Thomas Muir of Huntershill; Edward Albert, who wrote a number of novels based on episodes in Scottish history; and Roderick Watson Kerr whose volume of war poems *War Daubs* attracted some interest on publication.

It was Kerr who, together with his fellow student John Gould and George Malcolm Thomson, in 1922 set up the Porpoise Press with the express intention of publishing Scottish poets and novelists. Among those to benefit were Lewis Spence, Neil Gunn and Grieve himself.

Grieve left Broughton just before the end of his three-year course. He claimed in his autobiography *Lucky Poet* that he had been forced to leave after the death of his father but his father in fact died eight days after Grieve's departure. The truth is more prosaic. Grieve had been involved in the theft of several books from his mentor, Ogilvie. Ogilvie, anxious to avoid a scandal, allowed Grieve to resign on 27 January, 1911, the school log recording that 'Christopher Grieve, Junior Student, resigned on grounds of health and mistaking his vocation'.

It was Ogilvie who helped Grieve obtain a job on the *Edinburgh Evening Dispatch* but he was unhappy and lasted less than a year. The editor dismissed him on discovering that the young journalist had been supporting himself by selling review copies. The scandal was to have repercussions throughout his life. Grieve's application to join *The Scotsman* was turned down because of it. Grieve had never liked Edinburgh and he gratefully took a journalism job in South Wales.

Though he vowed never again to live in Edinburgh, Grieve did return briefly in 1918 to be married at 3 East Castle Road to Margaret Skinner, whom he had met five years before while working on the *Forfar Review* in Angus. For six months during the winter of 1932–33, before moving to Shetland, he travelled in from Longniddry to his job as assistant editor of the Scottish nationalist paper, *Free Man*, then based in India Buildings in Victoria Street. A number of other writers have been educated at Broughton including the playwright and poet A. D. Mackie, J. K. Annand, Fred Urquhart and Alan Bold.

STEVENSON,
CARLYLE AND LEITH

Pilrig House in Pilrig Street was the 'pleasant gabled house set by the walkside among some brave young woods' to which David Balfour went in Stevenson's *Catriona* (1893) in order to talk to James Balfour. Stevenson was well acquainted with the area, often going to Leith Walk to consort with prostitutes or merely to escape the constrictions of his background. He must have been a strange sight in his blue-black flannel shirts, red tie, salt-and-pepper trousers and patent-leather shoes. He wrote warmly of such trips:

> I walk the streets smoking my pipe
> And I love the dallying shop-girl
> That leans with rounded stern to look at the fashions;
> And I hate the bustling citizen,
> The eager and hurrying man of affairs I hate,
> Because he wears his intolerance writ on his face
> And every movement and word of him tells me how
> Much he hates me.
>
> I love night in the city,
> The lighted streets and the swinging gait of harlots.
> I love cool pale morning,
> In the empty bye-streets,
> With only here and there a female figure,
> A slavey with lifted dress and the key in her hand,
> A girl or two at play in a corner of waste-land
> Tumbling and showing their legs and crying out to me loosely.

Another author who knew Leith Walk well was Thomas Carlyle, who took it as the model for his Rue St Thomas de l'Enfer in *Sartor Resartus*. It was in Leith Walk he later claimed that he realised God did not exist. Between 1822 and 1824 he lodged at 3 Spey Street (then called Moray Street), working on his Schiller translations and fighting off depression.

Between Leith and Cramond are the large council estates of Granton, Pilton and Muirhouse, built in the post-war period and the backdrop to Irvine Welsh's novels, all of which are marked by their linguistic energy and portraits of the drug culture of Edinburgh. His picture of Edinburgh is not of the Old and New Towns, which Welsh refers to derisively as 'shortbread disneyland', but the housing estates on the city's rim with their problems of crime, casual violence and sex, poverty, alcoholism and HIV infection. The narrator of *Marabou Stork Nightmares* (1995) remembers Edinburgh:

> as a dirty, cold, wet, rundown slum; a city of dull, black
> tenements and crass concrete housing schemes which were
> populated by scruffs, but the town still somehow being run
> by snobs for snobs.[14]

Welsh (1958–) was born in Leith and grew up in Muirhouse and artistically he has made the area his own, not least with his use of working-class vernacular. After leaving school he was a musician in London before returning to Edinburgh for an MBA at Heriot Watt University and a job in Edinburgh District Council's housing department. The phenomenal success of *Trainspotting* (1993), a series of tales about the junkies and disaffected youth of north Edinburgh, which was made into a film starring Ewan McGregor in 1996, allowed him to write full time.

His next book, a short story collection, *The Acid House* (1994), is written in an aggressively masculine Scots dialect which has since become a trademark of Welsh's fiction. One of the stories of the three that make up *Ecstasy* (1996) is set in the grim backstreets of modern Edinburgh while *Glue* (2001) follows the lives of four Edinburgh 'schemies' from the 1970s to the present day. Simon 'Sick Boy' Williamson, Begbie, Renton and Spud return in *Porno* (2002), the sequel to *Trainspotting*, set ten years on. Begbie is in Saughton Prison, Spud is planning a history of Leith, while Sick Boy, having failed as a pimp in London, has returned and is teaming up with Renton to produce a pornographic movie. One theme of the book is the increasing gentrification of the city and the vanishing of old communities:

> – Ah but, very soon, Franco, auld Leith will be gone. Look at Tollcross, man, it's a finance centre now. Look at the South Side: a student village. Stockbridge's been yuppiesville for donks, auld Stockeree. Us and Gorgie-Dalry'll soon be the only places left in the inner city for working-class cats, man, and that's just cause ay the fitba clubs.[15]

> It looks different doon here, man, aw redeveloped; the docks now aw smart bars and restaurants, loads ay yuppie converted warehouses. It wis sayin in the paper thit they moved the prossies fae whaire they eywis worked cause ay the complaints fae the residents. That tae me's pure no fair, cause thuv eywis worked thair n cats ken what the place is like before they move in.[16]

In *Marabou Stork Nightmares*, the memories of a football hooligan lying unconscious in hospital, there is a shocking scene on Silverknowes Beach where the central character attaches fireworks to a dog and sets them alight. *Fleshmarket Close* (2004), Rankin's novel about racism, immigration and asylum, sees Rebus investigating the stabbing of a Kurdish immigrant in a grotty underpass on an Edinburgh housing scheme called Knoxland, which bears a resemblance to the schemes between Pilton and Silverknowes.[17]

CRAMOND

Cramond began as a Pictish fort, and takes its name from the Gaelic for the fort on the Almond – Caer Almond. The Romans built a fort and harbour here as part of their defensive line stretching from the Forth to the Clyde. Later, the village grew up around the mills built to service a succession of industries including grain, nail manufacturing and paper-making. Now it is renowned for its sailing and pretty, white-washed quayside cottages.

Cramond was where the singing master Gordon Lowther in *The Prime of Miss Jean Brodie* lived, and where Miss Brodie used to spend her weekends in:

> A large gabled house with a folly-turret. There were so many twists and turns in the wooded path leading up from the road and the front lawn was so narrow, that the house could never be seen from the little distance that its size demanded and it was necessary to crane one's neck upward to see the turret at all.[18]

It was an area Stevenson knew well. Cramond House is supposed to have provided the setting for his House of Shaws and he describes the village in chapter thirty of *St Ives*. It was while walking along the Cramond seashore towards South Queensferry that he told his father of his intention of becoming a writer:

> After lunch, my father and I went down to the coast and walked a little way along the shore between Granton and Cramond. This has always been with me a very favourite walk. The firth closes gradually together before you, the coast runs in a series of the most beautifully moulded bays, hill after hill, wooded and softly outlined, trends away in front till the two shores join together. When the tide is out, there are great gleaming flats of wet sand, over which the gulls go flying and crying; and every cape runs down into them with its little spit of wall and trees.[19]

Cramond Island is supposed to have been the inspiration for *Treasure Island*. The central character of *Marabou Stork Nightmares* takes a more jaundiced view:

> Cramond Island is a small island less than a mile out in the Forth Estuary. You can walk out to it at certain times, before the incoming tide cuts it off from the mainland. There's fuck all to see over there, just a few old pill-boxes from World War Two, full ay beer cans and used condoms.[20]

With his friend Walter Simpson, the son of the famous doctor James Young Simpson, Stevenson often used to go canoeing in South Queensferry. It was with Simpson that Stevenson made his canoe trip through France, which became his book *Inland Voyage*. The Hawes Inn at South Queensferry has a number of literary associations: it is where Lovel and Jonathan Oldbuck dine in *The Antiquary*, and it provided the model for the Admiral Benbow where David Balfour is brought by his uncle Ebenezer in *Kidnapped* and handed over to Captain Hoseason of the brig *Covenant*. The ship then sets sail for America with David aboard to be sold as a slave in the Carolina plantations. The fictional school where Rebus's cousin is shot in Rankin's *A Question of Blood* (2003) is in South Queensferry.

Overshadowing the Hawes Inn are the Forth Rail Bridge (1890) and the Forth Road Bridge (1964), each of which have literary associations. In *1982, Janine* Alasdair Gray describes the 'railway bridge crawling across like a steel Loch Ness Monster into the distinctly hedged and wooded fields and hills of Fife' while the climax of Martin Claridge's *The Midnight Chill* (1992) takes place on the rail bridge. Both Edwin Morgan (1920–) and Sydney Goodsir Smith wrote poems to mark the opening of the Road Bridge.

'The Twa Brigs' by Sydney Goodsir Smith

> This braw new brig that streetches owre the Frith
> Wi a lichtsome streetch.
> Twa bonny airms o'lassies jynin owre the water,
> Wi their feet in the water tae –
> Didnae Venus rise frae the wave, for luve's sake?

Across the Forth at North Queensferry lives Iain Banks (1954–) who writes both fiction and, as Iain M. Banks, science fiction. His novels include *The Wasp Factory* (1984), *The Crow Road* (1992) and *Complicity* (1993), a moral thriller whose central character is an Edinburgh journalist and which owes something to the literary tradition of the 'divided self'.

A small residential street on the side of Corstorphine Hill makes an unlikely literary site. It was at Dinnieduff, 4 Hillview Terrace, that Helen Cruickshank (1886–1975) lived for over fifty years and where she entertained most of the members of the Scottish Literary Renaissance. On coming to Edinburgh in 1912 to work as a civil servant, first in a branch of the National Health Insurance on Dean Bridge and then in the Old Commercial Exchange buildings in the Grassmarket, Cruickshank lodged in Marchmont Crescent and then Shandwick Place. In the early 1920s she moved to Corstorphine about the same time she met Hugh MacDiarmid, an experience she later described as a 'watershed' in her life. MacDiarmid became a regular guest in her spare room, the 'Prophet's Chamber', and with her was actively involved in promoting Scottish PEN where she was Secretary from 1929 to 1934.

Herself a minor poet, she was a friend and confidante to many writers including Edwin and Willa Muir, Lewis Grassic Gibbon, Norman MacCaig, Sydney Goodsir Smith, Hamish Henderson, Donald and Catherine Carswell. MacDiarmid and Gibbon dedicated *Scottish Scene* (1934) to her. In 1973 she moved to Queensberry Lodge in the Canongate, where she died two years later.[21]

Ian Rankin's *Dead Souls* begins at Edinburgh Zoo which backs onto Corstorphine Hill. On the 529-feet summit is Clermiston Tower, now boarded up, which was built in 1871 to mark the centenary of Walter Scott's birth while on the Ravelston side of the hill is the viewpoint of 'Rest and Be Thankful' where David Balfour parted from Alan Breck in Stevenson's *Kidnapped*.

Below, off Craigcrook Road, is Craigcrook Castle which has a number of literary associations. Archibald Constable lived there at the beginning of the nineteenth century, selling it to Lord Jeffrey in 1815. Cockburn thought 'No unofficial house in Scotland has had a greater influence on literary or political opinion'. Certainly, most of the leading literary figures of the day visited it including Alfred Tennyson, Charles Dickens, Hans Christian Andersen, George Eliot, Washington Irving and William Thackeray.

Nearby in Ravelston Dykes Road, is New Ravelston House, which was built in 1791. Now part of the Mary Erskine School, its terraces, grass walks and statues once provided the inspiration for Tullyveolan in Scott's *Waverley.*

COLINTON

Colinton is remembered chiefly because of its associations with Stevenson. His maternal grandfather Lewis Balfour was the minister of Colinton parish church for thirty-seven years until his death in 1860 and Stevenson spent many holidays at the manse there. In later life he would remember:

> It was a place in that time like no other: the garden cut into provinces by a great hedge of beech, and overlooked by the church and the terrace of the churchyard, where the tombstones were thick, and after nightfall 'spunkies' might be seen to dance at least by children; flower-pots lying warm in sunshine; laurels and the great yew making elsewhere a pleasing horror of shade; the smell of water rising from all around, with an added tang of paper-mills; the sound of water everywhere, and the sound of mills – the wheel and the dam singing their alternate strain; the birds on every bush and from every corner of the overhanging woods pealing out their notes until the air throbbed with them; and in the midst of this, the manse.[22]

It was here at the manse, surrounded by scores of relations, that Stevenson was able to behave like any normal high-spirited young boy rather than the rather precocious child of the Edinburgh New Town. He writes about the village in *Pentland Essays.*

A derelict cottage at what used to be the Colinton train terminus, just before the descent into Colinton Village, was once rather grandly known as Colinton Bank House. A plaque records that Henry Mackenzie lived there.

The sixteenth-century Colinton Castle, the ruins of which form part of Merchiston Castle School, was owned by, among others, George

Drummond, the Lord Provost responsible for the building of the New Town, and Sir William Forbes of Pitsligo who married Walter Scott's sweetheart Williamina Stuart-Belsches. It is also the scene of Mrs Oliphant's famous ghost story 'The Open Door'. The school figures in Paul Johnston's *Water of Death*, after being set on fire by 'a particularly vicious drugs gang who called themselves the Boys in Blue'.[23]

Bonaly Tower, designed by William Playfair in 1836, was the home of Henry Cockburn. Evelyn Waugh attended a course there during the Second World War and, recognising the Cockburn coat of arms, realised it had been the home of his great-great-grandfather.

SWANSTON

Swanston also has numerous associations with Stevenson. A track just before the village leads to the eighteenth-century Swanston cottage which the Stevenson family leased between 1867 and 1880 in the hope that the country air would improve the boy's health. In his novel *St Ives* the hero Monsieur le Vicomte de Saint-Yves, after his escape from the Castle, makes for Swanston where he comes across a cottage that is the exact replica of the Stevenson home:

A single gable and chimney of the cottage peered over the shoulder of the hill: not far off, and a trifle higher on the mountain, a tall old white-washed farmhouse stood among the trees beside a falling brook . . . a little quaint place of many rough cast gables and grey roofs. It had something of the air of a rambling infinitesimal cathedral, the body of it rising in the midst two storeys high, with a steep-pitched roof and sending out up all hands (as it were chapter-houses, chapels and transepts) one storeyed and dwarfish projections. To add to this appearance it was grotesquely decorated with crockets and gargoyles, ravished from some medieval church. The place seemed hidden away being not only concealed in the trees of the garden, but on the side on which I approached it, buried as high as the eaves by the rising of the ground. About the walls of the garden there went a line of

well-grown elms and beeches, the first entirely bare, the last
still petty well covered with red leaves, and the centre was
occupied with a thicket of laurel and holly in which I could
see arches cut and paths winding . . . .[24]

If one carries on up the original path past a three-sided square of grey
one-storey buildings one comes to Swanston village, a cluster of cottages
with grey window surrounds and immaculate front gardens. Immediately
above, sheep graze contentedly, quite oblivious of the passing golfers
while 'straight above the hills climb 1,000 feet into the air'.

At the highest point of the green there is a teak bench with the
inscription:

TO THE MEMORY OF EDWIN MUIR 1887–1959
Poet, Novelist, Essayist, Teacher.
This seat is given by his friends to
The village of Swanston where the poet
Liked to linger and meditate.

Muir used to love coming up here and writes of his 'little paradise' in his
poem 'In Love for Long'. Born and brought up in Orkney, Muir spent
much of his early life abroad before eventually taking a job with the
British Council in Edinburgh in 1942 and later becoming Warden of
Newbattle Abbey College, an adult education college to the south-east of
Edinburgh where he was a mentor to writers such as George Mackay
Brown (1921–96) and Tom Scott (1918–95).

He was a prominent member of PEN and after its 1934 conference
wrote *Scottish Journey* (1935), whose first chapter on Edinburgh gives a
shrewd analysis of the divided nature of the city. He also wrote books on
John Knox and in *Scott and Scotland* (1936) reached the famous
conclusion that 'Scotland can only create a national literature by writing
in English'.

The Pentland Hills mark the southern limits of Edinburgh, and
form a convenient boundary for this companion. Stevenson knew them
intimately, calling them the 'Hills of Home' and even from Samoa he
would remember how:

The tropics vanish, and meseems that I,
From Halkerside, from topmost Allermuir,
Or steep Caerketton, dreaming gaze again.

Just before his death he wrote to Lord Rosebery describing how he wished he 'could be buried there – among the hills, say, on the head of Allermuir – with a table tombstone like a Cameronian'. His first book was a sixteen-page pamphlet privately printed by his father called *The Pentland Rising* which centred around the Covenanters' rising put down by the 1666 Battle of Rullion Green, and both his story 'The Body Snatchers' and *Weir of Hermiston* have scenes at Glencorse Church.

Stevenson is perhaps the most elegiac and lyrical writer about Edinburgh and it is appropriate that he should have the last word:

I was born likewise within the bonds of an earthly city
illustrious for her beauty, her tragic and picturesque
association, and for the credit of some of her brave sons.
Writing as I do in a strange quarter of the world, and a late
day of my age, I can still behold the profile of her towers and
chimneys, and the long trail of her smoke against the sunset;
I can still hear those strains of martial music that she goes to
bed with, ending each day like an act of an opera to the notes
of bugles: still recall with a grateful effort of memory, any one
of a thousand beautiful and spacious circumstances that
pleased me and that must have pleased any one in my half-
remembered past. It is the beautiful that I thus actually recall,
the august airs of the castle on its rock, nocturnal passages of
lights and trees, the sudden song of the blackbird in a
suburban lane, rosy and dusky winter sunsets, the
uninhabited splendours of the early dawn, the building up of
the city on a misty day, house upon house, spire above spire,
until it was received into a sky of softly glowing clouds, and
seemed to pass on and upwards by fresh grades and rises, city
upon city, a New Jerusalem bodily scaling heaven.[25]

Reference Notes

THE OLD TOWN

1. Neil McCallum, *A Scream in the Sky* (Cassell, 1964) p.20.
2. A number of novels have scenes at Waverley; e.g. Simon Brett, *So Much Blood* (Gollancz, 1976) p.9; Michael Bassi, *The Kilted Parrot* (The Molendivar Press, 1981) p.9; James Allen Ford, *A Statue for a Public Place* (Hodder & Stoughton, 1965) pp.173–174.
3. Quoted William Ruddick (ed.), *Peter's Letters to His Kinsfolk* (Scottish Academic Press, 1977) Letter XXVII. Cf Joanna McDonald, *Dubious Assets* (Headline, 1995) pp.64–65.
4. Quoted Rosaline Masson, *In Praise of Edinburgh* (Constable, 1912) p.205.
5. George Borrow, *Lavengro* (John Murray, 1888) chapter 7.
6. Eric Linklater, *Magnus Merriman* (Cape, 1934) p.138.
7. Owen John, *Festival* (Robert Hale, 1978) pp.92–3. Simon Brett, *So Much Blood* has a suicide from the Castle ramparts.
8. William Boyd, *The New Confessions* (Penguin, 1988) pp.17–18.
9. A dinner with Boswell and Dr Johnson figures in James Robertson's *Joseph Knight* (Fourth Estate, 2003) pp.174–176
10. Daniel Defoe, *A Tour Through the Whole Island of Great Britain*, G. D. H. Cole (ed.) (Peter Davies, 1927) p.692.
11. G. K. Chesterton, *Robert Louis Stevenson* (Hodder & Stoughton, 1929) pp.68–9. A good contemporary description of Brodie is given in Eric Linklater, *Edinburgh* (Newnes, 1960) p.168.
12. Tobias Smollett, *The Expedition of Humphrey Clinker* (OUP, 1985) p.218.
13. Thomas Carlyle, *Reminiscences* (Longman, 1881) vol. 2, pp.5–6.
14. Robert Louis Stevenson, *Edinburgh: Picturesque Notes* (Seeley & Co., 1900) pp.52–53.
15. W. D. Lyell, *The Justice-Clerk* (William Hodge, 1923); James Allen Ford, *A Judge of Men*, (Hodder & Stoughton, 1968); Magda Sweetland, *The Hermitage*, (Macmillan, 1988).
16. Ruddick, *Peter's Letters to His Kinsfolk*, Letter XXVIII.
17. Muriel Spark, *The Prime of Miss Jean Brodie* (Penguin, 1965) p.35
18. Ibid., p.108.
19. John Galt, *Ringan Gilhaize* (Scottish Academic Press, 1984) p.320.
20. Smollett, p.217.
21. Walter Scott, *Heart of Midlothian* (OUP, 1982) pp. 56–7.
22. Henry Cockburn, *Memorials of His Time* (Robert Grant, 1945) p.105.
23. A good account can be found in Alan J. Wilson et al, *Hidden and Haunted Underground Edinburgh* (Mercat Tours, 1999).
24. Linklater, *Magnus Merriman*, p.51.
25. Cockburn, pp.240–42.
26. Alexander Carlyle, *Autobiography* (Foulis, 1910) p.327.

27. Smollett, p.222.
28. Letter to Craibe Angus. Quoted Neil McCallum, *A Small Country* (Mercat Press, 1983) p.120; cf Robert Garioch's poem 'At Robert Fergusson's Grave'.
29. For a good description of Stewart see R. P. Gillies, *Reminiscences of a Literary Veteran* (Richard Bentley, 1851) vol. I pp.282–9.
30. Paul Johnston, *Water of Death* (NEL, 1999) pp.85–6. Kathleen Jamie's poem 'On the Design for the New Scottish Parliament Building by Architect Enric Miralles' is more succinct: An upturned boat – a watershed.
31. For descriptions of the area see Boyd, p.18 and Moray McLaren, *A Dinner with the Dead* (Serif, 1947), pp.11–12.
32. Quoted Masson, p.62.
33. Stevenson, *Picturesque Notes*, pp. 6–8.
34. Quoted Michael Turnbull, *Edinburgh Portraits* (John Donald, 1987). Simon Brett's *So Much Blood* revolves around a plot to bomb Holyrood.
35. Alexander Smith, *A Summer in Skye*, (Strahan, 1866) pp.19–20. Good descriptions can also be found in Stevenson, *Picturesque Notes*, p.39, and Alastair Alpin MacGregor, *Auld Reekie* (Methuen, 1943) p.137.
36. Ian Rankin, *Dead Souls* (Orion, 1999) p.263.
37. See for example John Wilson McLaren's *Weir the Wizard,* K. L. Montgomery's *Major Weir* and James Robertson's *The Fanatic.*
38. Another account of the riot can be found in Carlyle, *Autobiography*, chapter 2 and it figures in novels such as Josephine Delves-Broughton's *I Saw No Sun* and Duncan McLellan's *The Hanging of Captain Green.*
39. See I. Goodwin, *Bury me in Lead*, (Alan Wingate, 1952); Inga Dunbar's *Tanner's Close* and Elizabeth Byrd, *Rest Without Peace* (Macmillan, 1974) amongst many others. Hector Bryson's narrator in *Doctors, Bodies and Snatchers* is a pupil of Doctor Knox who was involved in obtaining bodies from Burke and Hare.

THE UNIVERSITY QUARTER

1. See William Watson, George Square 1766–1966, *University of Edinburgh Journal,* Spring 1966, vol. XXII pp.239–251.
2. Rebecca West, *The Judge* (Hutchinson, 1922) p.74.
3. Cf Sydney Goodsir Smith, 'Interim Report', *Gambit*, August 1957.
4. Paul Johnston, *Water of Death* (NEL edition, 1999) p.284
5. Lockhart, chapter 3.
6. A good description of MacGregor can be found in John Herdman *Poets, Pubs, Polls & Pillar Boxes* (Akris, 1999) p.27.
7. Stevenson, *Picturesque Notes*, pp.76–9.
8. A good portrait can be found in *Peter's Letters to His Kinsfolk,* Letter X.
9. Donald Low, 'Walter Scott and Williamina Belsches', *Times Literary Supplement,* 23 July 1971, pp.865–6.
10. Quoted Andrew Pennycook, *Literary and Artistic Landmarks of Edinburgh* (Charles Skilton, 1973) p.82.
11. Smollett, p.233.
12. *Letters of R. L. Stevenson,* vol. 2, p.276; *Letters of R. L. Stevenson* vol. 4, p.274.
13. 'A College Magazine' XXV in *Memories and Portraits* (Richard Drew, 1990) pp.46–7.
14. *Letters of R. L. Stevenson* vol. 2, pp.114–15.
15. Quoted Andrew Birkin, *The Lost Boys* (Futura, 1980) p.24.
16. Arthur Conan Doyle, *The Firm of Girdlestone* (Chatto & Windus, 1890) chapter 5.
17. See Owen Dudley Edwards, *The Edinburgh Stories of Arthur Conan Doyle* (Polygon, 1981).
18. Conan Doyle, *Memories and Adventures* (Hodder & Stoughton, 1924) p.25.

19. Borrow, *Lavengro*, chapter 4.
20. S. R. Crockett, *Kit Kennedy* (James Clarke, 1899); Stevenson, *Picturesque Notes*, p.5.

THE NEW TOWN

1. Rankin, *Dead Souls*, p.98.
2. Linklater, *Edinburgh*, pp.44–5; Joan Lingard, *The Prevailing Wind* (Hodder & Stoughton, 1964) p.47 and p.128.
3. Muriel Spark, 'What Images Return', in Karl Miller, ed. *Memoirs of a Modern Scotland* (Faber, 1970) p.151. The North British figures in Angus Ross *The Edinburgh Exercise* (Long, 1975) p.29, and Moray McLaren *The Pursuit* (Jarrolds, 1959) p.204.
4. Cockburn, *Memorials*, pp.104–5.
5. For a description of the Blackwood premises in Princes Street, see *Peter's Letters to His Kinsfolk*, Letter XLIV. cf F. Tredrey, *The House of Blackwood 1804–1954* (Blackwood, 1954).
6. Ford, *A Statue for a Public Place*, pp.13–14. A less romantic picture is given in Johnston, *Water of Death*, pp. 366–7.
7. Linklater, *Magnus Merriman*, p.40.
8. While working for the British Council in Edinburgh Muir lodged first at 47 Manor Place and then rented a flat at 8 Blantyre Terrace.
9. Linklater, *The Merry Muse*, pp.224–5. The club also figures in Moray McLaren's *The Unpossessed*, pp.32–8 as the New Athenian Club. Quintin Jardine's detective Bob Skinner is a member.
10. Tom Driberg, *Ruling Passions* (Quartet, 1978) p.144.
11. W. M. Parker, 'Catherine Sinclair', *Edinburgh Tatler*, May 1967.
12. Quoted Pennycook, p.83.
13. Ibid. Jane Oliver's *The Blue Heaven Bends Over All* and Allan Massie's *Ragged Lion* (Hutchinson, 1994) are novels about Scott, while in Elizabeth Scarborough's *The Lady in the Loch* Scott becomes a sleuth. 'Walter Scott, lawyer, romantic author and newly appointed sheriff of Edinburgh, finds a mystery on his hands. The slowly draining Nor' Loch is giving up a collection of bones and bodies – recent bodies – incomplete bodies. And, when women begin disappearing, snatched right off the street, it becomes very worrying indeed. Someone is up to something hideous and diabolical, and Scott needs to get to the bottom of it!'
14. Cf Patrick Chalmers, *Kenneth Grahame* (Methuen, 1933) and Eleanor Grahame, *Kenneth Grahame* (Bodley Head, 1963).
15. It now has its own website – www.oxfordbar.com – with all its references in the Rebus novels.
16. Bol.com internet interview for the publication of *Set in Darkness* (Orion, 2000). Marcel Berlins reviewing the book in *The Times* (5 February, 2000) began, 'In times to come, I suspect, we shall know more about Edinburgh through the novels of Ian Rankin than from the combined tomes of all the other writers who have written factually or fictionally about the city.'
17. Smith, *A Summer on Skye*, p.14. Cf Christopher Whyte, *The Gay Decameron* (Gollancz, 1999) p.343.
18. Quoted W. Forbes Gray, 'The Edinburgh Relations and Friends of Dickens', *The Dickensian*, September and December 1926.
19. Novels with a Festival setting include Robert Blyth's *Festival*, Simon Brett's *So Much Blood*, Dorothy Halliday's *Dolly and the Singing Bird*, Owen John's *Festival*, Robert Kemp's *The Maestro*, Ian Rankin's *Mortal Causes* and Quintin Jardine's *Skinner's Festival*.
20. Trederey, p.192.
21. Quoted ibid, p.168.

22. Quoted ibid, p.186.
23. Alasdair Gray, *1982, Janine* (Cape, 1984) p.282. The bar figures in Goodsir Smith's *Kynd Kittock's Land*, Abraham Adam's *Another Little Drink* and Norman MacCaig's poem 'Milne's Bar'.
24. See profile *Scotland on Sunday*, 4 November, 1990.
25. Hugh MacDiarmid, *The Company I've Kept* (Hutchinson, 1966) p.233.
26. See profile *Scotland on Sunday* 21 December, 1990, and in *Edinburgh University Alumni* Magazine,May 1990.
27. Alan Bold, *Hugh MacDiarmid*, (John Murray, 1988) p.413.
28. Linklater, *Magnus Merriman*, pp.69–70.
29. For a description of the house see Morris Rosenblum, *The Baker Street Journal*, vol. 13 no. 4, 1963.
30. A good account of the Heretics is given in Herdman pp.29–38.
31. Elizabeth Grant of Rothiemurchus, *Memoirs of a Highland Lady* (John May, 1911) p.284.
32. Moray McLaren, *The Capital of Scotland* (Douglas & Foulis, 1950) p.64; McLaren, *The Pursuit* (Jarrolds, 1959) p.148.
33. McLaren, *The Pursuit*, p.59.
34. Quoted Jenni Calder, *RLS: A Life Study* (Hamish Hamilton, 1980) pp.16–17.
35. Alexander McCall Smith, *44 Scotland Street* (Polygon, 2005) p.1
36. Ibid p.10

THE VILLA QUARTERS

1. Smith, *A Summer in Skye*, pp.13–14.
2. See Stevenson, *Memories and Portraits*, pp.149–158.
3. Jules Verne, *Backwards to Britain* (Chambers, 1992) p.100.
4. Linklater, *Edinburgh*, p.53.
5. Ian Miller, *School Tie* (Newnes, 1935), p.21.
6. *Edinburgh Review*, no. 102, pp.17–32.
7. Paul Johnston, *The Blood Tree* (Hodder & Stoughton, 2000) p.7.
8. Interview with John Connolly at www.johnconnollybooks.com/int-johnston.
9. Quintin Jardine, *Skinner's Rules* (Headline, 1993) p.3
10. See Andrew Kerr's pamphlet on Ann Street (Edinburgh City Library, 1982) and for Bannerman, Elizabeth Hay, *Sambo Sahib* (Paul Harris, 1981) p.132.
11. Linklater, *The Merry Muse*, pp.246–7.
12. Other Edinburgh addresses for Annand are 1 Silverknowes Loan, 174 Craigleith Road and 10 House o'Hill Row.
13. Linklater, *Magnus Merriman*, p.88.
14. Quoted Wilmot Harrison, *Memorable Edinburgh Houses* (Oliphant, Anderson & Ferrier, 1893) p.75.
15. Spark, *The Prime of Miss Jean Brodie*, p.39.
16. Bruce Marshall, *The Black Oxen* (Constable, 1972) p.19.
17. Smollett, p.226.
18. Spark, *The Prime of Miss Jean Brodie*, p.144.
19. Karl Miller (ed.), *Memoirs of Modern Scotland* (Faber, 1970) chapter 10 for Edinburgh's influence on Spark.
20. The various Edinburgh locations in the books are listed on her official website – www.dorothydunnett.co.uk – and in Elspeth Morrison's *The Dorothy Dunnett Companion* (Michael Joseph, 1994) and *The Dorothy Dunnett Companion II* (Michael Joseph, 2002).
21. Both Searle and Lee have written books about St Trinnean's.
22. Cf Hector Waugh (ed.) *George Watson's College 1724–1970* (1970).

23. Stephen Macdonald's play about Owen and Sassoon, *Not About Heroes*, was a hit of the 1982 Festival Fringe. Cf Pat Barker, *Regeneration* (Viking, 1991).
24. Siegfried Sassoon, *The Complete Memoirs of George Sherston* (Faber, 1937) p.638 and pp.679–80.
25. Stevenson, *Picturesque Notes*, p.118.
26. Robert Kemp, *The Maestro* (Duckworth, 1956) p.45.
27. Susan Buchan (ed.), *John Buchan by his Wife and Friends* (Hodder & Stoughton, 1947) p.40.
28. Quoted Trevor Royle, *Precipitous City* (Mainstream, 1980) p.171.

EDINBURGH'S VILLAGES

1. Stevenson, *Picturesque Notes,* pp.156–9.
2. Ibid, pp.159–60.
3. Johnston, *Water of Death,* p.131.
4. Ford, *A Judge of Men;* Jeremy Bruce Watt, *The Captive Summer* (Chambers, 1979) and Lingard, *The Prevailing Wind.*
5. Elspeth Davie, *Coming to Light* (Hamish Hamilton, 1989) p.35.
6. Dorothy Wordsworth, *Recollections of a Tour in Scotland 1803* (Edmonstone & Douglas, 1874) p.244. Cf Rosemary Kay, *Return Journey* (Headline, 1996) p.120, and Matthew Reid, *Blackstone's Pursuits* (Headline, 1996) p.67.
7. Scott, *Heart of Midlothian,* chapter 8.
8. Wilhelm de Greer, *Swede in Edinburgh* (William McLennan, 1965) p.64.
9. McGregor, *Portrait of a Lowland Boyhood* (Methuen, 1943) p.92.
10. Isla Dewar, *Women Talking Dirty* (Headline, 1996) p.168.
11. Davie, p.100.
12. Smollett, pp.225–6.
13. Quoted Bold, *MacDiarmid,* p.43.
14. Irvine Welsh, *Marabou Stork Nightmares* (Cape, 1995) p.75.
15. Irvine Welsh, *Porno* (Cape, 2002) p. 261
16. Ibid, p.351.
17. *Marabou Stork Nightmares,* p.164.
18. Spark, p.89.
19. Letter RLS to Frances Sitwell 13 September, 1873, quoted *Robert Louis Stevenson's Edinburgh,* p.57
20. Irvine Welsh, *Marabou Stork Nightmares* (Vintage edition, 1996) p.164.
21. Cf Cruickshank, *Octobiography* (Standard Press, 1976).
22. Stevenson, *Memories and Portraits,* p.76.
23. Johnston, *Water of Death,* p.190.
24. Stevenson, *St Ives,* pp.46–7.
25. Quoted Pennycook, pp.121–2.

Edinburgh Literary Figures

WILLIAM EDMONDSTOUNE AYTOUN (1813–65). Son-in-law of John Wilson, he is best remembered for his humorous short stories and satirical verse parodies.

R. M. BALLANTYNE (1825–94). Wrote adventure novels, of which the best known is *Coral Island* (1858).

HELEN BANNERMAN (1862–1946). The author of *Little Black Sambo* was born and educated in the city, returning to spend almost thirty years of her retirement there.

J. M. BARRIE (1860–1937). One of the Kailyard school of writers, now largely remembered for his plays *Peter Pan* and *The Admirable Crichton*.

JOSEPH BELL (1837–1911). Surgeon colleague of Conan Doyle and model for Sherlock Holmes.

WILLIAM BLACKWOOD (1776–1834). Publisher, who founded Tory *Blackwood's Magazine* in opposition to Whig *Edinburgh Review*.

ALAN BOLD (1943–98). Prodigious writer, journalist and poet often associated with the older members of the Scots Literary Renaissance.

GEORGE BORROW (1803–81). His best-known book *Lavengro* is based on his early life in Edinburgh.

JAMES BOSWELL (1740–95). Best known for his biography of Samuel Johnson and *The Journal of the Tour to the Hebrides*.

DEACON BRODIE (1741–88). Edinburgh town councillor by day and thief by night, an inspiration for numerous Edinburgh novels.

JOHN BUCHAN (1875–1940). Lived and worked in Edinburgh, returning as Lord High Commissioner and Chancellor of Edinburgh University.

GEORGE BUCHANAN (1506–82). A scholar and translator, he also wrote plays, poetry and a history of Scotland.

ROBERT BURNS (1759–96). Scotland's premier poet. During his two visits to Edinburgh he wrote some of his most famous poems and had his famous correspondence with 'Clarinda'.

ALEXANDER 'JUPITER' CARLYLE (1722–1805). His *Autobiography* provides a vivid picture of Scottish life during the late eighteenth century.

THOMAS CARLYLE (1795–1881). Writer and historian, whose best-known books are *The French Revolution* and *Sartor Resartus*.

JOYCE CARY (1888–1957). Author of *The Horse's Mouth* and *Mr Johnson*, his first book was published while at Edinburgh Art School.

HENRY COCKBURN (1779–1854). Solicitor General and contributor to *The Edinburgh Review*, his *Memorials of His Time* is a classic account of Edinburgh society during the first half of the nineteenth century. Great-great-grandfather of Evelyn Waugh.

STEWART CONN (1936–). Playwright, poet and Edinburgh's first Makar.

ARCHIBALD CONSTABLE (1774–1827). Publisher of *The Edinburgh Review* and Walter Scott.

WILLIAM CREECH (1745–1815). Lord Provost and publisher of Robert Burns.

SAMUEL RUTHERFORD CROCKETT (1859–1914). Free Church minister whose novel *Cleg Kelly* draws on his missionary work in Edinburgh slums.

HELEN CRUIKSHANK (1886–1975). Though a poet in her own right, she is now remembered for her support of Scottish PEN and writers like Hugh MacDiarmid.

DAVID DAICHES (1912–). Distinguished academic who has written widely about Edinburgh's history and literary figures.

ELSPETH DAVIE (1919–95). Novelist now best known for her short stories.

DANIEL DEFOE (1660–1731). The author of *Robinson Crusoe* lived in Edinburgh in 1707 and returned in 1724 on his *Tour Through the Whole Island*.

THOMAS DE QUINCEY (1785–1859). The author of *Confessions of an English Opium Eater* spent the last forty years of his life in debt and in various lodgings around the city.

CHARLES DICKENS (1812–70). His wife's family came from Edinburgh and the novelist made a number of successful reading tours to the city.

GAVIN DOUGLAS (*c.* 1476–1522). Provost of St Giles, best known for his loose translation of the Aeneid into Middle Scots.

ARTHUR CONAN DOYLE (1859–1930). He wrote a number of stories based on his youth in the capital and Sherlock Holmes was inspired by Joseph Bell, one of his teachers at the University.

WILLIAM DUNBAR (*c.* 1460–*c.* 1513). Medieval Makar whose poems criticise Edinburgh for its materialism, lack of spiritual values and corruption.

GEORGE ELIOT (1819–80). Visited Edinburgh in 1845 and 1852.

ROBERT FERGUSSON (1750–74). Poet who wrote about ordinary people and life in Edinburgh, much admired by Burns and Stevenson.

SUSAN FERRIER (1782–1854). One of Edinburgh's few nineteenth-century female novelists, she is often generously compared to Jane Austen.

JAMES ALLAN FORD (1920–). Former Registrar-General for Scotland, whose two Edinburgh novels cast a sharp eye on the Law and Civil Service.

JOHN GALT (1779–1839). Novelist whose work tended to trade on the Scottish nostalgia boom created by Scott.

ROBERT GARIOCH (1909–81). One of the most distinguished Edinburgh poets of the twentieth century.

JOHN GAY (1685–1732). The poet and playwright spent some time in Edinburgh.

OLIVER GOLDSMITH (1728–74). The author of *The Vicar of Wakefield* studied medicine at the University and subsequently wrote about the city's dancing assemblies.

KENNETH GRAHAME (1859–1932). The author of *The Wind in the Willows* was born and spent the first few years of his life in Edinburgh, without any noticeable effect on his writing.

ALASDAIR GRAY (1935–). Though strictly speaking a Glasgow writer, his novel *1982, Janine* has some marvellous Edinburgh scenes.

C. M. GRIEVE (1892–1978). As Hugh MacDiarmid, a leading figure in the Scots Literary Renaissance of the twentieth century. His most famous poem is 'A Drunk Man Looks at the Thistle'.

NEIL GUNN (1891–1973). Worked for the Civil Service in Edinburgh from 1909 to 1911 and writes about the city in his novel *The Drinking Well*.

HAMISH HENDERSON (1919–2002). Poet, folklorist and founder of the University School of Scottish Studies.

W. E. HENLEY (1849–1903). Friend and collaborator with R. L. Stevenson and J. M. Barrie. He was the inspiration for Long John Silver and his daughter for Wendy in *Peter Pan*.

JAMES HOGG (1770–1835). Known as 'The Ettrick Shepherd' and a friend of Scott, his *The Private Memoirs and Confessions of a Justified Sinner* is one of the great Scottish novels.

JOHN HOME (1722–1808). A minister whose play, *Douglas*, aroused opposition from colleagues in the Church thereby further delaying the establishment of a Scottish theatrical tradition.

DAVID HUME (1711–76). Major figure of the Scottish Enlightenment, who challenged in a series of books hitherto sacrosanct beliefs about religion and argued for the power of reason.

HENRY JAMES (1843–1916). A friend of Stevenson, he visited Edinburgh in 1876.

FRANCIS JEFFREY (1773–1850). Lord Advocate and first editor of *The Edinburgh Review*. He wrote the inscription for the foundation stone of the Scott Monument.

Dr SAMUEL JOHNSON (1709–84). Visited Edinburgh in 1771 and was highly critical of the city.

PAUL JOHNSTON (1957–). Old Fettesian who presents a chilling picture of a future Edinburgh in his Quintin Dalrymple crime novels.

JOHN KNOX (*c.* 1513–72). Writer and preacher whose influence on the intellectual, social and religious life of the city has lasted to the present day.

ROBERT KNOX (1791–1862). Anatomist to whom murderers Burke and Hare supplied bodies.

JOAN LINGARD (1932–). Many of her adult and children's novels are set in the city.

ERIC LINKLATER (1899–1974). Novelist and Scottish Nationalist who wrote a number of books about, or set in, Edinburgh.

JOHN GIBSON LOCKHART (1794–1854). Son-in-law and biographer of Walter Scott, he also wrote several novels and a series of sketches on Scottish life, *Peter's Letters to his Kinsfolk*.

DAVID LYNDSAY (*c.* 1486–1555). Chiefly remembered for *Ane Satyre of the Thrie Estaitis*, widely regarded as the first great play in Scottish drama.

NORMAN MacCAIG (1910–96). Poet who has written widely about Edinburgh.

ALEXANDER McCALL SMITH (1948–). Professor of Medical Law at the University and author of the Mma Ramotswe detective series and Edinburgh serial novel *44 Scotland Street*.

WILLIAM MacGONAGALL (1825–1902). Though generally associated with Dundee, Scotland's 'worst' poet was born and died in the Cowgate.

STEWART MacGREGOR (1935–73). Doctor whose two Edinburgh novels are set in university and medical circles.

DUNCAN BAN McINTYRE (1724–1812). Renowned for his Gaelic poetry, half his life was spent in Edinburgh.

COMPTON MACKENZIE (1883–1972). Prolific writer, often about himself, now principally remembered for his novel *Whisky Galore!*.

SIR GEORGE MACKENZIE (1636–91). Founder of the Advocates Library, he wrote Scotland's first novel as well as several books of law, history and poetry.

HENRY MACKENZIE (1745–1831). Lionised in his lifetime for his novel *The Man of Feeling*, his significance in retrospect is as a patron of Burns and elder statesman of the arts.

MORAY McLAREN (1901–71). Novelist who lived for many years in Inverleith Row.

SORLEY MACLEAN (1911–96). One of Scotland's greatest living Gaelic poets was educated, and then taught for several years, in the city.

BRUCE MARSHALL (1899–1987). Author of several satirical novels about Edinburgh, most notably *The Black Oxen*.

HUGH MILLER (1802–56). Geologist and essayist, who embodied the independence of the Scottish dissenting tradition.

NAOMI MITCHISON (1897–1999). Born in Edinburgh and author of countless books ranging from science fiction to feminism, she was also a chief of a Botswanan tribe.

EDWIN MUIR (1887–1959). Poet and stringent critic of Edinburgh, best exemplified in *Scottish Journey.*

WILFRED OWEN (1893–1918). While convalescing in Craiglockhart Hospital wrote some of his most memorable poetry.

ALLAN RAMSAY (1685–1758). Poet, publisher and founder of Edinburgh's first lending library.

IAN RANKIN (1960–). Novelist whose Rebus crime series has much to say about the state of modern Edinburgh.

JOHN RUSKIN (1819–1900). A frequent visitor to, and highly critical of, the New Town, much of his work was published in *The Edinburgh Review*.

SIEGFRIED SASSOON (1886–1967). First World War poet, who spent several months at Craiglockhart hospital.

WALTER SCOTT (1771–1832). Born, educated and most of his life resident in Edinburgh, he drew on the city and its history for many of his novels, with the result that he is probably the pre-eminent Edinburgh literary figure of all time.

PERCY BYSSHE SHELLEY (1792–1822). Paid visits to the city in 1811 and 1813, marrying the same person on each occasion.

CATHERINE SINCLAIR (1800–64). One of the most successful novelists of her day, she supposedly first guessed the identity of 'The Great Unknown'.

WILLIAM SMELLIE (1740–95). Friend of Burns and as editor of *The Encyclopaedia Britannica* made an important contribution to the Scottish Enlightenment.

ADAM SMITH (1723–90). Another major figure of the Scottish Enlightenment, who as a result of his *Inquiry into the Nature and Causes of the Wealth of Nations* is regarded as the founder of the modern study of political economy.

SYDNEY GOODSIR SMITH (1915–75). Poet and novelist, whose *Carotid Cornucopius* celebrates the capital, much as his hero Robert Fergusson did two centuries before.

TOBIAS SMOLLETT (1721–71). Wrote *The Expedition of Humphry Clinker*, which has many scenes set in Edinburgh while staying with his sister in the city.

MURIEL SPARK (1918–). Though choosing to exile herself from Edinburgh at an early age, her novel, *The Prime of Miss Jean Brodie*, is one of the best realisations of the city and its social nuances.

LEWIS SPENCE (1874–1955). Poet who championed the cause of writing in Scots.

ROBERT LOUIS STEVENSON (1850–94). Major writer whose life has sometimes overshadowed his writing, much of which is about the city in which he was born.

DUGALD STEWART (1753–1828). Professor of moral philosophy and influential figure of the Scottish Enlightenment.

WILLIAM THACKERAY (1811–63). Came to the city several times on lecture tours, despite being hissed on an early visit.

FRED URQUHART (1912–95). Novelist and short story writer who draws on his Edinburgh childhood for some of his work

JULES VERNE (1828–1905). French science-fiction author whose novel *Backwards to Britain* is a fictionalised account of his visit to Edinburgh in 1859.

IRVINE WELSH (1958–). Revolutionised perceptions of Edinburgh with his novel *Trainspotting* (1993).

JOHN WESLEY (1703–91). Preached several times on Calton Hill and leaves a picture of the city during the eighteenth century in his diaries.

REBECCA WEST (1892–1983). Though she left the city as a child, she gives a sharp portrait of the city in her novel *The Judge*.

JOHN WILSON (1785–1854). Author of the *Noctes Ambrosianae* for Blackwoods, he was also one of the first critics to do justice to Wordsworth.

WILLIAM WORDSWORTH (1770–1850). Came to Edinburgh in 1803, during which he paid a visit to Scott in Lasswade.

Edinburgh Novels

Aitken, Hannah, *In a Shaft of Sunlight* (Hodder & Stoughton, 1947)
– *Seven Napier Place* (Hodder, 1952)
Aitken, Mary Baird, *Soon Bright Day: a story of the Edinburgh of the French Revolution*
  (MacLellan, 1944)
Albert, Edward, *Man's Chief End* (Cassell, 1928)
– *The Grey Wind* (Cassell, 1929)
– *Herrin' Jennie* (Nicolson & Watson, 1931)
Allan, Mabel Esher, *A Formidable Enemy* (Nelson, 1975)
Anderson, Dawn, *Futon Fever* (Black Ace Books, 1998)
Andrews, Lucilla, *Edinburgh Excursion* (Harrap, 1970)
– *One Night in London* (Heinemann, 1979)
– *In an Edinburgh Drawing Room* (Heinemann, 1983)
– *A Weekend in the Garden* (Heinemann, 1981)
Andrews, Val, *Sherlock Holmes and The Theatre of Death* (Breese Books, 1997)
Arbuthnot, Gill, *The Chaos Clock* (Floris, 2003)
– *The Chaos Quest* (Floris, 2004)
Armour, Margaret, *The Professor's Impropriety* (1895)
– *Agnes of Edinburgh* (Andrew Melrose, 1911)
Arnette, Lamb, *Betrayed* (Simon & Schuster, 1995)
– *Beguiled* (Simon & Schuster, 1996)
Arundel, Honor, *Green Street* (Hamish Hamilton, 1966)
– *The High House* (Hamish Hamilton, 1967)
– *The Amazing Mr Prothero* (Hamish Hamilton, 1968)
– *The Two Sisters* (Heinemann, 1968)
– *Emma in Love* (Hamish Hamilton, 1970)
Aycliffe, Jonathan, *The Matrix* (Collins, 1994)
Bailey, Henry, *The Master of Gray* (Longman, 1903)
Baillie, Jamieson, *Walter Crighton or Reminiscences of George Heriot's Hospital*
  (Livingstone, 1898)
Balfour, Andrew, *To Arms!* (Methuen, 1898)
Balman, James, *The Meek Inheritance* (Cranston House, 1993)
Banks, Iain, *Complicity* (Little Brown, 1993)
Barke, J., *The Song in the Green Thorn Tree: A Novel of the Life and Loves of Robert Burns*
  (Collins, 1947)
– *Wonder of all the Gay World* (Collins, 1949)
Barker, Pat, *Regeneration* (Viking, 1991)
Bassi, Michael, *The Kilted Parrot* (The Molendinar Press, 1981)
Begg, Ken, *The Anvil Agreement* (Pluto Press, 1985)
Bell, J.J., *Wee MacGregor Enlists* (Hodder, nd)
– *Wee Macgregor* (Moray Press, 1953)
Bigland, Eileen, *Doctor's Child* (Arthur Barker, 1934)
Blair, Joan, *Sister of Nelson Ward* (Mills & Boon, 1937)

Blyth, Robert, *Festival* (Canongate, 1977)
Bold, Alan, *East is West* (Keith Murray Publishing, 1991)
Bone, Florence, *The Lass with a Lantern* (Stanley Paul, 1934)
Borrow, George, *Lavengro* (OUP, 1982)
Bosanko, Abigail, *Lazy Ways to Make a Living* (Time Warner, 2002)
– *A Nice Girl Like Me* (Time Warner, 2004)
Bowen, John, *The Truth Will Not Help Us* (Chatto & Windus, 1956)
Boxer, Charlie, *The Cloud of Dust* (Cape, 2000)
Boyd, Albert, *Kinmont Willie* (Moray Press, 1934)
Boyd, William, *The New Confessions* (Penguin, 1988)
Bramble, Forbes, *The Strange Case of Deacon Brodie* (Hamish Hamilton, 1975)
Brett, Simon, *So Much Blood* (Gollancz, 1976)
Bright, Pamela, *Breakfast at Night* (MacGibbon & Kee, 1956)
Brink, Carol, *Lad with a Whistle* (Macmillan, 1941)
Brookmyre, Christopher, *Quite Ugly One Morning* (Little Brown, 1996)
– *Country of the Blind,* (Little Brown, 1997)
– *Boiling a Frog* (Little Brown, 2000)
Broomfield, Janet, *Fallen Land* (Bodley Head, 1990)
Bruce, Dorita, *A Lavercock Lilting* (OUP, 1945)
Bruce-Watt, Jeremy, *Captive Summer* (Chambers, 1979)
Bryson, Hector, *Doctors,Bodies and Snatchers* (Canongate, 1978)
Buchan, John, *John Burnet of Barns* (John Lane, 1898)
– *A Lost Lady of Old Years* (John Lane, 1899)
Buckland, Paul, *Chorus of Witches* (WH Allen, 1959)
Butlin, Ron, *Night Visits* (Serpent's Tale, 2003)
Byrd, Elizabeth, *Rest Without Peace* (Macmillan, 1974)
Caird, Janet, *In a Glass Darkly* (Morrow, 1966)
Campsie, Alistair, *The Clarinda Conspiracy* (Mainstream, 1989)
Carr, Caleb, *The Italian Secretary* (Time Warner, 2005)
Chalmers, H., *Before the Wars* (International Publishing, 1947)
Christie, Anna, *First Act* (Piatkus, 1983)
Claraso, Mercedes, *Langwheeple: A Novel* (Black Ace Books, 1997)
Claridge, Marten, *Nobody's Fool* (Headline, 1991), *The Midnight Chill* (Headline, 1992)
Clarke, Brenda, *Under Heaven* (Bantam, 1988)
Clavering, Molly, *Near Neighbours* (Hodder, 1956)
Cleaton, Irene, *The Outsider* (Little Brown, 1944)
Cockburn, Sir Antrobus, *Cockburn's Oath* (John Sutherland, 1839)
Cohen, William, *One-Eyed Kings* (Bantam, 1991)
Connell, John, *David Go Back* (Cassell, 1935)
Corbett, The Misses, *The Busy-Bodies* (Longman, 1827)
Cost, March, *After the Festival* (Cassell, 1966)
Cowan, Torquil, *Dagger at Dawn* (Pentland Press, 1999)
Craig, Bill, *Scobie in September* (Hutchinson, 1971)
– *September can be Dangerous in Edinburgh* (Walker, 1971)
Craig, Robert, *Traitor's Gait* (Porpoise Press, 1934)
Crampsey, Robert, *The Edinburgh Pirate* (Canongate, 1979)
Crawford, F. Marion, *A Cigarette Smoker's Romance* (Macmillan, 1892)
Crockett, Samuel Rutherford, *Cleg Kelly, Arab of the City* (Smith Elder, 1896)
– *The Black Douglas* (Smith, Elder, 1899)
– *Kit Kennedy* (James Clarke, 1899)
– *Kid McGhie: A Nugget of Dim Gold* (James Clarke, 1906)
Cunningham, Jane, *The Baker's Window* (Edinburgh Press, 1933)
– *Clearance* (Simpkin Marshall, 1934)

Dallas, Oswald, *Blinker* (Eldon Press, 1934)
Davie, Elspeth, *Creating a Scene* (Calder & Boyars, 1971)
– *Climbers on a Stair* (Hamish Hamilton, 1978)
– *Coming to Light* (Hamish Hamilton, 1989)
Davis, Carol Anne, *Shrouded* (The Do-Not Press, 1997)
– *Safe as Houses* (The Do-Not Press, 1999)
– *Noise Abatement* (The Do-Not-Press, 2001)
Davis, Margaret Thomson, *Light and Dark* (Century, 1984)
– *Burning Ambition* (B&W, 1997)
Delves-Broughton, Josephine, *I Saw No Sun* (Faber, 1952)
Demarco, Gordon, *Murder at the Fringe* (Polygon, 1987)
De Quincey, Thomas, *Confessions of an English Opium Eater* (OUP, 1985)
Devereux, Jude, *Temptation* (Simon & Schuster, 2001)
Dewar, Isla, *Women Talking Dirty* (Headline, 1996)
– *Women Giving up on Ordinary* (Headline, 1997)
– *Two Kinds of Wonderful* (Headline, 2000)
Dhondy, Farrukh, *Bombay Duck* (Cape, 1990)
Douglas, Anne, *Catherine's Land* (Piatkus, 1997)
– *As the Years Go By* (Piatkus, 1999)
Douglas, Colin, *The Houseman's Tale* (Canongate, 1975)
– *The Greatest Breakthrough Since Lunchtime* (Canongate, 1977)
– *Bleeders Come First* (Canongate, 1979)
– *For Services to Medicine* (Hutchinson, 1985)
– *Ethics Made Easy* (Mainstream, 1986)
– *Sickness & Health* (Heinemann, 1991)
Downe, Walmer, *The Bloom of Faded Years* (McKelvie, 1896)
Doyle, Arthur Conan, *The Firm of Girdleston* (Chatto & Windus, 1890)
– *A Duet with an Occasional Chorus* (Grant Richards, 1899)
Dunbar, Inga, *Scarlet Lady, White Bride* (Mills & Boon, 1988)
– *Candle Maker Row* (Simon & Schuster, 1992)
– *Tanner's Close* (Simon & Schuster, 1993)
Duncan, J. R., *Switchback City* (Hale, 1985)
Dunlop, Eileen, *The House on Mayferry Street* (Holt, 1976)
– *A Flute in Mayferry Street* (Richard Drew, 1987)
Dunne, Colin, *Ratcatcher* (Secker, 1985)
Dunwoodie, Helen, *Solo Act* (Corgi, 1997)
Eccott, W. J., *The Background* (Blackwood, 1909)
Engel, Howard, *Mr Doyle & Dr Bell: A Victorian Mystery* (Viking, 1997)
Ferguson, Ruby, *Lady Rose and Mrs Memmary* (Hodder & Stoughton, 1937)
Fergusson, Adam, *Scone: A Likely Tale* (Sinclair-Stevenson, 2004)
Ferrier, Susan, *Marriage* (OUP, 1997)
Fetterless, Arthur, *The Career of Kembole* (Blackwood, 1912)
Findlater, Jane, *Rachel* (Methuen, 1899)
Findlater, Mary, *Over the Hills* (Methue, 1897)
Findlater, Jane and Mary, *Crossriggs* (Smith Elder, 1908)
– *Penny Moneypenny* (Smith Elder, 1911)
– *Beneath the Visiting Moon* (Hurst & Blackett, 1923)
Findlay, Jessie, *Norman Reid* (Oliphant Anderson, 1890)
Fitzsimons, Christopher, *Early Warning* (Hodder & Stoughton, 1978)
Ford, James Allen, *A Statue for a Public Place* (Hodder & Stoughton, 1965)
– *A Judge of Men* (Hodder & Stoughton, 1968)
Gala, James, *Take It While It's There* (The Pentland Press, 1992)
Galbraith, Douglas, *The Rising Sun* (Picador, 2001)

Galford, Ellen, *Queendom Come* (Virago, 1990)

Galt, John, *Ringan Gilhaize* (Scottish Academic Press, 1984)

Geikie, Mary, *Sleeve o silk* (Hutchinson, 1935)

Goodwin, I., *Bury me in Lead* (Alan Wingate, 1952)

Gordon, Richard, *The Sleep of Life* (Heinemann, 1975)

Grant, Anne, *Kathleen* (1900)

– *Road to Tarfe* (Simkin Marshall, 1928)

Grant, James, *The Romance of War* (Routledge, 1850)

– *Harry Ogilvie* (London, 1856)

– *Jane Seton* (London, 1857)

– *Mary of Lorraine* (London, 1860)

– *Oliver Ellis* (London, 1861)

– *The Captain of the Guard* (London, 1862)

– *The White Cockade* (London, 1870)

Graves, Frederick, *Ombra: the mystery* (Morton, 1904)

Gray, Alasdair, *1982 Janine* (Jonathan Cape, 1984)

Gray, Elizabeth, *Meggy MacIntosh* (Doubleday, 1930)

Grayson, Richard, *The Tartan Conspiracy* (Macmillan, 1992)

Green, Evelyn Everett, *Ringed by Fire: A Story of the Franco– Prussian War* (Nelson, 1904)

Grey, Cyril, *Under the Upas Tree: a Romance of Scotland in the 16th Century* (Marshall, 1915)

Groome, Francis, *Hindes Kriegspiel* (Ward Lock, 1896)

Guinness, Peter, *Hidden Agenda* (Premier Fois, 1999)

Gunn, Neil, *The Drinking Well* (Faber & Faber, 1946)

Gutteridge, Peter, *No Laughing Matter* (Headline, 1997)

Halliday, Dorothy, *Dolly and the Singing Bird* (Cassell, 1968)

Hamilton, Julia, *Forbidden Fruits* (Harper Collins, 2002)

Hammond, Gerald, *The Game* (Macmillan, 1982)

Hanagan, Eva, *Upas Tree* (Constable, 1979)

Hanley, Clifford, *Love from Everybody* (Hutchinson, 1959)

Hardy, Robina, *Jock Halliday: a Grassmarket Hero* (Oliphant, 1883)

– *Tom Telfer's Shadow* (Oliphant, 1884)

– *Katie: An Edinburgh Lassie* (Oliphant, 1886)

– *Within a Mile o' Edinburgh Town* (Oliphant, 1886)

– *Johnnie* (Oliphant, 1889)

Harker, Lizzie Allen, *Marigold* (French's, 1928)

Harris, Wilson, *Black Marsden* (Faber, 1972)

Harrison, John, *The Laird of Restalrig's Daughter* (Edinburgh, 1857)

Hay, Ian, *The Right Stuff* (Blackwood, 1908)

Hely, Elizabeth, *Mark of Displeasure* (Heinemann, 1961)

Henderson, Francis, *Under the Cardinal* (Gardner, 1913)

Herdman, John, *Three Novellas* (Polygon, 1987)

Hewlett, Maurice, *The Queen's Quair* (Macmillan, 1904)

Hird, Laura, *Born Free* (Rebel, 1999)

Hodge, Merton, *The Wind and the Rain* (Gollancz, 1934)

Hogg, James, *Private Memoirs and Confessions of a Justified Sinner* (Canongate Classics, 1983)

Holland, Elizabeth, *The House in the North* (Macmillan, 1963)

– *The House by the Sea* (Chatto & Windus, 1965)

– *The Adding Up* (Chatto, 1968)

Holms, Joyce, *Payment Deferred* (Headline, 1996)

– *Foreign Body* (Headline, 1997)

– *Bad Vibes* (Headline, 1998)

- *Thin Ice* (Headline, 1999)
- *Mr Big* (Headline, 2000)
- *Bitter End* (Headline, 2001)
- *Hot Potato* (Allison & Busby, 2003)
- *Hidden Depths* (Allison & Busby, 2004)

Holt, Victoria, *Snare of Serpents* (Collins, 1990)

Honeyman, William, *Jock Howieson or the Lass o' Cramond Brigg* (Menzie, 1893)

Houston, Terry, *The Wounded Stone* (Argyll, 1998)

Hunter, J. D., *The Allerton Affair* (Jordanbooks, 1992)

Hunter, Mollie, *The Spanish Letters* (Floris Books, 2003)
- *The Lothian Run* (Floris Books, 2003)
- *A Sound of Chariots* (Trophy Press, 1994)

Hunter, Peter, *Bible and Sword* (Hodder & Stoughton, 1904)

Irvine, Helen, *Torchlight Procession* (Longmans, 1945)

Jacob, Violet, *Flemington* (John Murray, 1911)

Jardine, Quintin, *Skinner's Rules* (Headline, 1993)
- *Skinner's Festival* (Headline, 1994)
- *Skinner's Trail* (Headline, 1994)
- *Skinner's Round* (Headline, 1995)
- *Skinner's Ordeal* (Headline, 1996)
- *Skinner's Mission* (Headline, 1997)
- *Skinner's Ghosts* (Headline, 1998)
- *Murmuring the Judges* (Headline, 1998)
- *Gallery Whispers* (Headline, 1999)
- *Thursday Legends* (Headline, 2000)
- *Autographs in the Rain* (Headline, 2001)
- *Head Shot* (Headline, 2002)
- *Fallen Gods* (Headline, 2003)
- *Stay of Execution* (Headline, 2004)
- *Lethal Intent* (Headline, 2005)
- *Blackstone's Pursuits* (Headline, 1996)
- *A Coffin for Two* (Headline, 1997)
- *Poisoned Cherries* (Headline, 2002)
- *Unnatural Justice* (Headline, 2004)

Jinks, Peter, *Hallam Foe* (Headline, 2001)
- *Intuition* (Headline, 2003)

John, Owen, *Festival* (Hale, 1978)

Johnston, Paul, *Body Politic* (Hodder & Stoughton, 1997)
- *The Bone Yard* (Hodder & Stoughton, 1998)
- *Water of Death* (Hodder & Stoughton, 1999)
- *The Blood Tree* (Hodder & Stoughton, 2000)
- *The House of Dust* (Hodder, 2001)

Johnstone, Christine, *Elizabeth de Bruce* (Blackwood, 1827)

Kay, Rosemary, *Return Journey* (Headline, 1996)

Keeton, George, *The Speedy Return* (G Bell, 1938)

Kelly, Mary, *Dead Man's Riddle* (Secker & Warburg, 1957)

Kemp, Robert, *The Malacca Cane* (Duckworth, 1954)
- *The Maestro* (Duckworth, 1956)
- *The Highlander* (Duckworth, 1957)
- *Gretna Green* (Chambers, 1961)

Kent, Nora, *I am a Wanderer* (Macdonald, 1952)

Kirk, Russell, *Lord of the Hollow Dark* (St Martin's, 1979)

Knight, Alanna,
Inspector Faro series:
– *Enter Second Murderer* (Macmillan, 1988)
– *Blood Line* (Macmillan, 1989)
– *Deadly Beloved* (Macmillan, 1990)
– *Killing Cousins* (Macmillan, 1990)
– *A Quiet Death* (Macmillan, 1991)
– *To Kill a Queen* (Macmillan, 1992)
– *The Evil That Men Do* (Macmillan, 1993)
– *The Missing Duchess* (Macmillan, 1994)
– *The Bull Slayers* (Macmillan, 1995)
– *Murder by Appointment* (Macmillan, 1996)
– *The Coffin Lane Murders* (Macmillan, 1998)
– *The Final Enemy* (Macmillan, 2001)
– *Unholy Trinity* (B&W, 2004)
– *Faro and the Royals* (B&W, 2005)
Tam Eildor series;
– *The Dagger in the Crown* (Macmillan, 2001)
– *The Gowrie Conspiracy* (Allison & Busby, 2004)
Rose McQuinn series:
– *Dangerous Pursuits* (Constable, 2002)
– *The Inspector's Daughter* (Constable, 2000)
– *Ghost Walk* (Allison & Busby, 2004)
– *The Black Duchess* (Macdonald, 1980)
– *The Royal Park Murder* (McGraw Hill, 2001)
Knox, Bill, *A Killing in Antiques* (Hutchinson, 1981)
Koning, Christina, *A Mild Suicide* (Lime Tree, 1992)
Kyle, Elisabeth, *Mally Lee* (Peter Davies, 1947)
– *The House of the Pelican* (Nelson, 1954)
– *The Stark Inheritance* (Peter Davies, 1978)
Laird, Elizabeth, *Arcadia* (Macmillan, 1990)
Lane, Elinor, *Nancy Stair* (Heinemann, 1905)
Lane, Jane, *Parcel of Rogues* (Andrew Dakers, 1948)
Lindsay, Frederic, *A Charm Against Drowning* (Carlton, 1988)
– *After the Stranger Came* (Deutsch, 1992)
– *Kissing Judas* (Hodder & Stoughton, 1997)
– *A Kind of Dying* (Hodder & Stoughton, 1998)
– *Idle Hands* (Hodder & Stoughton, 1999)
– *Death Knock* (Hodder, 2000)
– *Darkness in My Hand* (Hodder, 2001)
Lingard, Joan, *The Prevailing Wind* (Hodder & Stoughton, 1964)
– *The Headmaster* (Hodder & Stoughton, 1967)
– *A Sort of Freedom* (Hodder & Stoughton, 1969)
– *The Gooseberry* (Hamish Hamilton, 1978)
– *The Second Flowering of Emily Montgomery* (Paul Harris, 1979)
– *Strangers in the House* (Hamish Hamilton, 1981)
– *Reasonable Doubts* (Hamish Hamilton, 1986)
– *Rags & Riches* (Hamish Hamilton, 1988)
– *Glad Rags* (Hamish Hamilton, 1990)
– *After Colette* (Sinclair Stevenson, 1993)
– *The Kiss* (Allison & Busby, 2003)
– *Encarnita's Journey* (Allison & Busby, 2005)
Linklater, Eric, *Magnus Merriman* (Cape, 1934)

– *The Impregnable Women* (Cape, 1938)
– *The Merry Muse* (Cape, 1959)
Logan, Eliza, *Restalrig* (1829)
Lorimer, James, *The Red Sergeant* (Nelson, 1931)
– *The Green Brigade* (Blackwood, 1935)
Lyell, W. D. *The House in Queen Anne Square* (Blackwood, 1920)
– *The Justice-Clerk* (W. Hodge, 1923)
MacAndrew, Richard, *Inspector Logan*: Cambridge English Reader Level 1 (CUP, 2002)
– *Logan's Choice*: Cambridge English Reader Level 2 (CUP, 2000)
– *A Puzzle for Logan* : Cambridge English Reader Level 3 (CUP, 2001)
– *The University Murders*: Cambridge English Reader Level 4 (CUP, 2003)
McAulay, Allan, *The Rhymer* (Unwin, 1900)
McCabe, Brian, *The Other McCoy* (Mainstream, 1990)
McCall Smith, Alexander, *The Sunday Philosophy Club* (Little Brown, 2004)
– *Friends, Lovers, Chocolate* (Little Brown, 2005)
– *44 Scotland Street* (Polygon, 2005)
– *Espresso Tales* (Polygon, 2005)
McCallum, Neil, *A Scream in the Sky* (Cassell, 1964)
McClure, Ken, *Fenton's Winter* (Harper Collins, 1989)
– *Crisis* (Simon & Schuster, 1993)
– *Trauma* (Simon & Schuster, 1995)
– *Resurrection* (Simon & Schuster, 1999)
– *Deception* (Simon & Schuster, 2001)
– *Eye of the Raven* (Allison & Busby, 2005)
McDonald, Joanna, *Dubious Assets* (Headline, 1995)
McDonnell, Virginia, *Dixie Cline* (Nelson, 1966)
McEwen, Todd, *McX* (Secker & Warburg, 1990)
Macfarlane, Hamish, *Threeplay* (Aspire, 1998)
McGregor, Iona, *An Edinburgh Reel* (Faber, 1968)
– *Death Wore a Diadem* (Women's Press, 1989)
MacGregor, Stuart, *The Myrtle and the Ivy* (Macdonald, 1967)
– *The Sinner* (Calder & Boyars, 1973)
McInnes, Betty, *The Alexander Inheritance* (Headline, 1994)
McIntosh, Isobel, *Men Love Affairs* (Marionette Books, 1997)
Mackay, Colin, *The Sound of the Sea* (Canongate, 1989)
Mackay, John *Criminal Camera* (Pentland Press, 1996)
McKelway, St Clair, *The Edinburgh Caper* (Gollancz, 1963)
Mackenzie, Agnes Mure, *Without Condition* (Heinemann, 1923)
McKenzie, John *Are You Boys Cyclists* (Serpent's Tale, 1997)
McKinlay, Margaret, *Double Entry* (Harper Collins, 1992)
– *The Caring Game* (Harper Collins, 1993)
– *Legacy* (Collins, 1993)
McLaren, John, *Tibbie and Tam* (Baillie, 1894)
McLaren, Moray (as Michael Murray), *The Noblest Prospect* (Duckworth, 1934)
– *The Unpossessed* (Chapman & Hall, 1949)
– *The Pursuit* (Jarrolds, 1959)
McLellan, Duncan, *The Hanging of Captain Green* (Murray, 1932)
McNeill, Elisabeth, *A Woman of Gallantry* (Century, 1989)
– *Perseverance Place* (Century, 1991)
– *Money Troubles* (Severn House, 1999)
– *Press Relations* (Severn House, 2003)
Maconachie, Aileen, *No Rest for the Sole of My Foot* (Book Guild, 1992)
McWilliam, Candia, *Debatable Land* (Bloomsbury, 1994)

Mann, Jessica, *Charitable End* (Collins, 1971)
– *The Sticking Place* (Macmillan, 1974)
Marchbank, Agnes, *Some Edinburgh Bohemians* (Torani, 1891)
Marshall, Bruce, *Crumpled Silk* (1921)
– *Teacup Terrace* (Hurst & Blackett, 1926)
– *Father Malachy's Miracle* (Heinemann, 1931)
– *The Word, the Flesh and Father Smith* (Houghton Miflin, 1945)
– *George Brown's Schooldays* (Constable, 1946)
– *Thread of Scarlet* (Collins, 1959)
– *The Black Oxen* (Constable, 1972)
Martin, Graham Dunstan, *Time-slip* (Unwin, 1986)
Masefield, Muriel, *Seven Against Edinburgh* (Heinemann, 1951)
Masson, Rosaline, *The Transgressors* (Hodder & Stoughton, 1899)
– *In Our Town* (Hodder & Stoughton, 1901)
Matheson, Jean, *The Little Green Bird* (Hodder, 1963)
Miller, Ian, *School Tie* (Newnes, 1935)
Millington, Mil, *A Certain Chemistry* (Hodder, 2003)
Mitchell, Weir, *Characteristics* (Century, 1892)
Moir, David, *The Life of Mansie Wauch, tailor in Dalkeith* (Blackwood, 1828)
Montgomery, K. L., *Major Weir* (Fisher Unwin, 1904)
Morgan, Morgan, *Part of the Price: a story of Edinburgh Life in Lent* (St Giles, 1883)
Morrison, Morag, *Operation Code-Name Cavalier* (Book Guild, 1988)
Muir, Augustus, *The Blue Bonnet* (Methuen, 1926)
– *Castles in the Air* (Methuen, 1938)
Munro, Hugh, *Brain Robbers* (Hale, 1977)
Murray, David, *Commander of the Mists* (Hodder & Stoughton, 1938)
Mylechreest, Winifred, *The Fairest of the Stuarts* (Sampson Low, 1912)
Nairne, Campbell, *One Stair Up* (Tauchnitz, 1933)
Niven, Frederick, *The Paisley Shawl* (Collins, 1931)
Norman, Nicole, *Heather Song* (Simon & Schuster, 1980)
Oliver, Jane, *Mine is the Kingdom* (Collins, 1937)
– *Not Peace but a Sword* (Collins, 1939)
– *In No Strange Land* (Collins, 1944)
– *Blue Heaven Bends Over All: A Novel of the Life of Sir Walter Scott* (Collins, 1971)
Oliver, Lawrence, *Jamie Simpson* (Nicolson & Watson, 1935)
Olmis, Elizabeth, *Jack's Hymn* (Oliphant Anderson, 1891)
O'Neill, Anthony, *The Lamplighter* (Headline, 2003)
Orr, Christine, *The Glorious Thing* (Hodder & Stoughton, 1919)
– *Kate Curlew* (Hodder & Stoughton, 1922)
– *Hogmany* (Hodder & Stoughton, 1928)
– *The Player King* (Hodder & Stoughton, 1931)
– *Immortal Memory* (Hodder & Stoughton, 1933)
– *Gentle Eagle: A life of James IV* (International Publishing Company, 1937)
– *The Happy Woman* (Rich & Cowan, 1947)
– *You Can't Give Them Presents* (Rich & Cowan, 1949)
Oswald, Andrena, *The Edinburgh Lions* (Dent, 1956)
Paterson, Aileen, *Maisie's Festival Adventure* (Glowworm, 1988)
– *Maisie & the Space Invader* (Amaising Publishing Co, 1988)
– *Maisie Loves Paris* (Amaising Publishing House, 1989)
– *Maisie's Merry Christmas* (Amaising Publishing Co, 1995)
Pat, David, *The Double Sacrifice: An Edinburgh Tale* (unknown, 1856)
– *The Fatal Error: A Story of the Burke & Hare Murders* (Fred Farrah, 1866)
Paul, William, *The Lion Rampant* (Macdonald, 1989)

– *Dance of Death* (Severn House, 1991)
– *Sleeping Dogs* (Constable, 1994)
– *Sleeping Pretty* (Constable, 1995)
– *Sleeping Partner* (Constable, 1996)
– *Stranger Things* (Constable, 1997)
Paull, Mary Anna, *The Flower of the Grassmarket* (Hodder & Stoughton, 1909)
Peck, Winifred, *The Warielaw Jewel* (Faber, 1933)
– *Clear Dawn* (Faber, 1949)
Pelton, Sonya, *Windswept Passion* (Kensington, 1984)
Peters, Elizabeth, *Ghost in Green Velvet* (Cassell, 1976)
– *Legend in Green Velvet* (Dodd Mead, 1976)
Piper, Peter, *Death in the Canongate* (Hodder & Stoughton, 1952)
Pirie, David, *The Patient's Eyes: The Dark Beginnings of Sherlock Holmes* (Century, 2001)
– *The Night Calls* (Arrow, 2003)
Pollatschek, Stefan, *The Strange Story of John Law* (Hutchinson, 1936)
Pottinger, George, *Whisky Sour* (Paul Harris, 1979)
Preedy, George, *Double Dallilay* (Cassell, 1933)
Primrose, Hilda, *Marjolaine* (Moray Press, 1935)
Pugh, Marshall, *Stranger Any Place* (Hutchinson, 1962)
Rankin, Ian, *Knots and Crosses* (Bodley Head, 1987)
– *Hide & Seek* (Barrie & Jenkins, 1991)
– *Strip Jack* (Orion, 1992)
– *The Black Book* (Orion, 1993)
– *Mortal Causes* (Orion, 1994)
– *Let it Bleed* (Orion, 1995)
– *Black & Blue* (Orion, 1997)
– *Death is not the End* (Orion, 1998)
– *The Hanging Garden* (Orion, 1998)
– *Dead Souls* (Orion, 1999)
– *Set in Darkness* (Orion, 2000)
– *The Falls* (Orion, 2001)
– *Resurrection Men* (Orion, 2002)
– *A Question of Blood* (Orion, 2003)
– *Fleshmarket Close* (Orion, 2004)
Reade, Charles, *Christie Johnstone* (Sisley Books, 1907)
Reed, Paul, *The One* (Mercat, 2003)
Ritchings, Rev. B., *The Wanderer Brought Home: The Life and Adventures of Colin* (Seeley
    Jackson, 1866)
Robb, Candace, *A Trust Betrayed* (Heinemann, 2000)
– *The Fire in the Flint* (Heinemann, 2003)
Robertson, Dirk, *Highland T'ing* (The X Press, 1998)
Robertson, James, *The Fanatic* (Fourth Estate, 2000)
– *Joseph Knight* (Fourth Estate, 2003)
Robertson, M, *Evil Enchantment* (Nash & Grayson, 1930)
Ross, Angus, *The Edinburgh Exercise* (Long, 1975)
Ross, Clarissa, *Face in the Pond* (Avon, 1970)
Ross, Jean, *The Martlet Box* (Canongate, 1987)
Roxburgh, R. A., *Robin Bide-a-Wee* (Blackwood, 1928)
– *Ninian Herd* (Blackwood, 1929)
Saxby, Jessie, *Ben Hanson: A Story of George Watson's College* (Oliphant Anderson, 1884)
Scarborough, Elizabeth Ann, *The Lady in the Loch* (Ace Books, 1998)
Scott, Honoria, *A Winter in Edinburgh* (unknown, 1810)
Scott, John Dick, *The End of an Old Song* (Eyre & Spottiswoode, 1954)

Scott, Sir Walter, *Waverley* (Constable, 1814)
– *Guy Mannering* (1815)
– *The Heart of Midlothian* (1818)
– *Redgauntlet* (Constable, 1824)
– *The Abbot* (Cadell, 1831)
Scott-Moncrieff, George *Burke Street* (Richard Patterson, 1956)
– *Tinker's Wind* (Wishart, 1933)
Seger, Maura, *The Lady and the Laird* (Mills & Boon, 1999)
Sellick, George, *The Rebels of Fairmilehead* (Boys Own Paper, 1927)
Setoun, Gabriel, *Robert Urquhart* (Bliss, Sands & Foster, 1896)
Sheridan, Sara, *Ma Polinski's Pockets* (Heinemann, 1999*)*
Simon, Edith, *Sable Coat* (Cassell, 1958)
Sinclair, Catherine, *Holiday House* (James Wood, 1865)
Slater, Catherine, *Margaret Pow Looks Back* (Hodder & Stoughton, 1920)
Sligh, Nigel, *Traitor's Bridge* (Werner Laurie, 1952)
Smart, Harriet, *A Garland of Vows* (Headline, 1991)
– *Green Grow the Rushes* (Headline, 1992)
– *The Daughters of Blane* (Headline, 1994)
– *The Lark Ascending* (Headline, 1995)
Smith, Janet Mary, *While the Candles Burn* (William Maclellan, 1951)
Smith, Sydney Goodsir, *Carotid Cornucopius* (Macdonald, 1964)
Smollett, Tobias, *The Expedition of Humphry Clinker* (1771)
Sommerfield, Sylvie, *Fires of Surrender* (Kensington, 1990)
Spark, Muriel, *The Prime of Miss Jean Brodie* (Penguin, 1965)
Steele, Hunter, *The Wishdoctor's Song* (Black Ace Books, 2005)
Stevens, Riccardo, *The Cruciform Mark* (Chatto, 1896)
– *Mr Peters* (Bliss Sands, 1897)
Stevenson, Dorothy, *The Story of Rosabelle Shaw* (Chambers, 1937)
Stevenson, Robert Louis *Catriona* (Cassell, 1893)
– *Master of Ballantrae* (Cassell, 1896)
– *St Ives* (Heinemann, 1898)
– *Weir of Hermiston* (Chatto, 1896)
– 'The Misadventures of John Nicholson' in *The Scottish Stories and Essays*, Kenneth
    Gelder (ed.) (Edinburgh University Press, 1989)
– *Dr. Jekyll and Mr. Hyde* and *The Bodysnatcher* (OUP, 1990)
Stevenson, William, *Puddin'* (1894)
Stewart, Andrew, *One False Step* (Oliphant, 1888)
Stodart-Walker, Archibald, *The Well-Intentioned* (Andrew Melrose, 1912)
Stubbs, Jean, *The Case of Kitty Ogilvie* (Macmillan, 1970)
Sutcliff, Rosemary, *The Shining Company* (Bodley Head, 1990)
Swan, Annie, *Bess: The Story of a Waif* (Marr, 1880)
– *Adam Hepburn's Vow* (Cassell, 1885)
Sweet, Lucy, *Have Love Will Travel* (Black Swan, 2005)
Sweetland, Magda, *Eightsome Reel* (Macmillan, 1985)
– *The Hermitage* (Macmillan, 1988)
Tate, Joan, *The Runners* (David & Charles, 1974)
Taylor, Vincent, *Sunray* (Macdonald, 1982)
Thirkell, Angela, *Now the King's Come* (Hale, 1981)
Thomas, Dylan, *Doctor and the Devils* (New Directions, 1953)
Thomson, George Malcolm, *The Ball at Glenkerran* (Secker & Warburg, 1982)
Todd, Margaret, *Windy Laugh* (1899)
– *The Way of Escape* (Blackwood, 1902)
Torriggia, Count of, *Martyrs and the Hero* (Anglo-Italian, 1953)

Trapido, Barbara, *The Travelling Hornplayer* (Hamish Hamilton, 1998)
Trocchi, Alexander, *Young Adam* (Olympia Press, 1957)
Trotter, Janet, *The Beltane Fires* (Lochar, 1989)
Tytler, Sarah, *The Diamond Rose* (Ward Lock, 1867)
– *Lady Jean's Son* (Jarrold, 1897)
Urquhart, Fred, *Jezebel's Dust* (Methuen, 1951)
– *Palace of Green Days* (Quartet, 1979)
– *Time Will Knit* (Richard Drew, 1988)
Verne, Jules, *Backwards to Britain* (Chambers, 1992)
Wallace, Christopher, *The Resurrection Club* (Collins, 1999)
Ware, Ciji, *Island of the Swans* (Bantam, 1989)
Warner, Alan, *The Sopranos* (Cape, 1998)
Watt, Margaret, *The House in the Square* (Grant & Murray, 1931)
Waugh, Joseph, *Betty Grier* (Chambers, 1915)
Webster, Mary Morison, *Everygreen* (1929)
– *The Schoolhouse* (Constable, 1933)
Welsh, Irvine *Trainspotting* (Secker & Warburg, 1993)
– *Marabou Stork Nightmares* (Cape, 1995)
– *Ecstasy* (Cape, 1996)
– *Filth* (Cape, 1998)
– *Glue* (Cape, 2001)
– *Porno* (Cape, 2002)
West, Rebecca, *The Judge* (Hutchinson, 1922)
Whyte, Christopher, *The Gay Decameron* (Gollancz, 1998)
Whyte-Melville, George, *The Queen's Maries: A Romance of Holyrood* (Tauchnitz, 1862)
Wiggin, Kate, *Penelope's Experiences in Scotland* (Gay & Bird, 1898)
Williams, Harley, *Fingal's Box* (Cape, 1941)
Williamson, Charles, *The Heather Moon* (Methuen, 1912)
Wilson, John, *The Trials of Margaret Lyndsay* (London, 1823)
Wilson, William, *Forsyth* (Houghton & Scott-Snell, 1937)
Wynd, Oswald, *Summer Can't Last* (Cassell, 1960)

SOME SHORT STORY COLLECTIONS
FEATURING EDINBURGH

Butlin, Ron, *Vivaldi and the Number 3* (Serpent's Tale, 2004)
Edwards, Owen Dudley, *The Edinburgh Stories of Arthur Conan Doyle* (Polygon, 1981)
Ferrars, Elizabeth, *Designs on Life* (Collins, 1980)
Greenberg, Joanne, *Summering* (Gollancz, 1967)
Hendry, J. F., *Penguin Book of Scottish Short Stories* (Penguin, 1970)
Hird, Laura, *Nail & Other Stories* (Canongate, 1997)
Kravitz, Peter (ed.) *The Picador Book of Contemporary Scottish Fiction* (Picador, 1997)
McCabe, Brian, *Lipstick Circus and Other Stories* (Mainstream, 1985)
– *In a Dark Room with a Stranger* (Penguin, 1995)
– *Body Parts* (Canongate, 1999)
– *A Date with My Wife* (Canongate, 2001)
MacDougall, Carl, *The Devil & the Giro* (Canongate, 1989)
McLaren, Moray, *A Dinner with the Dead* (Serif, 1947)
MacLaverty, Bernard, *A Time to Dance and Other Stories* (Cape, 1982)
Meek, James, *Last Orders* (Polygon, 1992)
– *McFarlane Boils the Sea* (Polygon, 1989)
Miller, William (ed.), *Two Streets and a Castle: A Collection of Short Stories by Leith and Edinburgh Writers* (Perserverance Writers' Club, nd)

Rankin, Ian, *A Good Hanging* (Century, 1992)
– *Herbert in Motion and other Stories* (Revolver, 1997)
– *Beggars Banquet* (Orion, 2002)
Reid, J. M. (ed.), *Classic Scottish Short Stories* (OUP, 1989)
Robertson, James, *The Ragged Man's Complaint* (B&W, 1993)
Stewart, J. I. M., *Parlour 4 and other stories* (Gollancz, 1984)
Urquhart, Fred, *The Year of the Short Corn* (Methuen, 1949)
Urquhart, Fred and Giles Gordon, *Modern Scottish Short Stories* (Hamish Hamilton, 1978)
Welsh, Irvine, *The Acid House* (Cape, 1994)
Williamson, Kevin, *Children of Albion Rovers* (Rebel Inc., 1997)
– *Rover Returns* (Rebel Inc, 1998)

SOME POETRY COLLECTIONS
FEATURING EDINBURGH

Byrne, Michael (ed.), *George Campbell Hay: Collected Poems and Songs* (Edinburgh University Press, 2000)
Conn, Stewart, *Stolen Light* (Bloodaxe, 1999)
– *Ghosts at Cockcrow* (Bloodaxe, 2005)
Fraser, Bashabi and Elaine Greig, *Edinburgh: An Intimate City* (City of Edinburgh Council, 2000)
Fraser, Douglas, *Rhymes o' Auld Reekie* (Macdonald, 1988)
Fulton, Robin (ed.), *Robert Garioch: Complete Poetical Works* (Macdonald, 1983)
Garioch, Robert, *The Masque of Edinburgh* (M. McDonald, 1954)
– *Doktor Faust in Rose St* (Macdonald, 1973)
– *Collected Poems* (Macdonald, 1977)
Lewis, Roger (ed.), *The Collected Poems of Robert Louis Stevenson* (Edinburgh University Press, 2003)
McCaig, Ewen (ed.), *The Poems of Norman MacCaig* (Polygon, 2005)
Maclean, Sorley, *From Wood to Ridge: Collected Poems in Gaelic and English Translation* (Birlinn, 2000)
Massie, Allan, *Edinburgh and the Borders in Verse* (Secker & Warburg, 1983)
Mitchell, Ross, *Rhymes & Verses of Edinburgh Town* (Albyn Press, 1985)
Morgan, Edwin, *Today Tomorrow; The Collected Poems of George Bruce 1933–2000* (Edinburgh University Press, 2001)
Ransford, Tessa, *Shadows from the Greater Hill* (Ramsay Head Press, 1987)
Robertson, James (ed.), *Robert Fergusson Selected Poems* (Birlinn, 2000)
Smith, Sydney Goodsir, *Collected Poems* (Calder, 1978)
Spence, Lewis, *Collected Poems of Lewis Spence* (Serif, 1953)
Todd, Ruthven, *Until Now* (Fortune Press, 1942)

Bibliography

Adam Smith, Janet, *John Buchan* (Hart Davis, 1965)
– *John Buchan & His World* (Thames & Hudson, 1979)
Adams, Abraham, *Another Little Drink: Story of an Alcoholic's Decline, Fall and Return to Life* (Scotia, 1973)
Bamford, Francis, *Edinburgh* (Faber, 1938)
Barclay, J. B., *Edinburgh from the Earliest Days to the Present Day* (A. & C. Black, 1965)
Barrie, J. M., *An Edinburgh Eleven* (Hodder & Stoughton, 1896)
Benton, Jill, *Naomi Mitchison* (Pandora, 1990)
Bertram, James, *Some Memories of Books Authors and Events* (Constable, 1893)
Birkin, Andrew, *The Lost Boys* (Futura, 1980)
Birrell, J. F., *An Edinburgh Alphabet* (The Mercat Press, 1980)
Bishop, Alan, *Joyce Cary* (Michael Joseph, 1988)
Bold, Alan, *Smollett* (Vision, 1982)
– *Modern Scottish Literature* (Longmans, 1983)
– *Muriel Spark* (Methuen, 1986)
– *Hugh MacDiarmid* (John Murray, 1988)
– *Scotland: A Literary Guide* (Routledge, 1989)
Brown, L. J., and D. Forrest, *Letters of John Brown* (A. & C. Black, 1907)
Bruce, George, *Festival in the North* (Robert Hale, 1975)
– *To Foster and Enrich: The First Fifty Years of the Saltire Society* (Saltire Society, 1986)
Buchan, James, *Capital of the Mind* (John Murray, 2003)
Buchan, Susan, *John Buchan* (Hodder & Stoughton, 1947)
Calder, Jenni, *A Robert Louis Stevenson Companion* (Paul Harris, 1980)
– *RLS: A Life Study* (Hamish Hamilton, 1980)
Campbell, Donald, *A Brighter Sunshine: A Hundred Years of the Royal Lyceum* (Polygon, 1983)
– *Edinburgh: A Cultural and Literary History* (Signal Books, 2003)
Campbell, Ian, *Thomas Carlyle* (Hamish Hamilton, 1974)
Cant, Malcolm, *Marchmont in Edinburgh* (John Donald, 1984)
– *Villages of Edinburgh* (John Donald, 1986)
– *Villages of Edinburgh, vol. 2* (John Donald, 1987)
– *Sciennes and the Grange* (John Donald, 1990)
– *Gorgie & Dalry* (privately published, 1995)
– *The District of Greenbank in Edinburgh* (Malcolm Cant publications, 1998)
Carlyle, Alexander, *Autobiography* (Foulis, 1910)
Carlyle, Thomas, *Reminiscences* (Longman, 1881)
Carroll, David, *Edinburgh: Literary Lives and Landscape* (Sutton, 2004)
Catford, E. F., *Edinburgh: The Story of a City* (Hutchinson, 1975)
Chalmers, Patrick, *Kenneth Grahame* (Methuen, 1933)
Chambers, Robert, *Traditions of Edinburgh* (Chambers, 1824)
Chesterton, G. K., *Robert Louis Stevenson* (Hodder & Stoughton, 1929)
Cochrane, Robert, *Pentland Walks: Their Literary & Historic Associations* (Andrew Eliot, 1908)
Cockburn, Henry, *Memorials of His Time* (Robert Grant, 1945)

Cockburn, Harry, *A History of the New Club 1787–1937* (Chambers, 1938)

Coghill, Hamish, *Discovering The Water of Leith* (John Donald, 1988)

Cole, G. D. H. (ed.), *A Tour Through The Whole Island* (Peter Davies, 1927)

Collie, Michael, *George Borrow Eccentric* (OUP, 1982)

Collis, John Stewart, *The Carlyles* (Sidgwick & Jackson, 1971)

Conan Doyle, Arthur, *Memories & Adventures* (Hodder & Stoughton, 1924)

Cowper, A. S., *Historic Corstorphine* vol. 2 (privately published, 1992)

Craig, Cairns, *The Modern Scottish Novel* (Edinburgh University Press, 1999)

– *Iain Banks' Complicity: A Reader's Guide* (Continuum, 2002)

Cruickshank, Helen, *Octobiography* (Standard Press, 1976)

Daiches, David, *Walter Scott & His World* (Thames & Hudson, 1971)

– *Edinburgh* (Hamish Hamilton, 1978)

– *Robert Fergusson* (Scottish Academic Press, 1982)

– *Edinburgh: A Traveller's Companion* (Constable, 1986)

– *Two Worlds* (Canongate, 1987)

Darlington, W. A., *J. M. Barrie* (Blackie, 1938)

De Greer, Wilhelm, *Swede in Edinburgh* (William McLennan, 1965)

Dick, David, *Capital Walks in Edinburgh: The New Town* (Neil Wilson, 1994)

Donaldson, Islay, *Samuel Rutherford Crockett* (Aberdeen University Press, 1989)

Douglas, Hugh, *Robert Burns* (Robert Hale, 1976)

Dunlop, Eileen and Kamm, Anthony, *A Book of Old Edinburgh* (Macdonald, 1983)

Edwards, Owen Dudley, *Edinburgh: A Literary Anthology* (Canongate, 1983)

Fairley, A, *The Queensferry Companion* (Albyn Press, 1981)

Fitzhugh, Robert, *Robert Burns* (W.H. Allen, 1971)

Geddie, John, *The Water of Leith from Source to Sea* (W. H. White, 1896)

Gibson, John Sibbald, *Deacon Brodie Father to Jekyll and Hyde* (Saltire, 1993)

Gillies, R. P., *Reminiscences of a Literary Veteran* (Richard Bentley, 1851, vol. I)

Glen, Duncan, *Makar's Walk: Walks in the Old Town of Edinburgh with an Anthology of Poetry* (The Scottish Poetry Library, 1990)

Gordon, Ian, *John Galt* (Oliver & Boyd, 1972)

Grahame, Eleanor, *Kenneth Grahame* (Bodley Head, 1963)

Grant, Aline, *Susan Ferrier of Edinburgh* (Alan Swallow, 1957)

Grant, Elizabeth of Rothiemurchus, *Memoirs of a Highland Lady* (Canongate, 1988)

Gray, Alasdair, *Saltire Self-Portraits* (Saltire Society, 1988)

Gray, John and Charles Smith, *A Walk on the Southside in the footsteps of Robert Burns* (John Gray, 1998)

Gray, W. Forbes, *An Edinburgh Miscellany* (Robert Grant, 1925)

– *A Literary Centre of a Literary Capital* (Robert Grant, 1946)

Groves, David, *James Hogg* (Scottish Academic Press, 1988)

Haight, Gordon (ed.), *The George Eliot Letters vols 1–7* (OUP, 1954–56)

Hamilton, Alan, *Essential Edinburgh* (Andre Deutsch, 1977)

Hammerton, J. A., *Barrie: The Story of a Genius* (Sampson Low, Marston, 1929)

Harris, Paul (ed.), *Scotland: An Anthology* (Cadogan, 1985)

Harris, Stuart, *The Place Names of Edinburgh* (Gordon Wright Publishing, 1996)

Harrison, Wilmot, *Memorable Edinburgh Houses* (Oliphant, Anderson & Ferrier, 1893)

Hay, Elizabeth, *Sambo Sahib* (Paul Harris, 1981)

Henderson, Jan-Andrew, *The Town Below the Ground* (Mainstream, 1999)

Herdman, John, *The Double in Romantic and Post-Romantic Fiction* (Palgrave, 1990)

– *Poets, Pubs, Polls & Pillar Boxes* (Akros, 1999)

Holland, Lady, *A Memoir of the Rev Sydney Smith* (Longmans, 1878)

Holmes, Heather and David Finkelstein (eds.), *Thomas Nelson and Sons* (Tuckwell, 2001)

Hughes, Gillian (ed.), *The Spy: The Collected Works of James Hogg* (Edinburgh University Press, 2000)

Hutton, Lawrence, *Literary Landmarks of Edinburgh* (Osgood McIlvaine, 1891)

Johnson, Edgar, *Charles Dickens* (Allen Lane, 1977)

Jones, Ken, *With Gold and Honey Blest: Edinburgh in Autumn* (Volturna, 1979)

Joyce, Michael, *Edinburgh: The Golden Age 1769–1832* (Longmans, Green, 1951)

Lang, Theo, *Edinburgh & the Lothians* (Hodder & Stoughton, 1952)

Lindrop, Grevel, *The Opium-Eater: A Life of Thomas De Quincey* (Dent, 1981)

Lindsay, Ian, *Georgian Edinburgh* (Oliver & Boyd, 1948)

Lindsay, Maurice, *The Scottish Renaissance* (Serif Books, 1948)

– *Robert Burns* (McGibbon & Kee, 1968)

– *Scotland: An Anthology* (Hale, 1974)

– *The Lowlands of Scotland* (Hale, 1977)

Lindsay, Maurice, and David Bruce *Edinburgh: Past & Present* (Hale, 1990)

Linklater, Andro, *Compton Mackenzie* (Chatto, 1987)

Linklater, Eric, *The Man on My Back* (Macmillan, 1941)

– *A Year of Space* (Macmillan, 1953)

– *Edinburgh* (Newnes, 1960)

Lochhead, Marion, *Edinburgh Lore & Legend* (Robert Hale, 1986)

Lockhart, John Gibson, *The Life of Sir Walter Scott* (A. & C. Black, 1896)

Lorimer, R. L., *Edinburgh: Scotland's Capital* (Oliver & Boyd, 1967)

Lownie, Ralph, *Auld Reekie: An Edinburgh Anthology* (Timewell, 2004)

MacCallum, Neil, *It's an Old Scottish Custom* (Dennis Dobson, 1951)

McClevy, Alastair, *The Porpoise Press 1922–39* (Merchiston Publishing, 1988)

MacDiarmid, Hugh, *Scottish Scene* (Jarrolds, 1934)

– *The Company I've Kept* (Hutchinson, 1966)

MacDonald, Malcolm, *Edinburgh* (Pevensey, 1985)

MacGregor, Alasdair Alpin, *Auld Reekie* (Methuen, 1943)

– *The Turbulent Years* (Methuen, 1945)

Macgregor, Forbes, *The Story of Greyfriars Bobby* (S Savage, 2000)

McIntosh, Elspeth, *Edinburgh* (Hale, 1987)

MacIver, Mary and Hector, *Pilgrim Souls* (Aberdeen U.P., 1990)

Mackail, Denis, *The Story of J.M.B.* (Peter Davies, 1941)

Mckean, Charles, *Edinburgh: Portrait of a City* (Century, 1991)

Mackenzie, R. F., *A Search for Scotland* (Collins, 1989)

Mackie, Albert, *Edinburgh* (Blackie, 1951)

McLaren, Moray, *Return to Scotland* (Duckworth, 1932)

– *Escape and Return* (Chapman & Hall, 1947)

– *A New Scottish Journey* (Chapman & Hall, 1948)

– *The Capital of Scotland* (Douglas & Foulis, 1950)

McNally, Raymond and Radu Florescu, *In Search of Dr Jekyll and Mr Hyde* (Robson, 2001)

McNeil, Margery, *Norman McCaig: A Study of his Life and Work* (Mercat, 1996)

Magnusson, Magnus, *The Clacken & the Slate* (Collins, 1974)

Mair, William, *Historic Morningside* (Macmillan & Wallace, 1947)

Marshall, James Scott, *The Life and Times of Leith* (John Donald, 1986)

Martine, Roddy, *The Lowlands and Borders of Scotland* (Michael Joseph, 1989)

Marwick, Sandra, *Capital Writers: Robert Louis Stevenson* (City of Edinburgh Museums, 1994)

Massie, Alan, *Edinburgh* (Sinclair-Stevenson, 1994)

Masson, David, *Edinburgh Sketches and Memories* (A. & C. Black, 1892)

Masson, Rosaline, *In Praise of Edinburgh: An Anthology in Prose and Verse* (Constable, 1912)

– *Edinburgh* (A. & C. Black, 1912)

Mehew, Ernest (ed.), *Selected Letters of Robert Louis Stevenson* (Yale University Press, 2001)

Miller, Eileen, *The Edinburgh International Festival* (Scolar, 1996)

Miller, Hugh, *Edinburgh & Its Neighbourhood* (Nimmo, 1889)

Miller, Karl (ed.), *Memoirs of a Modern Scotland* (Faber, 1970)

Milne, Hugh, *Boswell's Edinburgh Journals* (Mercat Press, 2001)
Mitchell, Ann, *The People of Carlton Hill* (Mercat, 1993)
Mitchison, Naomi, *Small Talk: Memories of an Edwardian Childhood* (Bodley Head, 1973)
Moir, D. G., *Pentland Walks: Their Literary and Historical Associations* (Bartholomew, 1977)
Morace, Robert Irvine, *Welsh's 'Trainspotting': A Reader's Guide* (Continuum, 2001)
Muir, Edwin, *Scottish Journey* (Heinemann, 1935)
– *Scott and Scotland* (Routledge, 1936)
Mullay, Sandy, *The Edinburgh Encyclopedia* (Mainstream, 1996)
– *The Illustrated History of Edinburgh's Suburbs* (Breedon Books, 2002)
Napier, George, *The Homes and Haunts of Sir Walter Scott* (MacLehose, 1897)
Nimmo, Ian, *Portrait of Edinburgh* (Robert Hale, 1975)
– *The New Town* (John Donald, 1991)
Oman, Carola, *The Wizard of the North* (Hodder & Stoughton, 1973)
Parker, W. M., *The House of Oliver & Boyd 1788–1948* (Unpublished manuscript,
   Edinburgh City Public Library)
Parnell, Michael, *Eric Linklater* (John Murray, 1984)
Pennycook, Andrew, *Literary & Artistic Landmarks of Edinburgh* (The Albyn Press, 1973)
Plain, Gill, *Ian Rankin's 'Black and Blue': A Reader's Guide* (Continuum, 2002)
Rankin, Ian, *Rebus's Scotland* (Orion, 2005)
Rankin, Nicholas, *Dead Man's Chest: Travels After Robert Louis Stevenson* (Faber, 1987)
Reid, Alan and Brian Osborne (eds.), *Discovering Scottish Writers* (Scottish Cultural Press, 1997)
Rosie, George, *Hugh Miller* (Mainstream, 1981)
Ross, Raymond and Joy Hendry (eds.), *Sorley Maclean* (Scottish Academic Press, 1987)
Royle, Trevor, *Precipitous City: The Story of Literary Edinburgh* (Mainstream, 1980)
– *A Diary of Edinburgh* (Polygon, 1981)
– *The Mainstream Companion to Scottish Literature* (Mainstream, 1993)
Ruddick, William (ed.), *Peter's Letters to His Kinsfolk* (Scottish Academic Press, 1977)
Sassoon, Siegfried, *The Complete Memoirs of George Sherston* (Faber, 1937)
Scott, Paul Henderson, *Walter Scott & Scotland* (Blackwood, 1981)
– *John Galt* (Scottish Academic Press, 1985)
– *'Defoe in Edinburgh' and other Papers* (Tuckwell, 1995)
– *A Mad God's Dream: The Story of Literary Edinburgh* (City Art Centre, 1997)
Scott, Sir Walter, *An Edinburgh Keepsake* (Edinburgh University Press, 1971)
Scott-Moncrieff, George, *Edinburgh* (Batsford, 1947)
Simpson, E. Blantyre, *Robert Louis Stevenson's Edinburgh Days* (Hodder & Stoughton, 1898)
Skinner, Robert T., *The Royal Mile* (Oliver & Boyd, 1947)
Smeaton, Oliphant, *Famous Edinburgh Students* (Forbes, 1914)
Smith, Alexander, *A Summer in Skye* (Strahan, 1866)
Smith, Charles J., *Historic South Edinburgh: vol. 3* (Charles Skilton, 1986)
– *Historic South Edinburgh: vol. 4* (Charles Skilton, 1988)
Smith, Sean, *J.K. Rowling* (Michael O'Mara Books, 2001)
Smith, Sydney Goodsir (ed.), *Robert Fergusson* (Nelson, 1952)
Steven, W., *History of the High School of Edinburgh* (Maclachlan, 1849)
Stevenson, Robert Louis, *Edinburgh: Picturesque Notes* (Seeley & Co. 1879)
– *Memories & Portraits* (Richard Drew, 1990)
Swearingen, Roger, *Robert Louis Stevenson's Edinburgh* (City of Edinburgh Council, 2001)
Thompson, Harold, *A Scottish Man of Feeling* (OUP, 1931)
Thomson, James, *Edinburgh Curiosities* (John Donald, 1996)
– *Edinburgh Curiosities 2* (John Donald, 1997)
Topham, Edward, *Letters from Edinburgh* (1776)
Tredrey, F. D., *The House of Blackwood 1804–1954* (Blackwood, 1954)
Turnbull, Michael, *Edinburgh Portraits* (John Donald, 1987)
Walker, Marshall, *Scottish Literature Since 1707* (Longman, 1997)

Wallace, Gavin and Randall Stevenson (eds), *The Scottish Novel Since the Seventies* (Edinburgh University Press)
Wallace, Joyce M., *Traditions of Trinity and Leith* (John Donald, 1985)
– *Historic Houses of Edinburgh* (John Donald, 1987)
– *Canonmills and Inverleith* (John Donald, 1994)
– *Further Traditions of Trinity and Leith* (John Donald, 1997)
Ward, Robin, *The Spirit of Edinburgh* (Richard Drew, 1985)
Watson, Roderick, *The Literature of Scotland* (Macmillan, 1984)
Waugh, Hector (ed.), *George Watson's College 1724–1970* (1970)
Williams, David, *A World of his Own: The Double Life of George Borrow* (OUP, 1982)
Wilson, A. N., *Walter Scott: The Laird of Abbotsford* (OUP, 1980)
Wilson, Alan, *Ghostly Tales and Sinister Stories of Old Edinburgh* (Mainstream, 1991)
Wilson, Alan *et al*, *Hidden and Haunted Underground Edinburgh* (Mercat Tours, 1999)
Wordsworth, Dorothy, *Recollections of a Tour Made in Scotland AD 1803* (Edmonston & Douglas, 1874)
Yee, Chiang *The Silent Traveller in Edinburgh* (Methuen, 1948)
Youngson, A. J., *The Making of Classical Edinburgh 1750–1840* (Edinburgh University Press, 1966)
– *Companion Guide to Edinburgh and the Border Country* (Collins, 1993)

WEBSITES

Organisations/tours

Chapman magazine www.chapman-pub.co.uk
Edinburgh City of Literature www.cityofliterature.com
Edinburgh International Book Festival www.edbookfest.co.uk
Edinburgh Literary Pub Tours www.edinburghliterarypubtour.co.uk
National Library of Scotland www.nls.uk
Rebus Tours www.rebustours.com
Saltire Society www.saltiresociety.org.uk
Scottish Arts Council www.scottisharts.org.uk
Scottish Book Trust www.scottishbooktrust.com
Scottish Poetry Library www.spl.org.uk
Scottish Storytelling Centre www.scottishstorytellingcentre.co.uk
Trainspotting Tours www.leithwalks.co.uk
Writers' Museum www.cac.org.uk/venues/writers_museum

Authors

Iain Banks www.iainbanks.net
Christopher Brookmyre www.brookmyre.co.uk
Carol Anne Davis www.carolannedavis.co.uk
Dorothy Dunnett www.dorothydunnett.co.uk
John Herdman www.johnherdman.co.uk
Laura Hird www.laurahird.com
Joyce Holms www.joyceholms.com
Quintin Jardine www.quintinjardine.com
Paul Johnston www.paul-johnston.co.uk
Alanna Knight www.alannaknight.com
Joan Lingard www.joanlingard.com
Ken McClure www.KenMcClure.com
Ian Rankin www.ianrankin.net
JK Rowling www.jkrowling.co.uk
Irvine Welsh www.irvinewelsh.com

Index